Robert Steele

Huon of Bordeaux

Done into English by Sir John Bourchier, Lord Berners, and now retold by Robert

Steele

Robert Steele

Huon of Bordeaux
Done into English by Sir John Bourchier, Lord Berners, and now retold by Robert Steele

ISBN/EAN: 9783337399955

Printed in Europe, USA, Canada, Australia, Japan

Cover: Foto ©Andreas Hilbeck / pixelio.de

More available books at **www.hansebooks.com**

HUON OF BORDEAUX : DONE
INTO ENGLISH BY SIR JOHN
BOURCHIER, LORD BERNERS : AND
NOW RETOLD BY ROBERT STEELE

PUBLISHED BY GEORGE ALLEN
RUSKIN HOUSE : CHARING CROSS
ROAD : LONDON : MDCCCXCV

DEAR DR. FURNIVALL,

If I put your name at the head of this book it is not primarily because its publication is in a manner due to you, nor because of the friendly kindness you have shown me in common with many another beginner in literature : it is to mark my grateful sense of the obligation which the younger men among us owe to those who have opened the stores of Early English Literature to them, and pre-eminently among them all, to you.

No doubt there were brave men before Agamemnon, and there were lovers and printers of our earliest literature before you and your allies ; but it was rarely available to those who needed it and enjoyed it most, while the Early English Text Society has, on the other hand, given us, practically in its entirety, the literature of our forefathers from the first days when the gleeman's song was written down to the hour when the printing press had firmly established itself in the land. The list of two hundred and more works, printed for the first time or reprinted from unique and inaccessible originals, is a monument to which no words from any of us can add dignity : we can but testify our gratitude to and respect for him who has devoted his life to the task of raising it.

Nor is the book to which I have put your name unworthy of you—except for my part in it, small as it is. One of the finest of the Chansons de Geste, it had the good fortune to be put into English by Berners, and save for alterations which have brought the story nearer to its original form, little change has been made, and nothing has been added to it.

I need not, I believe, justify to you my wish to open these stories to a wider public. Among the many kind notices of former work in this direction that I have received, a few critics have regretted that my alterations have taken away the philological value of the work. May I assure these friends that the story is intended to appeal to them as story only, and that I should be jealous on its behalf of anything else, however beautiful or valuable, if it seemed to take the foremost place. Those who wish to subject these stories to scientific study and cold analysis will do well to seek them out in the editions of the Early English Text Society. To that edition of this story, I would refer all those who desire information on the many points of interest raised in it, since Mr. Lee's introduction deals so fully with them that any additional discussion would be entirely beyond the province of a story book.

ROBERT STEELE.

"PRAISE WE THEN
TALES OF OLD TIME, WHEREBY ALONE
THE FAIRNESS OF THE WORLD IS SHOWN."

CONTENTS

xi

the story of Duke Huon of Bordeaux now retold by Robert Steele with drawings by Fred Mason

HERE BEGINS THE STORY OF
HUON OF BORDEAUX, TRANS-
LATED FROM THE FRENCH
BY JOHN BOURCHIER, LORD
BERNERS, AND NOW RETOLD
BY ME, ROBERT STEELE.

N THE TIME AC
COUNTED THE
YEAR OF OUR
LORD, SEVEN
HUNDRED &
NINETY - SIX,
THERE REIGN
ED IN FRANCE
THAT RIGHT GLORIOUS AND
VALIANT PRINCE, CHARLES
THE GREAT, NAMED OF ALL
MEN CHARLEMAGNE, WHO
IN HIS TIME ACHIEVED AND

brought to an end many high deeds and great enterprises by the grace that our Lord God had given him in this transitory world, for God had given him the grace to have the wit and conduct so to do. God sent to aid him, to accomplish and bring to an end his noble enterprises, many a prince and baron, so that by the aid of their forces, with the valour that God had given them, he conquered Germany, Sclave-land, and Spain, part of Africa, and Saxony, wherein he had much ado: but at the end, by the aid of his noble barons and chivalry, he subdued and put them to open flight, and was crowned with the crown of the Holy Empire of Rome. The renown of him and of his valiant chivalry stretched out of the east into the west in such wise that for ever there shall be made of him perpetual memory, as hereafter ye shall hear.

So it was, after that this right noble Emperor Charlemagne had lost his dear nephews Roland and Oliver and divers other barons and knights in the right piteous and dolorous battle that was at Roncesvalles, where there was so great and so piteous a loss that all the twelve peers of France were there slain except the good Duke Naymes of Bavaria: on a day the noble Emperor held open court at his noble city of Paris, where were many dukes, earls, and barons, sons and nephews and kinsmen of the princes dead in the foresaid battle, by the falsehood

2   and

and great treason done and contrived by Duke
Ganelon, the noble Emperor ever after being in
dolour and grief by reason of the great annoyance
and displeasure that he suffered by this loss, and
also because that he was sore feeble for the great age
that he felt himself in. Thus when the King and
the princes had dined, the Emperor called his lords
before him, he sitting on a bench richly apparelled,
and beside him sat his barons and knights.

Then the King called to him Duke Naymes, and
said: "Sir Duke Naymes, and all ye my barons being
here present, ye know right well the great time and
space that I have been King of France and Emperor
of Rome, during the which time I have been served
and obeyed of you all. For this I thank you, and
render grace and praise to God my sweet Creator.
Now because I know certainly that my life in course
of nature cannot long endure, for this cause I have
caused you all to be assembled here together, to
declare to you my pleasure and will. I require you
all, and humbly desire you, that ye will take counsel
together, and advise which of you may and will have
the government of my realm, for I can no longer
bear the travail and pain of the government thereof;
I will from henceforth live the residue of mine age
in peace, and serve our Lord God : wherefore, as
much as I may, I desire you to advise which of
you all shall be thereto most able. Ye know all that
I have two sons, that is to say, Lewis, who is too
3   young

young, and Charlot, whom I love well, and he is of age sufficient to rule. But his manners and conditions are not meet to have the governance of two such noble empires as the realm of France, and the Holy Empire of Rome. Ye know well in days past, by reason of his pride, my realm was like to have been destroyed, and I to have had war against you all, when by his felony he slew Baldwin, son to the good Ogier the Dane, whereby so many ills have come about, that it shall never be out of remembrance. As long as I live, I will not consent that he shall have the governance, though he be rightful inheritor, and that after me he ought to have the seignory. Thus I desire you to advise me what I shall do."

Forthwith, Duke Naymes and all the barons assembled in a corner of the palace, and there were long together. At last they all concluded that the governing of the said realms appertained to Charlot, the King's eldest son. Then they returned to the King, and shewed him the conclusion whereupon they were agreed, at the which the Emperor was right joyful. So he called before him his son, and shewed him many fair reasons before his barons. Thereupon advanced forth a felon traitor in whom the Emperor had great trust, he had the governance of Charlot, the King's son, who did nothing but by his advice : he was called Earl Amaury, son to one of the nephews of the traitor Ganelon. Then he said to the King and noble Emperor :

4   " How

"How is it that ye haste so sore to deliver your lands to govern to Charlot your son? Sire, be not yet so hasty: but, Sire, to prove his governing, give him a land that ought to be your own, wherein you are neither honoured nor served. Two proud boys keep this land, who these seven years past have not served you, nor since their father Duke Seguin died would do you any reverence: the eldest is named Huon, and the other Gerard. They keep Bordeaux and all the land of Aquitaine, and think scorn to hold their lands from you. But, Sire, if you will give me men, I will bring them prisoners to your palace to do your will with them, and then you may give the land they hold to Charlot your son."

"Amaury," quoth the Emperor, "I owe you great thanks that you have warned me of this matter. I bid you take your best friends, and beside them you shall have of mine three thousand knights, well chosen and proved men of war, and I will that you bring to me the two sons of Duke Seguin, that is to say, Huon and Gerard, who in their pride set nothing by me."

When Duke Naymes, being there present, heard the words of Amaury, and saw how the Emperor consented to his desire, he stepped forth boldly, and looked on Amaury, and said openly:

"Sir Emperor, great ill and great sin it is that you lightly believe such men as you know well were never certain nor true. Sire, Duke Seguin served

5   you

you all his days well and truly, and never did thing wherefore you ought to disinherit his children : the cause that they have not come to your presence before now to serve you is none other than that they be so young. Also their mother, who loves them entirely, will not suffer them to depart from her, by reason of their young age. Sire, if you will believe me, you shall not be so hasty to take from them their lands : but, Sire, do as a noble prince ought to do for the love of their father who so truly hath served you, send two of your knights to the duchess their mother, and let them say to her from you, that she should send her two sons to your court to serve you and to do their homage. If it so be that she or they will not obey your commandment, then shall you have a just cause to provide a remedy : but, Sire, I know for certain the duchess will send them to you ; the long space of time that they have been absent is for no reason but for the love that the mother hath unto her children."

When the Emperor Charles had heard Duke Naymes speak, he said :

"Sir Duke, I know certainly that Duke Seguin hath served us truly, and the reason you have shewed is just, therefore I grant it shall be as you have spoken."

"Sire," quoth the duke, "I thank your Grace."

Then straightway the King sent for two knights, and gave them charge to go to Bordeaux, to do

his

his message to the duchess, and to the sons of Duke Seguin ; the which they did. So they departed from Paris, not resting past one night in a place till they arrived at Bordeaux, and then forthwith they went to the palace, where they found the duchess newly risen from her dinner. When she was advertised of their coming she came in haste to meet them, accompanied by Huon her son, who was by her, and Gerard came after with a sparrow-hawk on his fist. When the messengers saw the duchess and her two goodly sons, they kneeled down and saluted her and her two sons from King Charlemagne, and said :

"Lady, we be sent to you from our Emperor Charles, who by us sendeth to you his salutation with honour and amity."

When the noble lady understood that they were messengers sent from the noble Emperor Charles, she advanced and embraced them, and said how they were right welcome.

"Dame," quoth they, "our Emperor hath sent us to you, and commandeth you to send to him your two sons to serve him in his court, for there are few in his realm but are come to his service except your sons : and, lady, since you know that the land you hold pertaining to your sons is holden of the Emperor Charles, by reason of his realm of France, he hath great marvel that you have not sent them ere this time to do him service

7   as

as other dukes and princes have done : wherefore, lady, he commandeth you for your wealth and conservation of your lands, that you send them to him ; or, if you do not, know for certain he will take from you such lands as you hold, and give them to Charlot his son. Wherefore may it please you to shew us your good will."

Now when the good lady had well understood the messengers, she answered them sweetly, and said :

"Sirs, know for certain the cause that I have not sent my sons to the court ere this time to serve the King, as reason is, was because I saw them so young; and also for the love of Duke Seguin their father, because I knew certainly that my rightful lord, the Emperor Charlemagne, loved always the Duke Seguin, wishing always that he would take no displeasure with the children ; these things have been the principal cause that I have not sent them before this to serve the King. Wherefore, Sirs, I require you, as much as I can, to be my means to the Emperor and to all the other barons to have me and my children excused, for the fault is only in me and not in them."

Then Huon stepped forth before his mother and said : "Madame, if it had been your pleasure you might have sent us before this time."

"That is true," quoth Gerard, "for we be great enough to be made knights."

The lady beheld her two sons, and said weeping :

"Sirs,

"Sirs, you may return to the King, howbeit you shall rest you this night in my house, and to-morrow return at your pleasure. Recommend me and my sons to the King's good grace, and to the barons and knights, and among other salute Duke Naymes, who is a near kinsman to my sons, and desire him for the love of Duke Seguin to have my sons as friends."

"Dame," quoth the messengers, "have you no doubt, for Duke Naymes is a noble man and a true knight, nor will he ever be in a place where any ill judgment should be given."

So the duchess commanded her sons that they should make the King's messengers good cheer, and bring them into their chamber to rest them, the which they did, and there they were served and feasted as they should be. Then the next morning they returned to the palace where they found the duchess and her two sons, and they humbly saluted the lady.

When the duchess saw them she called Huon and Gerard, and said:

"Children, here in the presence of these two knights, I say that at Easter you shall go to our sovereign lord, the Emperor Charlemagne. And, when ye be in the court, serve your sovereign lord well and truly, as subjects ought to do; be diligent at all times to serve him truly, and keep company with noble men such as you see that be of good conditions; be not in the place where any ill words

9   be

be spoken, or ill counsel given ; fly from the company of them that love not honour and truth ; open not your ears to hear liars, or false reporters, or flatterers ; be often at church, and give largely for God's sake ; be liberal and courteous, and give to poor knights ; fly the company of janglers ; and all goodness shall follow. Now I will that there be given to each of these knights a courser, and a rich gown, as appertaineth to the messengers of a noble Emperor like Charlemagne ; and also each of them shall have a hundred florins."

"Madame," quoth Huon, "your pleasure shall be accomplished."

The two sons caused to be brought before the palace two goodly horses, and presented them to the two knights, and gave each of them a rich gown and a hundred florins ; whereof the messengers were joyful, and thanked the duchess and her two sons, and said that their courtesy should be remembered in time to come; howbeit they knew well it was done for the honour of the King. Then they took leave of the duchess and of her two sons, and so departed and rode without let or hindrance till they came to Paris, where they found the Emperor in his palace sitting among his barons. So the King perceived them and straightway called them to his presence, and, before they had leisure to speak, bade them welcome home, and asked of them if they had been at Bordeaux, and spoken with the duchess and the

two

two sons of Duke Seguin, and whether they would come and serve him in his court or not.

"Sire," quoth they, "we have been at Bordeaux and done your message to the duchess ; who right humbly received us, and made us great feast and cheer. When she had heard us speak, and knew that we were your messengers, she made us the best cheer that she could devise, and said that the cause why she had not sent her sons to your court before this time, was because of their youth : and she humblyrequireth your Grace to have her and her two sons excused, and at this next Easter she will send them to your court. And, Sire, the two children are so goodly that it is pleasure to behold them : specially Huon the older is so fair and so well formed that nature cannot amend him. Also, Sire, for the love of you she hath given each of us a goodly horse, and a rich gown, and a hundred florins of gold. Sire, the goodness, the valour, and the courtesy that is in the duchess and in her sons cannot be recounted. Sire, the duchess and her two sons entreat your Grace to retain them always in your favour and good grace, and to pardon the fault of their long absence."

When the Emperor had heard the messengers speak, he was right joyful, and said :

"Always I have heard say that a good branch brings forth good fruit. I say it for Duke Seguin, who in his time was a valiant and true knight, and by that I see and hear the two children resemble

11   their

their good father. I see they have received my messengers right honourably, and with great reverence have given them great gifts, the which shall be to them profitable in time to come. They shall no sooner be come to my court but in the despite of them that will speak against them, I shall treat them in such wise that it shall be an example to all other to do well; for I will make them, for love of their father, of my privy council."

Then the Emperor beheld Duke Naymes, and said: " Sir Duke, always your kindred have been good and true, and certainly I will that Amaury be banished my court, for neither he nor one of his lineage gave ever any good counsel."

" Sire," quoth the duke, " I knew well the long absence of Duke Seguin's sons was for none other cause but by reason of their youth."

So when the Earl Amaury had heard the King speak, and saw how he was chafed against him, he was sorrowful, and departed secretly from the court, and swore that he would provide for the two sons of Duke Seguin such a device that they should both die in dolour, and would do so much that he would bring all France into heaviness and trouble. So he went to his lodging sorrowful and in great displeasure, and then he imagined and studied on the matter, and how to bring about his enterprise. At the last he departed from his lodging, and went to Charlot the King's son, with whom he was right

privy

privy. He found him sitting on a rich couch, chatting with a young knight, and, with a piteous visage and his eyes full of water, Amaury entered into the chamber, and kneeled down before Charlot, who had great pity to see him in that case. Then Charlot took him up and asked wherefore he was in that sorrow, and whether any man had displeased him.

"Sir," quoth Amaury, "I shall shew you. True it is that the two sons of Duke Seguin of Bordeaux will come to the court, and, as I have heard say, the King hath said that at their coming they shall be made of his privy council, so that none other about the King shall have any profit or winning but they. And I can see nought else but if they thus come, all other that be now great about the King shall be chased away, so that within two years they shall have the best quarter of the realm of France. As for you, if you suffer it, they shall bring you clear out of the Emperor your father's favour. Therefore, Sir, I require you to help me now in this business, for in time past Duke Seguin their father by great wrong and treason took from me a strong castle of my own, and I never did him displeasure. Sir, you ought to aid me in this matter, for I am of your lineage, by reason of the noble queen, your mother."

When Charlot had well understood the Earl Amaury, he asked in what manner he might aid him.

"Sir," quoth he, "I shall shew you. I shall assemble the best of my lineage, and you shall let me me have of yours sixty knights well armed. I shall lie in the way to meet with the two boys, and I shall lay an ambush in a little wood a league from Montleherault on the way to Orleans, by the which way they must needs come. Then we shall set on them and slay them, so that none shall speak thereof: and if it be known hereafter, who dare speak against you, or wear helm in field?"

"Sir," quoth Charlot, "cease and appease your sorrow, for I shall never have joy in my heart till I be revenged of these two boys. Go and make ready your men, and I shall prepare mine, and I will go myself with you the sooner to make an end of this business."

When Amaury heard Charlot offer himself so liberally to go in his aid he thanked him, and embraced his legs, and would have kissed his shoe. But Charlot would not suffer him, and took him up and said: "Sir, haste you, and do your best that this matter may come to a good end."

Amaury departed from Charlot right joyous, and, till the day appointed, he ceased not day nor night to assemble his men and his next friends: and in the evening before he came to Charlot, who was then out of Paris, all armed, and stayed not till they came to the place appointed to tarry the coming of the two sons of Duke Seguin. Now will I leave to speak of them, and return to speak of the two sons of Duke Seguin, Huon and Gerard.

14   CHAP. II.

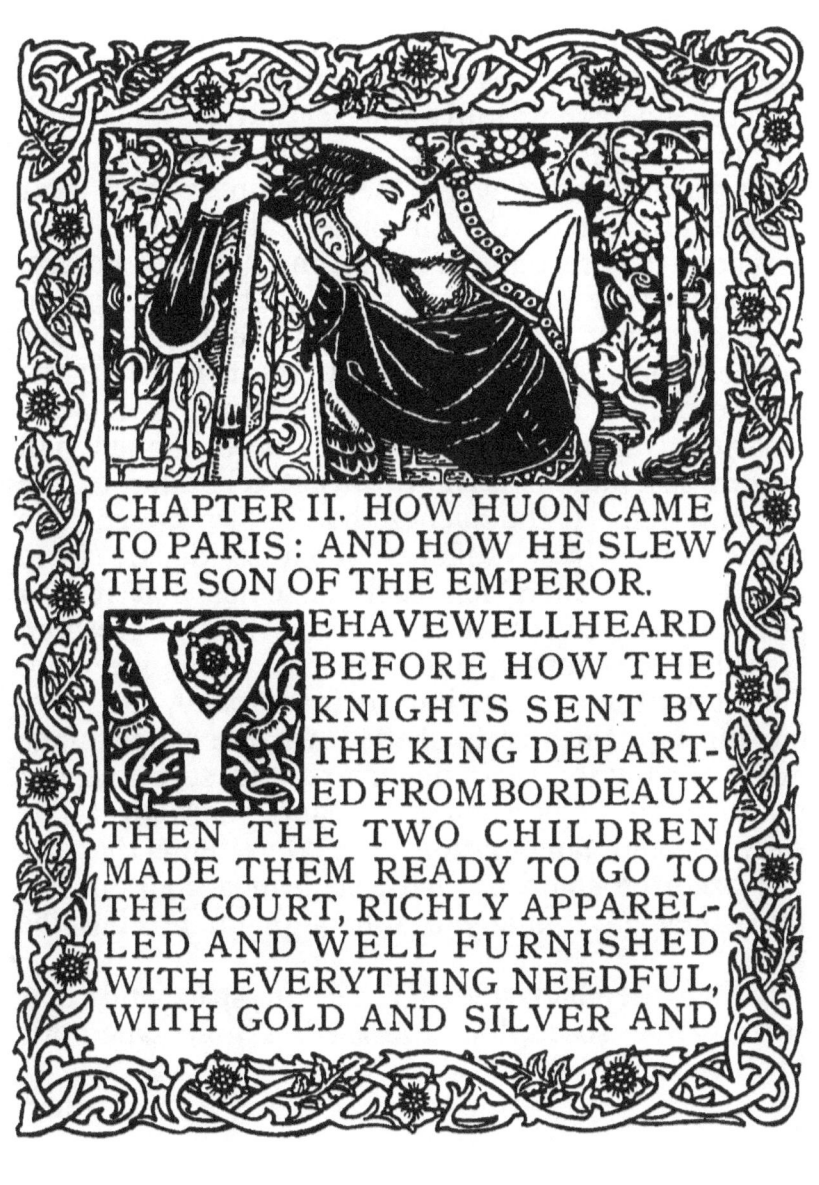

CHAPTER II. HOW HUON CAME
TO PARIS : AND HOW HE SLEW
THE SON OF THE EMPEROR.
YE HAVE WELL HEARD
BEFORE HOW THE
KNIGHTS SENT BY
THE KING DEPART-
ED FROM BORDEAUX
THEN THE TWO CHILDREN
MADE THEM READY TO GO TO
THE COURT, RICHLY APPAREL-
LED AND WELL FURNISHED
WITH EVERYTHING NEEDFUL,
WITH GOLD AND SILVER AND

apparel of silk as to their estate appertained. They
assembled the barons of the country, to whom they
recommended their lords and seignories, and chose
out ten knights and four counsellors to ride with
them to aid and govern their business and sent
for the provost of the Garonne, called Sir Guyer,
to whom they recommended all the deeds of justice,
and when they had chosen them that should go in
their company, they took leave of the duchess their
mother, and of the barons of the country. Sore was
the weeping because of their departure, and good
occasion was there thereof, and more if men had
known the piteous adventure that fell after to the
two children ; if the duchess had known thereof, she
would never have suffered them to depart from
her, for after there fell such mischief that it is a
piteous thing to recount it. Thus the two brethren
kissed their mother, and departed, sore weeping.
They took their horses and their company, and passing through the streets of the town, the people made
great sorrow for their departure, and sore weeping
prayed God to be their guide and guardian. The
weeping and lamentation were so extreme that the
two brethren could not have so firm a courage but
that they gave many a sore sigh on leaving the
town.

When they had ridden a certain space and their
sorrow was somewhat appeased, Huon called his
brother Gerard and said :
16   " Brother.

"Brother, we go to the court to serve the King, wherefore we have cause to be joyful. Let us two sing a song to refresh us."

"Brother," quoth Gerard, "my heart is not very joyful to sing or to make feast, for this night I dreamed a marvellous dream. Methought three leopards assailed me, and drew my heart out of my body. But you, methought, escaped safe and sound, and turned back. Wherefore, dear brother, if it be your pleasure not to withstand my dream, by which I reckon our voyage to be a dangerous journey, I would desire you let us return again to Bordeaux to our mother. She will be joyful of our return."

"Brother," quoth Huon, "if God will we shall not return for fear of a dream, it would be for ever our reproach and shame: I will not return to Bordeaux till I have seen the King. Therefore, sweet brother, dismay you not, but rather make good cheer: our Lord Jesus Christ shall guide and conduct us in safe-guard."

Thus these two brethren rode night and day till they perceived before them the Abbot of Cluny with thirty horse in his company, and he was going to the King's court.

So Huon perceived that company and called his brother Gerard, and said:

"Lo, yonder I see men of religion holding the way to Paris: you know well that when we departed from the duchess our mother, she charged us that we should always company with good people, therefore it is good that we hasten to overtake them."

"Brother," quoth Gerard, "your pleasure be fulfilled."

So they rode so long that they overtook the Abbot, who looked round to the right, and saw the two brethren coming to overtake him, and stood still till he saw Huon who came riding on before. Huon saluted him humbly, and the Abbot in like manner to him, and demanded whither he rode so hastily, from whence he came, what he was, and who was his father.

"Sir," quoth Huon, "since it is your pleasure to know, Duke Seguin of Bordeaux was our father, it is seven years since he departed this life. And, Sir, behold here my brother, who is younger than I, and we are going to noble King Charlemagne's court, to do homage for our lands and country. He hath sent for us by two noble knights, and, Sir, we are in doubt of some trouble by the way."

When the good Abbot understood that they were sons to Duke Seguin, he was right joyful and in token of true amity he embraced them one after another, and said:

"Dear friends, have no doubt, for by the grace of Jesus Christ I shall conduct you safely to Paris. Duke Seguin your father was a cousin of mine, wherefore I am bound to aid you : and know for truth that I am sworn of the great council of King

Charlemagne, and if there be any that will move or stir against you, I shall aid you to the extent of my power ; wherefore you may ride securely in my company without any doubt."

" Sir," quoth Huon, " I thank you."

Thus they rode talking with the Abbot their kinsman, and that night they came to Montleherault. The next day they rose betimes and heard Mass, and afterwards took their horses, and they were in all two score horses. They rode so long that they came to a little woodside where Charlot and the Earl Amaury lay in ambush, and they spied Huon and Gerard riding before, whereof they were joyful. Then Amaury said to Charlot :

" Sir, now is the time come to be revenged of the damage that Duke Seguin did to me ; yonder I see his two sons coming : if they be not forthwith slain by us, we are not worthy to have any land. And, Sir, by their death you shall be lord of Bordeaux, and of all the duchy of Aquitaine."

When that Charlot understood the Earl Amaury, he stretched him in his stirrups, and took a spear with a sharp head, and issued alone out of the wood. When Amaury saw that Charlot went out of the wood alone, he drew a little out of the way, and said to his men :

" Suffer Charlot alone, there need none go to aid him."

This said the false traitor because he desired
19   nothing

nothing else but that one of the sons of Duke Seguin might slay Charlot, and they should be destroyed for his murder.

The Abbot of Cluny saw Charlot coming all armed, and in the wood a great number of armed men, so he stood still, and called Huon and Gerard, and said:

"Dear nephews, I perceive in yonder wood a knight all armed, and the wood full of horsemen. I cannot tell what they mean. Have ye done a wrong to any man? If you have, or if you hold anything that is not your own, step forth and offer him reason, and promise to make amends."

"Sir," quoth Huon, "I know no man living that I or my brother have done any displeasure to, nor do we know any creature who hates us."

Then Huon said to his brother:

"Sir, ride on before and meet with yonder knight, and ask him what is his pleasure."

Gerard rode forth and met Charlot and demanded what his pleasure was to have, or whether he was keeper of that passage or not, and asked any tribute or not; if he did he was ready to pay it. Charlot answered him fiercely and said:

"What art thou?"

Gerard answered:

"Sir, I am of the city of Bordeaux, and son to Duke Seguin, whom God pardon, and hereafter cometh Huon mine elder brother; we are going

to

to Paris to the King's court, to take up our lands and our fees, and to serve him; if there be any that desire anything from us, let him come to Paris, and we shall satisfy him."

"Hold thy tongue," quoth Charlot, "whether thou will or no, I will have satisfaction for what Seguin thy father took from me. He had three of my castles, and I could never have revenge. But now since thou art here, I will be avenged of the wrong thy father did me, for as long as thou and thy brother be alive, I shall never have joy in my heart. Beware, for ere it be night, I shall make thy life depart from thy body."

"Sir," quoth Gerard, "have pity of me; you may see I am but naked, without armour. It shall be greatly to your shame and reproach if I be thus slain by you; it never comes of a gentle heart, or knightly, to assail a person without armour or weapon. Howbeit, Sir, I cry you mercy; well you see that I have neither sword, shield, nor spear to defend myself withal; you may see yonder coming my elder brother who shall be ready to make you amends if any harm hath been done you."

"Peace," quoth Charlot, "there is now no thing so dear to me as to change my mind, for I shall put thee shamefully to death, beware!"

Gerard, who was but young, was in great fear, and called upon our Lord God, and turned his horse to come again to his brother, but Charlot, who was in

his

his headstrong mood, couched his spear and ran after Gerard, and struck him on the side with such force that the spear ran through part of his body, and so bore him to the earth, weening he had been slain. Howbeit the stroke was not mortal, our Lord God saved him at that time, but he was so sore hurt that he could not move for the pain he felt.

The good Abbot of Cluny beheld Gerard, and saw him borne to the ground, and piteously weeping said to Huon:

" Ha, cousin, I see yonder your brother Gerard slain, the which slayeth my heart."

" Ah, Sir," quoth Huon, " for God's sake counsel me. Alas, what shall the duchess our mother, who so sweetly hath nourished us, say when she knoweth that my brother is slain? Ah, my dear brother Gerard, now I see well your dream is true. Alas that I had not believed you ; if I had, this had not fortuned. Sir, I require you succour me : for if I should be slain I will go and demand of yonder knight for what occasion he hath slain my brother, nor shall I ever return till I have slain him or he me."

" Ah, fair nephew," quoth the Abbot, " beware what you do : have no trust to be succoured by me, for you know well I cannot aid you in this case; I am a priest and serve God, I may not be where any man is slain."

Quoth

Quoth Huon, " Such company as yours is we might well forbear."

Then Huon beheld piteously the ten knights that came with him from Bordeaux and said :

" Sirs, ye that are come hither with me, and have been nourished in my house, how say you ? Will you aid me to revenge the death of my brother, and succour me against these false murderers that have lain in wait, and slain my brother Gerard ? "

" Sir," quoth they, " we shall die in your quarrel to aid and succour you : go forth and have no fear." And they rode forth with such small defence as they had. Then Huon spurred forth his horse with such fierceness that he made the earth tremble under him, and his knights followed him with a hardy courage determined to do valiantly.

The good Abbot saw his nephew and his company depart with great pity, and prayed our Lord God to defend them from death, then he followed softly after Huon to see what the end of the matter should be. Huon rode until he came to where his brother lay sore wounded, then he cried aloud :

" My right dear brother, if there be any life in your body, answer me and show me how you feel yourself."

" Brother," quoth Gerard, " I am sore wounded, I cannot tell if I may escape alive ; think on yourself, it is no loss of me : flee you away yonder ; you may see how the wood is full of armed men and they

abide

abide for nothing but to slay you as they have done me."

When Huon understood his brother he was very sorrowful and said that he had rather die than depart without revenging him. "An God will, I shall not depart till I have slain him that hath brought you to this point." Then he spurred his horse and followed after Charlot, who was returning to the wood to his company ; but when he perceived how Huon was following him, Charlot turned his horse and beheld him fiercely. Then Huon cried with a loud voice, and said :

" Villain, who art thou that hath slain my brother ? Where wert thou born ? "

Charlot answered and said :

" I was born in Almaine, and I am son to Duke Thierry."

Huon believed he had said truth, because Charlot had a strange shield that he might not be known.

"Ah," quoth Huon, "God give thee hindrance ; why hast thou slain my brother ? "

Then Charlot answered boldly and said:

" Thy father Duke Seguin took three castles from me, and would never do me right ; therefore I have slain thy brother, and so shall I thee."

Huon in great ire said :

" False and untrue knight and murderer, ere it be

night

night I shall quit you for the dolour that thou hast brought me into."

And Charlot said: "Beware thee of me, for I defy thee."

Huon, who had but small armour, took his cloak of scarlet and wrapped it about his arm, and drew his sword, and spurred his horse, and came against Charlot with his sword in his hand. Charlot on the other part came against him with his spear in rest, and struck Huon about the right arm, so that the stroke passed through the thickness of the cloak, and through his gown and shirt, and missed the flesh; thus Huon escaped that stroke, and thanked God therefor. Then he lift up his sword with both his hands, and let the bridle of his horse go, and so with all his might and manhood he struck Charlot on the helm in such wise that neither the circlet nor coif of steel could defend him, but that the sword went into his brain, and he fell to the earth and never rose after: thus Charlot was miserably slain.

Then the traitor Amaury being in the wood, perceived how Charlot was slain, and thanked God, and said:

"Charlot is dead, God be thanked; by that stroke I shall bring France into such a trouble, that I shall attain to all my desires."

Huon, seeing Charlot dead, returned to Gerard his brother, lying still upon the earth, and brought

him

him Charlot's horse, and asked whether he could ride or no."

"Brother," quoth Gerard, "I think yes, if my wound was bound fast I would assay."

Then Huon alighted, and took a piece of his shirt, and therewith bound his brother's wound, and Huon's knights came to him and aided him to set Gerard on his horse, though for the pain he suffered he swooned twice. When he came to himself again, they set him on an ambling palfrey, and a knight behind him to hold him upright, and he said to Huon:

"Brother, I desire you let us depart from hence without going any further forward, rather let us return to Bordeaux to the duchess our mother, for I doubt if we go any further that some great ill should come to us. I promise you if we be perceived by them that be in the wood, and they know that you have slain him that hurt me, they will slay us all."

"Brother," quoth Huon, "by the grace of God I shall not turn back for fear of death, till I have seen the King to charge him with treason, since under his conduct and commandment we be betrayed, and watched by the way to murder us."

"Brother," quoth Gerard, "as your pleasure is, so be it."

Then they rode forth on the way to Paris fair and easily, because of Gerard who was sore hurt.

The

The knights who were ambushed in the wood said to Sir Amaury:

"Sir, what shall we do? See, Charlot is slain and lieth in the plain. If we go after them that have done this deed, it shall be ill done if they escape away alive."

Then Sir Amaury answered and said:

"Let them go, God curse them, let us follow them afar off till they come to Paris and we will carry with us the body of Charlot and bring it to the King. I will make you all so rich that you shall never be poor after."

They answered that they would do his pleasure, and then they went out of the wood, and came to where Charlot lay dead, and took him up and laid him before the Earl Amaury on his horse's neck, and so rode forth that, God confound their plans, forasmuch as in them lay, they laboured to have Huon judged to death.

Thus they rode the highway to Paris, and the Abbot of Cluny, who was riding on before, looked behind him and saw the two brethren coming after him. Then he tarried, and demanded of Huon what adventure he had found.

"Sir," quoth he, "I have slain him that hath sore hurt my brother, where he thought to have slain me, but, thanked be God, I have left him dead in the place."

"Fair nephew," quoth the Abbot, "I am sorry

thereof

thereof, but seeing it is done, if any plea come thereby and ye be accused before the King, I shall aid you with all my power."

"Sir," quoth Huon, "for that I thank you."

Then Huon looked behind him and saw where the Earl Amaury with all his power came fair and easily after him. Therewith all his blood trembled, and he said to the Abbot:

"Sir, what shall I do, yonder I see those approach that desire my death ; they be the same that lay in the wood watching for us."

"Fair nephew," quoth the Abbot, "have no fear, for they that come after us ride at a soft pace, and make no shew of overtaking us. Let us ride on at a good pace, we shall soon be at Paris ; it is but two miles thither."

Then they rode on and rested not till they came to the palace, and there they alighted and went up, Huon holding his brother by one hand, and the Abbot by the other.

The King was sitting among his barons, and Huon saluted Duke Naymes and all the other barons and said:

"God, that for us died on a cross, save all these noble barons and confound the King whom I see there sitting. Never was there heard of a greater treason than the King has practised against us: seeing that by his messengers and his letters patent he hath sent for us to do him homage, the which

commandment

commandment we have obeyed as to our sovereign lord. But he by great treason hath set spies upon us and laid a great ambush to murder us by the way, and his men have assailed my brother here present and left him for dead. They set on me, too, to have slain me, but by the aid of our Lord Jesus Christ with my sword I so defended me that I slew him who thought to have slain us."

When the King had heard Huon he said:

"Vassal, beware and think well what thou sayest here before all my barons, for never in all my life have I done or consented to any treason. By the faith that I owe to Saint Denis, and by my beard, if it so be that thou canst not prove this that thou layest to my charge, I shall cause both thee and thy brother to die an evil death."

When Huon heard how the King took his words, he stepped forth and said:

"O thou King, behold here my brother, who by thee is sore hurt and in jeopardy of his life," and so did off his brother's gown and doublet to the shirt, and thus opened the great wound so that the blood ran out, and Gerard fell in a swoon before the King and the barons for the great pain that he felt.

Seeing this, the Emperor had such pity that his heart grew tender. Incontinently he sent for his surgeons, causing them to search the wound and asking them if they could save the youth's life. When they had well visited the wound they said:

" Sire,

" Sire, by the pleasure of God he shall be whole and sound within this month."

The King was glad of that answer and looked on Huon and said :

" Seeing thou layest this deed to my charge, by the faith that I owe to God and to Saint Denis, never in my life I sought to do this treason. By the glorious Saint James, and by the crown that I bear on my head, if I may know who hath done this I shall do so great justice that it shall be for ever a perpetual memory, and I shall do you such right that you shall have no cause to complain."

" Sire," quoth Huon, "I thank you, for in obeying your commandment this mischief has fallen to us, for I cannot think or know that at any time in my life my brother or I did wrong to any creature. Now, Sire, I shall show at length the manner of this deed."

"After that we departed from Bordeaux we found no adventure till when we came to Montleherault we met with our uncle, the Abbot of Cluny, and so fell in company with him to conduct us to your court. We rode together till we came on this side Montleherault near a little wood, where by the brightness of the sun we saw the helms and spears and shields of them that were ambushed in the wood. One came out of the wood all armed, his spear in his hand and his shield about his neck, and he came soft apace towards us. Then we all stood still, and

I sent

I sent my brother to the knight to know whether they were spies or men to keep the passage, to the intent that if they demanded any tribute they should have right of us, if they wished any from us. When my brother came near the knight he demanded what we were, and my brother said how we were the children of the Duke of Bordeaux and were coming by your commandment to your court to do homage for our lands and fees to your Grace. Then the knight said that we were the persons he sought for, since that seven years ago Duke Seguin our father had taken from him three castles; the which was never so. My brother offered him that if he would come to Paris before you and your barons, he should have right done to him, if he had suffered any wrong, but he answered that he would not do so, and therewith suddenly couched his spear, and struck my brother as you see; he being unarmed fell to the earth, and then the knight rode again fair and easily toward the wood, weening that he had slain him.

"When I saw my brother borne to the earth, I had such sorrow at my heart that I could tarry no longer to be avenged, so I asked of my uncle if he would aid me. He answered and said no, because he was a priest, so he and all his monks departed and left me alone. Then I took ten knights that came with me out of my country, and rode as fast as I could to the intent that he should not escape who had so wounded my brother, and as soon as he saw that I
31   followed

followed him he returned against me. I demanded
of him what he was, he said he pertained to Duke
Thierry of Ardayne: then I demanded why he had
slain my brother, and he answered that in like wise
he would serve me, and therewith he couched his
spear and struck me on the side through my gown
and doublet, and hurt not my flesh, as it was the
pleasure of God, so I wrapped my mantle about my
arm and drew out my sword, and with both my
hands, as he passed by me, gave him such a
stroke that I clove his head near to the teeth, and
he fell down to the earth dead. I know not what
he is, but whosoever he be I have slain him, and if
there be any that will demand right in this case, let
him come into your royal court before all your
peers, and I shall do him reason if it be found that
I have done any wrong. When I had slain him I
laid my brother on the dead man's horse and overtook the Abbot, mine uncle. As I rode I saw those
behind me that were ambushed in the wood come
riding after, and one knight came before and brought
upon his horse the said dead knight. I know well
they will soon be here, if they be not come."

When King Charlemagne understood Huon, he
had great marvel what knight it was that was slain,
and said to Huon:

"Know for truth I shall do you reason, for I
know none so great in my realm, whosoever it be,
if I can prove on him any point of treason, but I
32   shall

shall cause him to die an ill death. The matter toucheth me right near, since under my assurance and by my commandment ye are come hither."

Then the King commanded that Gerard should be taken to a goodly chamber and well looked to, the which was done.

As soon as Huon of Bordeaux and the Abbot of Cluny, his uncle, heard the goodwill of the King, and the offer that he had made, they kneeled down as to kiss his foot, and thanked him for his courtesy, but the King took them up. Then the Abbot said : "Sire, all that my nephew hath said is true."

The King said :

" I believe you well," and did to them honour and feasted them ; but he had a great desire to know the truth of this case and said :

" Huon and you, Abbot of Cluny, know for truth I have a son whom I entirely love : if you have slain him in doing such a vile deed as to break my safe-conduct, I do pardon you, so that it be as you say."

" Sire," quoth Huon, "for that I thank your Grace, and surely the truth is as I have shewed you."

Then the King sent for Charlot his son, so he was searched for in his lodging, and there it was said how he had departed out of the town the night before. So the messengers turned back, and when they came into the street they saw where the Earl Amaury came riding, with Charlot dead on his

33   c   horse's

horse's neck, and they heard in the streets lords, knights, ladies, and damsels making great cries and piteous complaints for Charlot, the King's son, whom they saw dead. By reason of the cry that the people made the noise thereof came to the palace, and King Charlemagne heard his son named. Then he said to Duke Naymes:

"Sir, I have great marvel what noise is it that is made in the town, and as methinks I hear my son Charlot named, certainly my heart misgiveth me that it is my son that Huon hath slain, wherefore I require you to go and know what the matter is."

Straightway Duke Naymes departed, and encountered Charlot borne dead on a shield between four knights. When he saw that, he was right sorrowful so that he could speak no word while the unhappy Earl Amaury went up into the hall, and came before the King and all his barons, and there he laid down Charlot. When Charles saw his son so slain the dolour and sorrow he made was unspeakable, it was pity to see him. Then Duke Naymes, seeing the pitiful adventure, and also the sorrow that the lords made, came to the King and said:

"Sire, strengthen yourself in this evil case; by taking this dolour you can win nothing, nor recover your child again. Sire, you know well that my cousin Ogier the Dane slew my son Bertrand, who bore your message of defiance to the King of Pavia,

yet

yet I did suffer it without any great sorrow-making, because I knew well that sorrow could not recover him again."

"Naymes," quoth the King, "I cannot forget this: I have great desire to know the cause of this deed."

Then Duke Naymes said to Earl Amaury:

"Sir, know you who hath slain Charlot, and for what cause?"

Then Earl Amaury stepped forth, and said with a loud voice:

"Sir King Charlemagne, what demand you any further when you have him before you that hath slain your son? and that is Huon of Bordeaux, who is sitting there in your presence."

When the King heard what the Earl Amaury had said, he looked fiercely on Huon, and would have struck him down with his knife had not Duke Naymes been there, who blamed the King and said:

"Ah, Sire, what think you to do this day, to receive the children of Duke Seguin into your court, and promise to do them right and reason, and you would slay them? So shall all such as hear of the matter say that you have sent for them to murder and to slay them, and that you sent your son to lie in wait for them to have them slain. Sire, by this I see in you now, you bear yourself not like a man, but rather like a child. Sire,

demand

demand of Earl Amaury the cause why he led forth Charlot your son, and why he assailed the two brethren."

Now Huon was greatly abashed at the King, who had received him so kindly, and now would slay him; and was in great fear, and as much as he might he drew back from the King, since he had slain his son unwittingly: and it was no marvel that he was sore troubled, for he saw near him no man of his kindred to aid him or to maintain his right except the Abbot of Cluny, his uncle, who could give him no aid but with his words. Then he took courage, and right humbly said to the King:

" Sire, I require your Grace touch me not, for, Sire, know for truth, I slew him that lieth there before you in my own defence, not knowing that he was your son Charlot. If I had known him I would in no wise have touched him, and, Sire, you may well think if I had known it had been he I would not have come to you for justice; I would rather have fled away so far that no man should have had any tidings of me. I submit my body to the judgment of your noble peers, and if it can be proved that I slew Charlot knowing him to be your son, then, Sire, let me have a shameful death."

Then all the peers and barons there present said with a loud voice that he had spoken reasonably, and that if the Earl Amaury would say anything to the contrary, it was time to speak and shew it.

CHAP. III.

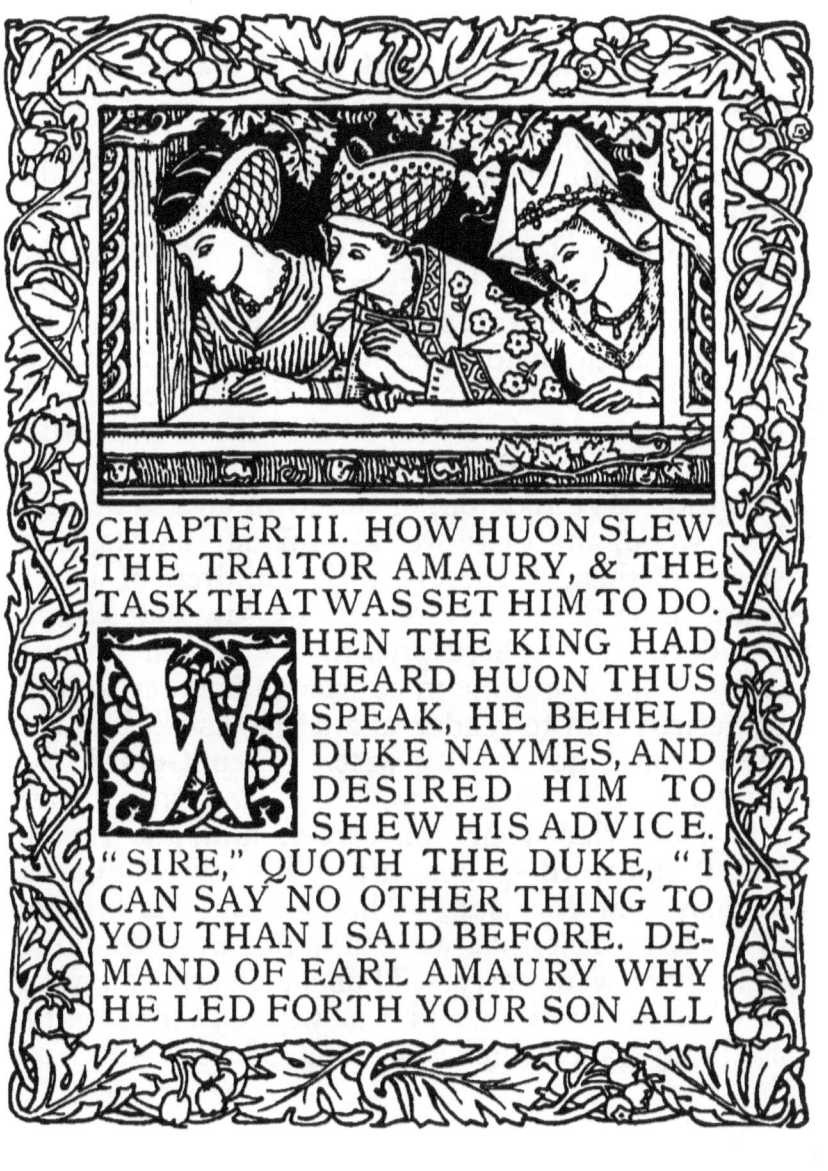

CHAPTER III. HOW HUON SLEW THE TRAITOR AMAURY, & THE TASK THAT WAS SET HIM TO DO.

WHEN THE KING HAD HEARD HUON THUS SPEAK, HE BEHELD DUKE NAYMES, AND DESIRED HIM TO SHEW HIS ADVICE. "SIRE," QUOTH THE DUKE, "I CAN SAY NO OTHER THING TO YOU THAN I SAID BEFORE. DEMAND OF EARL AMAURY WHY HE LED FORTH YOUR SON ALL armed, and laid an ambush in the wood to set on the two brethren, or else what was it that he sought for there."

Then Earl Amaury said:

"Sire, I shall shew you the truth, and if I do otherwise let me die a shameful death. This past night your son sent for me, desiring me to ride with him a-hawking, and I desired him to abide till the morning, but he said that he would needs go before night. Then I granted to go with him, so that he would ride armed, for I doubted the men of Arden, so that if we met with any of them we might be able to resist them; and so we did. We rode out of the town and came into a little wood, and there we cast off our hawks, and lost one of them. Therewith the children of Duke Seguin came the same way, and we saw that Huon, the eldest, who is here present, had taken up our hawk. Your son came in courteous manner to him and desired him to render again his hawk, but the traitor would not in any wise. Then Gerard, the younger brother, came to your son, and they strove so together that your son struck him, and Huon, without any word spoken, lift up his sword, and so piteously slew your son. Then he and his brother ran away so fast that we could not overtake him, whereof we were sorry. Thus he knew well your son when he slew him, and if he will say the contrary, here is my gage, which I lay down before you, and

if

if he be so hardy as to lift up my gage I shall make him confess it ere it be night that what I have said is true: and this I will prove, my body against his."

After that Earl Amaury had ended his tale, the Abbot of Cluny stepped forth and said to the King:

"Sire, you never heard so false a tale before as this traitor Amaury hath spoken, for I and four more of my monks, being priests here present, are ready to make solemn oath that the saying of this traitor is false, and therefore there ought no gage to be laid in the case, since there is true witness of the matter."

"Sir," quoth the King, "the witness is to be believed. Sir Amaury, how say you thereto?"

"Ah, Sire," quoth he, "I would be loth to speak against the Abbot, but the truth is as I have said. The Abbot may say as it please him, but if Huon be so hardy as to deny this that I have said before you, let him come into the field against me, and ere it be night I shall cause him to confess it openly."

When the Abbot heard that, he had great marvel, and beheld Huon and said:

"Fair nephew, offer your gage, for the right is with thee. If thou be vanquished in this quarrel, if ever I return to my abbey, there is no saint in my church but I shall with a staff beat and break to pieces; for if God will suffer such a wrong, I

shall

shall give such strokes upon the shrine of Saint Peter that I shall leave neither gold nor precious stone whole upon it."

"Sir," quoth Huon, "if God will I shall not hesitate to lift up his gage, for I shall prove that falsely and untruly Sir Amaury lieth, as a wicked and false traitor, and shall make him to confess that I never knew that he that I slew was the King's son."

Then the King said that Huon must give hostages.

"Sire," quoth Huon, "you shall have my brother; I cannot deliver you any that is so near me as he is, for I have neither cousin nor kinsman here that will lie in hostage for me."

"Fair nephew," quoth the Abbot, "say not so, for I and my monks will be pledges for you, and if anything shall fall to you otherwise than well, which God forbid, then shame have King Charlemagne, without he hang on the gallows both me and all my monks."

"Ah, Sir," quoth the King, "you say ill, for I would never do that;" then said the King to Amaury: "Sir, lay pledges for your part."

The traitor answered, "Sir, here be two of my nephews who shall be pledge for me."

"I am content," quoth the King, "on the condition that if thou be vanquished or discomfited I shall cause them to die an ill death."

40   Then

Then the pledges said they would be no pledges on that condition ; let others be pledges who would : but they said if the King would take them on the condition of losing their lands, they were content, and the King granted it them.

Thus as you have heard both parties delivered pledges, and the King to be in the more surety put them both in a tower till the time of battle ; then the field was prepared, for he had sworn that his son should not be buried until he that was vanquished was hanged, if he was not slain in the field. Duke Naymes was commanded to keep the field with a hundred knights, to see that no treason should be done, for the King said that he had rather lose the best city of his realm.

"Sire," quoth Duke Naymes, "by the pleasure of God the matter shall be ordered for the safety of both parties, so that none shall have wrong ; " the which thing was done so diligently that everything was ready.

So both parties were brought into the Church of Our Lady in Paris, accompanied by their friends, as is in such a case required, and with Amaury were all the genealogy of Ganelon. When they had both heard Mass they took a sup of wine, and then, richly armed and mounted on good horses, took their way to the field. The stages were ready, and the King and his barons there waiting for the two champions, who came one after another through

the

the streets. First came the Earl Amaury, and he rode till he came to the field, where he alighted and saluted the King and all his barons; then Huon came after accompanied by a goodly sort.

There were ladies and damsels a great number, leaning in windows, who all prayed our Lord Jesus Christ to aid and defend Huon from the traitor Amaury; the people complained, and thought it impossible that Huon should resist Earl Amaury, because he was so fair and young, but of the age of four and twenty years. Now Huon was so fair and well made of body that he could not be amended, therefore he was sore bemoaned both of men and women that saw him pass by, because Earl Amaury was a big man and a valiant, and an expert man in arms, none stronger in all the King's court: pity it was that he was such a traitor, for a worse could not be found in any realm. He had great trust in his own strength, and little appraised Huon of Bordeaux, thinking he should not long endure before him: but there is a common proverb, which hath beguiled many a man, "A little rain abateth a great wind." If our Lord Jesus Christ will save Huon, the force and puissance of Earl Amaury shall do Huon but small hurt; and the right excellent properties and great courage that was in Huon defended him, as you shall hereafter hear.

So Huon came into the field and saluted the King and all the barons right humbly, and approached
the

the relics, and there made his solemn oath, in the presence of Duke Naymes of Bavaria, who was keeper of the field, affirming that never in his life did he know Charlot the King's son before he had slain him, and all that Earl Amaury had said was false and untrue, and that he lied like a false traitor; and so he kissed the relics. When Huon had thus made his oath, Earl Amaury stepped forth all afraid, and swore that Huon's oath was false, and that he knew that it was Charlot when he slew him, because he claimed his hawk which Huon had taken up, and that, he said, he would cause him to confess ere night. When he had sworn he thought to have returned to his horse, and stumbled so that he had near hand fallen to the earth: and all that saw it took it for an evil sign, and judged in their minds that the matter was like to go ill against the Earl Amaury.

When both the champions had made their oaths, and Duke Naymes had caused the field to be cleared, and had set the keepers of the field in due order as it appertained, the champions leaped on their horses, their spears in their hands, and their shields about their necks: and a cry was made that none should be so hardy as to move or make any token to either of the parties, upon pain of death. After that, the noble Emperor Charlemagne, full of ire and displeasure, caused it to be cried that if the vanquisher should slay his enemy in the field before he confessed

43   the

the treason of the death of his son, the conqueror should lose all his lands, and be banished from the realm of France and the empire of Rome for ever. Then Duke Naymes and the other peers and barons came to the King and said:

"Ah, Sire, what will you do? This thing is against the statute of the noble realm of France and of the empire of Rome; ofttimes it happeth that one of the champions is slain and hath no puissance to speak. Your great renown, which so long time has been spread abroad, shall be quenched or blemished; it shall be said that you, who have lived in so great triumph all the days of your life, now, in your latter days, are become a child."

But of these words the King took small regard, for when he had heard Duke Naymes, he swore by Saint Denis of France, and by his crown and beard, that it should be as he had said, nor otherwise would he do it. Then the noble barons were sorry and sore displeased, and they departed from the King, saying that by all likelihood right should have no place in his court from thenceforth: and many noble princes and barons murmured sore at the cry that was made.

Meanwhile these two champions drew apart, and each of them fiercely looked on the other: then Earl Amaury spake aloud and said:

"Thou Huon of Bordeaux, false traitor knight, this day I shall cause thee to confess thy falseness; how-

beit

beit I have great pity on thee, I see thee so young. If thou wilt confess this murder that thou hast done, I shall desire King Charlemagne to have mercy upon thee."

When Huon heard the traitor so speak, he blushed red for anger, and said :

"Ah, thou false glutton and evil traitor, thy venemous words full of bitterness do no whit abash me, for the good right that I am in shall aid me by the help of our Lord Jesus Christ; I shall so punish thy trespass that this day I shall make thee to confess thy falseness, have thereof no doubt."

Therewith they couched their spears and dashed at each other with their horses, so that it seemed like thunder had fallen from heaven ; and with their sharp spears they encountered in such wise that their spears brake to their hands, so that the slivers flew high into the air, and on to the King's seat, and both their horses fell to the ground. Sore stunned as they were with their fall, both knights raised themselves with their swords in their hands, and approached each other, and so fought. But Huon's horse strangled Sir Amaury's, and when he saw his horse slain, the Earl stepped forward to kill Huon's. Then Huon stepped between them, and lifted up his sword and gave the Earl such a stroke that he was near stunned, and recoiled two paces and more, nearly falling to the earth. And all that saw them,

marvelled

marvelled at Huon's courage and strength seeing the great strength of Sir Amaury.

When the Earl felt himself in great pain he began to despise the name of God and of the glorious Virgin Mary; howbeit, as well as he might he approached Huon, and with his sword gave him such a stroke on the helm that all the flowers and precious stones there flew abroad on the field, and the circlet of the helm was all destroyed. The stroke was so mighty that Huon was therewith stunned, and by force was beaten to one knee on the earth. One of the Abbot of Cluny's servants, when he saw the great stroke that Huon had received, departed out of the field, and went into the church where he found his master the Abbot at prayers for the good speed of Huon his nephew. Then the varlet said :

"Ah, Sir, pray heartily to our Lord Jesus Christ to succour your nephew, for I saw him fain to kneel upon one of his knees in great doubt of death."

Then the good Abbot without any answer lifted up his hands devoutly to heaven, weeping and praying to God to aid and defend the honour of his nephew and to maintain his right.

Thus Huon, being in the field in great doubt of his life, feeling the force of the Earl Amaury, he called with a good heart to our Lord Jesus Christ, requiring Him to aid his right, the which He knew that it was true. But Earl Amaury, when he saw

that

that Huon had received such a heavy stroke, said to him :

"Huon, I believe thou wilt not endure long, it were better that thou confess the deed ere I slay thee. To-night thou shalt wave in the wind."

"Hold thy tongue, thou false traitor," quoth Huon, "thine evil shall not aid thee, for I shall bring thee to that point that all thy friends shall have shame of thee."

Then Huon advanced and made a show to have struck Amaury on the helm, so Amaury lifted up his shield to receive the stroke ; but when Huon saw that, he turned his stroke to a reverse, and struck Amaury under the arm with his sword, so that he cut off his arm, which fell down into the field, shield and all.

When Earl Amaury saw and felt that marvellous stroke, how he had lost his left arm, lying there in the field, he was full of pain and sorrow, and thought of a great treason. He spake to Huon, and said :

"Ah, noble knight, have pity on me, for wrong-fully and without cause I have accused you of the death of Charlot the King's son; but I know the truth, you knew him not, but he is dead by my means, for I brought him to the wood to murder you and your brother. I am ready to own this before the King and his barons, and to clear you thereof ; I pray you, slay me not, I yield me to you—here is my sword."

47   Then

Then Huon came to him and put out his arm to take it, but the false traitor Amaury, with a reverse stroke hit Huon on the arm, thinking to strike it off, but he failed. Howbeit, he gave him a great wound in the arm, so that the blood fell.

Then Huon lifted up his sword and gave the Earl such a marvellous stroke between the helm and the shoulder that he struck his head clean off from the body, so that the helm and head fell one way and the body another way. Alas, what hap it was to Huon that he did not remember the cry that the Emperor had made before he slew Amaury, for after he suffered so much pain and labour that there is no clerk can write it or bring it to memory. And thus Huon slew the Earl Amaury.

When Duke Naymes who kept the field saw how the Earl was slain by Huon, he was right joyful and came to Huon and asked him how he did.

" Sir," quoth he, " thanked be God I feel no pain or grief."

So they brought him to the palace to the King, who had departed out of the field when he saw the Earl slain, and was thereof right sorrowful. Charles demanded of Huon and of Duke Naymes if they had heard Earl Amaury confess the treason that he had laid to Huon for the deed of Charlot his son.

" Sire," said the duke, " I think he did confess it, but I heard it not for Huon pressed so sore on him that he had no leisure to do it."

48   Then

Then Charlemagne said :

" Ah, Earl Amaury, I know certainly thou never didst that treason, nor thought it, wherefore thou art slain wrongfully and without a cause : there was never a truer knight than thou wert, for I am sure if thou hadst done it, thou wouldst have confessed it before me."

Then turning to Huon, he said :

" I charge thee at once to leave my realm, out of which I banish thee for ever : thou shalt never enjoy one foot of land in Bordeaux nor in Aquitaine ; and also I forbid thee to go to Bordeaux, for by my lord Saint Denis, if I know that thou goest there I shall make thee to die an ill death.   And there is no man living, though he is never so near a friend to me, if he make any request for thee I shall never love him, nor shall he after come into my sight."

" Sire, how is it?" quoth Huon.   " Have I not done my duty, seeing that before you and all your barons I have discomfited in open battle him that brought you into all this trouble ?   Sire, certainly if you do to me as you say, I shall complain me to God, for never more wrong was done to any noble man.   Ill you remember the good service that the noble Duke Seguin my father hath done to you. By this you shew a great example to all your noble barons and knights for them to be well advised how from henceforth they should order themselves, and how to trust in you : since by your single opinion,

49   D   founded

founded on an evil ground and against all statutes royal and imperial, you would execute your own unreasonable will. Certainly if it were another prince beside you that would do me this great wrong, before I would consent to be so dealt with, many a castle and many a good town should be destroyed and brought to ruin, many poor men destroyed and disinherited, and many a knight brought to death."

When Huon had thus spoken to the King, Duke Naymes stepped forth and spake to him :

"Sire, what think you to do? You have seen that Huon had done his devoir when he had brought his enemy to outrance, and slain him. You may well think it is the work of God when such a youth should bring to outrance, and discomfit such a puissant knight as was the Earl Amaury. Sire, if you do as you have said, neither I nor any other man shall trust you, and every man, far and near, that heareth of thine extortion shall say that in the end of your days you are become childish, and more like a sot than a wise man."

Then Huon desired all the barons that were there present to require the King to have mercy on him, seeing they were all bound to do so, in that he was one of the peers of the realm, and all the princes and barons, holding Huon by the hand, kneeled down before the King, and Huon said :

"Sire, seeing your Grace to hate me so sore as you speak of, I require you here at the request of all

your

your barons, that you will grant me that I may abide in my own country for ever and never come into your sight, and in this I require your Grace of mercy."

" Avoid thee from my sight," quoth the Emperor, " for when I remember my son Charlot whom thou hast slain, I have no member on me but that trembleth for the enmity I bear thee, and I charge all my barons here present that they never speak to me more for thee."

When Duke Naymes heard the King thus speak, he said to all the barons :

" Sirs, ye that be here present have well heard the great unreasonableness the King offers to one of our peers—against right and reason, and not to be suffered. But because we know for certain the King is our sovereign lord, we must suffer his pleasure. From henceforth, since he will use himself to do things against reason and honour, I will not abide an hour longer with him, but will depart and never return again to a place where such extortion and unreasonableness is used : I will go into my country of Bavaria, and let the King do from henceforth as he listeth."

Then all the barons departed with the duke from the King without speaking any word, and so left the King alone in his palace.

When the King saw the duke depart with his other lords, he was right sorrowful and in great dis-

51   pleasure

pleasure, and said to the young knights that were left about him how that he ought greatly to be grieved for the death of his son, who was slain so piteously, and also for the way his barons had abandoned him and left him alone ; then he said openly :

"I see well I am forced somewhat to follow their wills," and therewith he wept piteously.

Incontinent he marched forth and followed them and said :

"Duke Naymes and all ye my barons, I require you to return again, for of force I must grant your desires, though it be against the promise that I made before."

Then the duke and all the others returned to the palace with the King, who sat down on a bench of gold, and his barons about him, and sent for Huon, who kneeled down before the King, requiring him humbly of mercy and pity.

The King said :

" Huon, seeing thou wouldst be agreed with me, it must behove thee to do what I command and ordain."

" Sire," quoth Huon, "to obey you there is no thing in this mortal world that any human body may do, but that I shall undertake to do it; not staying for fear of death, though it be to go to THE DRY TREE, yea, or to hell gates to fight with the fiends there, as once did Hercules, if I may thereby be reconciled with your Grace."

" Huon," quoth the King, " I think to send thee
into

into a worse place, for of fifteen messengers that I have sent, there was never one returned again. I shall shew thee whither thou shalt go, seeing thou wilt that I have mercy on thee."

"Thou must go to the city of Babylon to the Admiral Gaudys, and shew him what I shall declare to thee; beware on pain of thy life, fail not to do it. When thou art come there, mount up into his palace, and there tarry till he be at his dinner, and when thou seest him sit at the table, arm thyself with thy sword naked in thy hand, and look, the greatest lord that thou seest at his table, whether he be King or Admiral, thou must strike off his head, then thou shalt affiance and kiss three times the fair. Claramond, daughter to the Admiral Gaudys, openly in his presence and before all other there present, for I will that thou shouldst know she is the fairest maid now living; and after that thou shalt say to the Admiral Gaudys that I command him to send me a thousand hawks, a thousand bears, and a thousand boarhounds all chained, a thousand young varlets, and a thousand of the fairest maidens in the realm. Bring me also thy hand full of the hair of his beard, and four of his greatest teeth."

"Ah, Sire," quoth the barons, "we see well that you desire greatly his death when you charge him with such a message."

"That is true," quoth the King, "for without I have his beard and his great teeth without deceit or trick,

53   let

let him never return into France, nor come into my presence, for if he do he shall be hanged and drawn."

"Sire," quoth Huon, "have you shewed me all your pleasure?"

"Yea," quoth the King, "my will is as I have said, if thou wilt have peace with me."

"By the grace of God," quoth Huon, "I shall deliver your message, the fear of death shall not hinder me from doing it."

"Huon," quoth the King, "if God of his grace should suffer thee to return again into France, I charge thee, be not so bold as come to Bordeaux or to any part of thy country till thou hast spoken with me: if I find thee doing the contrary, I shall cause thee to die an ill death. And upon this I will that thou layest unto me good hostages."

"Sire," quoth Huon, " here be ten knights whom I shall leave with you for security, to the intent that thou shalt be content with me. Howbeit, Sire, I require your Grace to suffer the knights that came with me from Bordeaux to go with me to the Holy Sepulchre."

"I am content," quoth the King, "that they go with thee to the Red Sea."

"Sire," quoth Huon, "I thank your Grace."

Then Huon made him ready to furnish his voyage.

After that Charlemagne had given Huon the charge of his message, the King called Gerard before him, and delivered to him the governance of all his

brother's

brother's lands in his absence till his return. When Huon was ready he came to the King and to the ^T barons to take his leave, and the Abbot of Cluny said he would go with him part of his way, and twelve of the greatest princes and ladies conveyed him a two days' journey. When they came to the town of Troyes in Champagne Duke Naymes took leave of his cousin Huon, and gave him a sumpter charged with gold, and kissed him at their parting: then Gerard his brother took his leave, and also kissed him, but know for truth that the kiss he gave him was like the kiss that Judas gave to our Lord God; and dearly was it bought, as ye shall after hear. While Duke Naymes and Gerard departed and took their way to Paris the Abbot and Huon rested not till they came to the Abbey of Cluny, where they were received with great joy and well feasted. Next morning, Huon departed, and took leave of his uncle sore weeping, desiring him that he might be commended to his mother the duchess, and to Gerard his brother. The Abbot promised so to do, and gave Huon his nephew a mule charged with money current in France; thus he departed and took the way to Rome. Now leave we to speak of Huon, and tell of Duke Naymes and Gerard who returned to Paris.

There Gerard required the King that it would please him to receive his homage for the lands of Bordeaux, to the intent that he might be advanced

55   to

to the state of one of the peers of France, the which thing Duke Naymes would not consent unto nor agree to it. He said to the King:

"Sire, you ought not to suffer that Huon should be disinherited:" whereof Gerard was not content. But Duke Naymes set little thereby, for he believed Huon fully; so this homage was delayed, and Gerard returned to Bordeaux, where he was well received. When the duchess saw him return without Huon, she was sorrowful in her heart, and demanded of Gerard why Huon his brother did not return with him. Then Gerard showed her all the whole matter and adventure and the departure of Huon, and the manner of his voyage, whereof the duchess had such sorrow that she fell sick, and so lay twenty-nine days, and on the thirtieth day she died, and rendered up her soul to God, whereof all the country was sorrowful, and Gerard nobly buried her in the Church of Saint Severine beside the duke her husband. Soon after he married him to the daughter of Duke Guibert of Sicily, who was the greatest traitor, and most cruel, that might be heard of: and Gerard his son-in-law learned his ways and followed his condition, for he dealt so ill with the town of Bordeaux and with the country about, that it was pity to hear the poor people weep for the loss of Duke Seguin and the duchess, and pray to God for the good return of their lord Huon. Now we leave to speak of them, and speak of Huon.

CHAP. IV.

CHAPTER IV. HOW HUON PASSED
THE SEA AND MET OLD GERAMES.
EREBEFORE YE HAVE
HEARD HOW HUON
DEPARTED FROM HIS
UNCLE THE ABBOT OF
CLUNY, AND RODE
WITH HIS KNIGHTS
TILL HE CAME TO THE CITY OF
ROME, AND THERE HE WAS
LODGED IN A GOOD HOSTELRY.
HE ROSE IN THE MORNING AND

went to the Church of Saint Peter and heard Mass, accompanied by Guichard, whom he loved well, and with the other knights that came thither with him, and when the Mass was done, the Pope came out of the oratory. Then Huon came to him and humbly saluted him. The Pope beheld him and demanded who he was.

" Sir," quoth he," " my father was Duke Seguin of Bordeaux, who is deceased."

Then the Pope stepped to him and said :

" Fair nephew, you are welcome ; I pray you shew me how my sister, the duchess your mother, doth, and what adventure hath brought your hither."

" Sir," quoth he, " I require your holiness to hear my confession apart, for I have great need thereof."

" Fair nephew," quoth the Pope, " it pleases me right well to hear you :" and he took him by the hand and went with him into his oratory. There Huon showed him all that had happened since he came from Bordeaux, and of the voyage that Charlemagne had set him to do and to say to the Admiral Gaudys. When he had all shewed he required pardon and peace for his sins, and the Pope said that he would give him no other penance than what King Charles had given him, which was so great that no human body could suffer it, or durst think to do it ; and then gave him absolution for his sins.

After that the Pope led him into his palace, where he was honourably received with great joy : but

after

after they had dined and talked together a great space, the Pope said to Huon:

"Fair nephew, the way you must go is by the Port of Brindisi; there shall you find my brother Garyn of Saint Omers, who is your uncle, to whom I shall write a letter to the intent that he shall have knowledge of you, for I know well he shall have great joy of you. He hath the keeping of the Eastern Sea, and shall deliver you ships or galleys such as shall be necessary for you."

"Holy Father," quoth Huon, "for this I thank thee."

"Well," quoth the Pope, "this night you shall abide here with me."

"Sir," quoth he, "I require you to let me depart, for greatly I desire to see my uncle Garyn."

When the Pope saw that he would needs depart, he delivered him his letter, and said:

"Fair nephew, salute from me my brother Garyn, your uncle."

"Sir," quoth he, "I shall do your commandment."

Then the Pope gave great and rich presents to Huon, and to all that were with him, and kissed his nephew at parting. Huon took leave of him all weeping, and so departed, and entered into a rich ship in the river Tiber, which the Pope had well garnished for him.

He had good wind, and so arrived soon at Brindisi, but whilst he was on the water he wept sore and piteously complained that he was so driven out of

his

his country, but his men comforted him, and shewed him many fair examples to strengthen him.

"Sir," quoth Guichard, "leave your sorrow, for it cannot avail you. You must leave all to the mercy of our Lord God, who never forgetteth them that love Him. Shew yourself a man and no child, to the intent that we that be with you may be rejoiced, for the sorrow that we see you in doth sore trouble us."

"Sir," quoth Huon, "since it is so I shall follow your will."

When they arrived at the port of Brindisi, they issued out of their ship, and took out their horses, and there they saw Garyn before the gate, in a lodge well and richly hanged, sitting in a rich chair. When Huon saw him he saluted him, thinking he was lord of that country, but when Garyn beheld Huon he began to weep, and said:

"It pertaineth not to me, that you should do me so great honour as you do, for by that I see in you I am constrained to weep. You resemble much a prince of the realm of France called Duke Seguin, who was lord of the city of Bordeaux; and the great love I had to him causeth me to weep. I require you tell me where you were born, and who are your parents and friends, for Duke Seguin wedded my sister the Duchess Aclis."

"Sir," quoth Huon, "seeing you will know who I am, I may well shew it you, for the duke was my father and the Duchess Aclis was my mother,
60   and

and we be two brethren. I am the elder and the
younger is still at Bordeaux to keep the lands."

When Garyn understood that Huon was son to
Duke Seguin of Bordeaux the joy that he shewed
cannot be expressed, and he embraced Huon in
tears, and said :

" Right dear nephew, your coming is to me the
greatest joy in this world ;" then he kneeled down
and would have kissed Huon's feet, but Huon
raised him on the spot, and the joy that was between
them two was so great that all who saw it marvelled.
Then Garyn demanded of Huon, and said :

" Fair nephew, what adventure hath brought you
into these parts ?"

And Huon shewed him from point to point all his
business, and, the cause why he had entered on that
undertaking. When Garyn had heard all he began
to weep, and yet to comfort his nephew he said :

" Fair nephew, where lieth great peril, there lies
great honour. God aid you to achieve and finish
this great business; all is possible to God, and to
man by means of His grace. A man should never
be abashed for worldly matters."

Then Huon delivered his letters to his uncle
Garyn, who gladly received them, and read the
contents thereof at length, and said :

" Fair nephew, there needed none other recom-
mendation but the sight of your presence, for it
appeareth well that you be the same person that
61   our

our Holy Father maketh mention of : surely your coming seemeth to me fair and good, and you be arrived at a good port. I promise you faithfully I love well my wife and children, but for the great love I have to you on account of your father Duke Seguin and the duchess your mother, who was mine own dear sister, I abandon all that I have to serve you and keep you company, both with my body and all that I have. Know for truth I have three good galleys and three great ships well furnished for the wars, which I shall lead with you ; as long as life abideth in my body I shall not abandon you, but I shall aid you in all your enterprises."

" Fair uncle," quoth Huon, "for the great courtesy you offer me I thank you."

So Garyn took Huon by the hand and led him into his castle, where he was richly received, and Garyn's wife and four of her sons came to Huon, and he full courteously kissed the lady and her four children, his cousins. Great joy was made there in the hall, and the tables set for supper, and Garyn called the lady, his wife, and said to her :

" Dame, this young man that you see here is my nephew, and cousin to your children : he is come hither for refuge to have counsel and aid of me in a voyage and enterprise that he hath to do, and by the grace of God I shall go with him to aid and conduct him ; wherefore I pray and command that you take in rule all my affairs and keep your children."

" Sir,"

"Sir," quoth she, "seeing it is your pleasure so to do, and that you will go with him, your pleasure shall be mine, howbeit I rather you had abode than went:" and this she spoke sore weeping.

The next day in the morning Garyn, who had great will to serve and please his nephew, ordered a great ship to be made ready well furnished with biscuit, wines and flesh, and all other manner of victuals, and with munitions of war as it appertained, and put therein their horses and armour, gold and silver, and other riches necessary for them. Then they took leave of the lady, and so left her sore weeping. Thus Garyn and Huon entered into their ship, and all their company, being thirteen knights and two varlets to serve them ; they would have no greater number.

When Huon and Garyn were entered into their ship, they hoisted their sails and sailed night and day, so that they arrived safely at the port of Jaffa ; there they took land and drew out their horses, and rode forth, so the same day they came to Ramah, and the next day to the city of Jerusalem. That night they rested, and on the morrow they did their pilgrimage to the Holy Sepulchre, and there devoutly heard Mass and offered according to their devotion. When Huon came before the Holy Sepulchre he knelt down on his bare knees, and all weeping made his prayer to our Lord God, requiring Him to aid and comfort him in his voyage, so that

63   he

he might return again into France, and have peace with King Charlemagne. And when they had all made their prayers and offered, Huon and Garyn went into a little chapel on the Mount of Calvary, where now lyeth Godfrey of Bouillon and Baldwin his brother. Then Huon called to him all those that came with him out of France, and said :

"Sirs, ye that for the love of me have left fathers and mothers, wives and children, and lands and seignories, for this courtesy that ye have shewed me I thank you. Now ye may return into France, and recommend me to the King's good grace, and to all the other barons ; and when you come to Bordeaux, recommend me to the duchess my mother, and to Gerard my brother, and to the lords of my country."

Thereupon Guichard and all the other knights answered Huon and said :

"Sir, as yet we will not leave you, till we have brought you to the Red Sea."

"For the great service and courtesy ye offer me," quoth Huon, "I thank you."

Then Garyn called two of his servants and commanded them to return to his wife, and desire her to be of good cheer for shortly he would return : the which thing they did, and returned and did their message. When Huon understood that his uncle Garyn was disposed to abide with him he said :

"Fair uncle, you shall not need to travail so
64   much ;

much ; I would counsel you to return to your wife and children."

" Sir," quoth Garyn, " if God will, I shall not leave you till you return yourself."

" Uncle," quoth Huon, " I thank you for your courtesy."

So they went to their lodgings and dined, and after dinner took their horses and so rode by hills and dales, and many an adventure they found by the way ; and as the story telleth, they suffered much pain and travail, for they passed through deserts where they found but small sustenance. Thereof was Huon right sorrowful, for the love of them that were with him, and he began to weep and to remember his own country, saying :

" Alas, noble King of France, great wrong and great sin you have done, thus to drive me out of my country and send me into strange lands, to the intent to shorten my days. I pray God pardon you thereof."

Then Garyn and the other knights comforted him and said :

" Ah, Sir, dismay you not for us, God is puissant enough to aid us, He never failed them that love Him."

Thus they rode forth in the desert till at last they saw a little cottage, before which sat an old ancient man, with a long white beard, and his hair hanging over his shoulders. When Huon perceived him he

65   E   drew

drew thither and saluted the old man in the name of God and of the Blessed Virgin Saint Mary ; and the ancient man lifted up his eyes and beheld Huon, and had great marvel, for a great season before he had seen no man that spake of God. When he beheld Huon in the visage he began to weep sore, and stepping to him, he took him by the leg and kissed it more than twenty times.

"Friend," quoth Huon, "I require you shew me why you make this sorrow."

"Sir," quoth he, "thirty years past I came hither, and since that time I never saw man believing in the Christian faith. Now your visage causeth me to remember a noble prince that I have seen in France, who was called Duke Seguin of Bordeaux ; shew me, I require you, if ever you saw him, I pray you hide it not from me."

"Friend," quoth Huon, "I pray you shew me where you were born, and of what lineage and country you be."

"Nay, Sir," quoth he, "that will I not do first ; you shall shew me what ye be, and where ye were born, and why ye come hither."

"Friend," quoth Huon, "seeing it pleases you to know, I shall show you."

Then Huon and all his company alighted and tied their horses to trees.

When Huon was alighted, he sat down by the old man and said :

"Friend,

" Friend, seeing you will know my business, I will shew it you. Know for truth I was born in the city of Bordeaux, and am son to Duke Seguin."

Then Huon shewed him all his whole case, and the death of Charlot, and how he discomfited Earl Amaury, and how that Charlemagne had chased him out of France, and the message that he was charged with to the Admiral Gaudys : " This that I have shewed you is truth."

When the old man had well heard Huon, he began to weep.

" Sir," quoth Huon, " seeing it pleaseth you to know of my sorrow, Duke Seguin my father is dead seven years past, my mother I trust is alive, and a brother of mine whom I had left with her. And now, Sir, seeing you have heard of my affairs, I require you give me your counsel and advice, and also if it please you, shew me what ye be, and of what country, and how you came into these parts."

" Sir," quoth the old man, " know for truth I was born in Geronville, and was brother to the good provost Guyer.

" When I departed thence I was a young knight and haunted jousts and tourneys ; so that on a day it fortuned that at a tourney that was made at Poictiers I slew a knight of noble blood, wherfore I was banished out of the realm of France. But my brother the provost made such request to Duke Seguin your father, that by his means my peace was

made with the King, and my land saved on the condition that I should go a pilgrimage to the Holy
Sepulchre to pray for the soul of the knight that I
slew, and to forgive my sins. So I departed from
my country, and when I had done my pilgrimage I
thought to return, but as I came out of the city of
Jerusalem to take the way to Acre, passing by a
wood between Jerusalem and Nablous, there came
upon me ten Saracens, who took me and brought me
to the city of Babylon, where I was in prison two
years, and suffered much poverty and misery. But
our Lord God, Who never faileth them that serve
Him, and have in Him full trust, sent me the grace
that by the means of a right noble lady I was brought
out of prison by night, and so I fled into this forest,
where I have been these thirty years. In all this
time I have not seen nor heard man believing on
our Lord Jesus Christ. Thus I have shewed you
all my affair."

When Huon had heard the knight's tale, he had
great joy, and embraced him and said how often he
" had seen Guyer, his brother the provost, weep for
you ; and when I departed from Bordeaux I delivered
to him all my lands to govern, wherefore I require
you shew me your name."

" Sir," quoth he, " I am called Gerames, and now
I pray you shew me your name."

" Sir," quoth he, " I am named Huon, and my
younger brother is called Gerard. But, Sir, I pray
68   you

you shew me how you have so long lived here, and
what sustenance you have."

"Sir," quoth Gerames, "I have eaten none other thing but roots and fruits that I have found in the wood."

Then Huon demanded of him if he could speak the Saracen language.

"Yea, Sir," quoth he, "as well or better than any Saracen in the country, nor is there no way but I know it."

When Huon had heard Gerames he demanded further of him if they could go to Babylon.

"Yea, Sir," quoth Gerames, "I can go thither by two ways; the safest way is a forty days' journey, and the other is but fifteen days'. Yet I counsel you to take the long way, for if you take the shorter way you must pass through a wood, sixteen leagues in length; but the way is so full of magic and strange things that such as pass that way are lost. In that wood abideth the King of Fairyland named Oberon: he is but three feet high, and crooked shouldered, but he hath an angelic visage, so that there is no mortal man that seeth him but that taketh great pleasure in beholding his face. You shall no sooner be entered into that wood, if you go that way, but he will find the way to speak with you, and if you speak to him you are lost for ever: and you will ever find him before you so that it shall be in a manner impossible that you can escape from him without
69   speaking

speaking to him, for his words are so pleasant to hear that there is no mortal man that can well escape without speaking to him.

"If he see that you will not speak a word to him, he will be sore displeased with you, and ere you can get out of the wood he will cause rain and wind, hail and snow, and he will make marvellous tempests with thunder and lightning, so that it shall seem to you that all the world shall perish; and you shall see before you a great running river, black and deep. But you may pass it at your ease, and it shall not wet the feet of your horse, for all is but fantasy and enchantment that the dwarf has made, to the intent to have you with him, and if you can keep yourself without speaking to him, you may then well escape. But, Sir, to eschew all perils, I counsel you to take the longer way, for I think you cannot escape from him, and then are you lost for ever."

When Huon had well heard Gerames he had great marvel, and great desire in himself to see that dwarf king of the fairies, and the strange adventures that were in the wood : so he said to Gerames that for any fear of death he would not leave that way, seeing he might come to Babylon in fifteen days; for in taking the longer way he might perchance find more adventures, and since he was forewarned that with keeping his tongue from speaking he might abridge his journey, he said that he would surely go that way, whatsoever befell.

"Sir,"

"Sir," quoth Gerames, "you shall do your pleasure, for which ever way you take, it shall not be without me; I shall bring you to Babylon to the Admiral Gaudys, I know him right well, and when you be come thither you shall see there a damsel, the fairest in all India as I have heard say, and the sweetest and most courteous that ever was born: she it is that you seek, for she is daughter to the Admiral Gaudys."

When Huon had heard how Gerames was minded to go with him, he was thereof right joyful, and thanked him for his courtesy and service, and gave him a goodly horse, whereon he mounted. So they rode together until they came to the wood to the place which King Oberon haunted most. There Huon was weary of travail, and famine, and heat, for he and his company had endured two days without bread or meat, so that he was so feeble that he could ride no further. Then he began piteously to weep, and complained of the great wrong that King Charlemagne had done to him, but Garyn and Cerames comforted him and had great pity on him, for they knew well that by reason of his youth hunger oppressed him more than it did them of greater age, so they alighted under a great oak to search for some fruit to eat, and let their horses go to pasture.

While they were thus alighted, the dwarf of the fairies, King Oberon, came riding by, wearing a gown so rich that it were marvel to recount the

riches

riches and fashion thereof, and garnished with precious stones whose clearness shone like the sun. He had a goodly bow in his hand so rich that it could not be esteemed, and his arrows after the same sort, and these had such a property that they could hit any beast in the world he wished for. Moreover he had about his neck a rich horn, hung by two laces of gold so rich and fair that never was seen such a one: it was made by four fairies in the island of Cephalonia. One of them gave to the horn this power, that whosoever heard the sound thereof, if he were in the greatest sickness in the world, he should forthwith be whole and sound : the lady that gave this power to the horn was called Gloriande. The second lady was called Transeleyne; she gave to this horn the power that whosoever heard it, if he were in the greatest famine in the world, he should be satisfied as well as if he had eaten all that he could wish for, and likewise for drink as well as if he had drunk his fill of the best wine in the world. The third lady, named Margale, gave to this horn a yet greater gift, and that was that whosoever heard it, though he were never so poor or feeble or sick, he should have such joy in his heart that he should sing and dance. The fourth lady, named Lempatrix, gave to this horn such a gift, that whosoever heard it, if he were a hundred days' journey off, should come at the pleasure of him that blew it, far or near. So King Oberon, who knew well, and had seen the

fourteen

fourteen companions, set his horn to his mouth and blew so melodious a blast, that the fourteen, being under the tree, had so perfect a joy at their hearts that they all rose up and began to sing and dance.

"Ah," quoth Huon, "what fortune is come to us? Methinks we are in Paradise. Right now I could not sustain myself for lack of meat and drink, and now I feel myself neither hungry nor thirsty: from whence may this come?"

"Sir," quoth Gerames, "know for truth this is done by the dwarf of the fairies, whom ye shall soon see pass by you. But, Sir, I require you on jeopardy of your life that you speak to him no word, without you purpose to abide ever with him."

"Have you no doubt of me," quoth Huon, "seeing I know the jeopardy."

Therewith the dwarf began to cry aloud, and said:

"Ye fourteen men that pass by my wood, God keep you all. I desire you to speak with me, and I conjure you thereto by Almighty God, and by the Christendom that you have received, and by all that God has made, answer me."

CHAP. V.

CHAPTER V. HOW KING OBERON
GAVE HUON A CUP AND HORN, &
HOW HE MADE USE OF THEM.

HEARING THE DWARF
SPEAK, HUON AND
HIS COMPANY MOUN
TED THEIR HORSES,
AND RODE AWAY AS
FAST AS THEY WERE
ABLE, NOT SPEAKING ANY
WORD, AND THE DWARF WAS
SORROWFUL AND ANGRY, SEE-
ING THEM RIDE AWAY, SO HE

set one of his fingers on his horn, out of which there issued a wind and a tempest so great that it bore down the trees. Therewith came a great rain and hailstorm, and it seemed that heaven and earth had fought together, and that the world should be ended : the beasts in the woods brayed and cried, and the fowls of the air fell down dead for the fear that they were in ; all creatures were afraid in that great tempest. Then suddenly a great river appeared before them that ran swifter than the birds did fly ; and the water was black and perilous, and made such a noise that it might be heard ten leagues away.

"Alas," quoth Huon, "I see well that we be all lost, we shall here be oppressed without God have pity on us : I repent me that ever I entered into this wood, I had better have travelled a whole year than have come hither."

"Dismay you not," quoth Gerames, "all this is done by the dwarf of the fairies."

"Well," quoth Huon, "I think it best to alight from our horses, for we shall never escape from hence, but we shall all be oppressed."

Then Garyn and the other companions had great marvel, and were in fear.

"Ah, Gerames," quoth Huon, "you shewed me well that it was great peril to pass this wood, I repent me that I did not believe you."

Then they saw on the other side of the river a fair castle environed by fourteen towers, and on every

tower

tower was a belfry of fine gold by seeming, which they looked at a long time. By the time they had gone a little by the river side they lost sight of the castle which was clean vanished away, whereof Huon and his company were sore abashed.

"Huon," quoth Gerames, "be not dismayed at all this which you see, for it is done by the crooked dwarf of the fairies, and all to beguile you. He cannot harm you if you speak no word; howbeit, ere we depart from him he will make us all abashed, for soon he will come after us like a madman because you will not speak to him; but I require you, as in God's name, be not afraid, but ride forth securely, and ever beware of speaking to him a word."

Then they rode to pass the river, and found there nothing to hinder them, and so rode five leagues.

"Sir," quoth Huon, "we may well thank God that we be thus escaped this dwarf, who thought to have deceived us. I was never in such fear in my life, God guard us."

Thus they rode talking of the little dwarf who had done them so much trouble.

When Gerames understood that the company thought they were escaped from the dwarf, he began to smile, and said :

"Sirs, make no vaunt that ye be out of his power, for I believe you shall soon see him again."

As soon as Gerames had spoken the words, they saw before them a bridge which they must pass, and
they

they saw the dwarf on the other side. Huon saw him first, and said :

" I see the devil who hath done us so much trouble."

Oberon heard him, and said :

" Friend, thou dost me injury without cause, for I am neither devil nor evil creature. I am a man as others be, but I conjure thee by the Divine puissance to speak to me."

Then Gerames said :

" Sirs, for God's sake let him alone, nor speak a word to him, for by his fair language he may deceive us all, as he hath done many another ; it is a pity he hath lived so long."

Then they rode at a good pace, and left the dwarf alone sore displeased that they would not speak to him ; so he took his horn and set it to his mouth and blew it ; and when Huon and his company heard it they had no power to ride any further, but they all began to sing. Then Oberon the dwarf said :

" Yonder company are fools and proud, since for any salutation that I can give them they disdain to answer me. But by the God that made me, ere they escape me the refusal of my words shall be dear bought."

So he took again his horn and struck it three times on his bow, and cried out aloud :

" Ye my men, come appear before me."

77   Then

Then there came to him four hundred men of arms and demanded of Oberon what was his pleasure, and who had displeased him.

"Sirs," said Oberon, "I shall shew you, howbeit I am grieved to shew it. Here in this wood fourteen knights have passed who disdain to speak to me; but that they shall not mock me they shall dearly buy their refusal, wherefore I will that you go after them and slay them all, let none escape."

Then one of his knights said:

"Sir, for God's sake have pity of them."

"Certainly," quoth Oberon, "I cannot spare them seeing they disdain to speak to me."

"Sir," quoth Gloriande, "for God's sake do not as you say, but, Sir, work by my counsel, and after do as it please you. Sir, I counsel you, yet once again go after them, for if they do not speak we shall slay them all; for surely, Sir, if they see you return again to them, they shall be in great fear."

"Friend," quoth Oberon, "I shall do as you have counselled me."

All this while Huon and his company had ridden off again, and Huon said:

"Sirs, we are now about five leagues from the dwarf, I never in my life saw a creature so fair in the visage; I have great marvel how he can speak of God Almighty, if he is a devil of hell, and since he spake of God, methinks we ought to speak to him, for I think such a creature can have no power

78   to

to do us any ill. I think he is not past the age of five years."

"Sir," quoth Gerames, "as little as he seemeth, although you take him for a child, he was born forty years before the Nativity of our Lord Jesus Christ."

"Surely," quoth Huon, "I care not what age he be of, if he come again ill hap come to me if I keep my speech from him; I pray you be not displeased."

After they had ridden fifteen miles suddenly Oberon appeared to them, and said:

"Sirs, are ye not yet advised to speak to me? Yet again I am come to salute you in the name of the God that made and formed us, and I conjure you by the power that He hath given me that ye speak to me; for I repute you for fools to think thus to pass through my wood and disdain to speak to me. Ah, Huon, I know thee well enough, and whither thou wouldst go: I know all thy deeds, thou didst slay Charlot, and after discomfit Amaury: and I know the message that Charlemagne hath charged thee to say to the Admiral Gaudys, the which thing is impossible to be done without my aid, for without me thou shalt never accomplish this enterprise. Speak to me, and I shall cause thee to achieve thine enterprise, and when thou hast done thy message I shall bring thee again to France in safe-guard. I know the cause that thou wilt not speak to me, it is by reason of old Gerames who is there with thee. Therefore, Huon, beware of thyself, go no further,

79   for

for I know well it is three days past since thou didst eat any meat to profit thee : if thou wilt believe me, thou shalt have enough of such sustenance as thou wilt wish for. And so soon as thou hast dined I will give thee leave to depart, if it be thy pleasure, of this have no doubt."

"Sir," quoth Huon, "ye be welcome."

"Ah," quoth Oberon, "thy salutation shall be well rewarded. Know for truth thou didst never make salutation so profitable for myself : thou mayst thank God, that He hath sent thee that grace."

When Huon had well heard Oberon, he had great marvel, and demanded if it were true that he had said.

"Yea, truly," quoth Oberon, " of that make no doubt."

" Sir," quoth Huon, " I have great marvel for what cause you have desired to speak with us."

" Huon," quoth Oberon, " know that I love thee well because of the truth that is in thee, and since I naturally love thee, if thou wilt know who I am, I shall shew thee. My mother was the lady of the Secret Isle, sometime beloved of the fair Florimont of Albany. But because his mother spied on them, she departed and left Florimont her lover in great weeping, and never saw him after. Then she returned into her land and married after, and had a son who in his time was King of Egypt, named Anectanabus ; he it was who fostered Alexander the
80   Great

Great, and met his death by him. After many years Julius Cæsar passed by the sea as he went into Thessaly where he fought with Pompey. In his way he passed by Cephalonia, where he fell in love with my mother, because she shewed him that he should discomfit Pompey, as he did, and thus have I shewn you that Cæsar was my father. At my birth there was many a prince of the fairies, and many a noble lady that came to see my mother. But amongst them there was one who was not content, because she was not sent for as well as the others, and when I was born, she gave me a gift that when I should pass three years of age I should grow no more, but be as you see me now: and when she had thus done, and saw how she had served me by her words, she repented herself, and would recompense me another way. Then she gave me another gift that I should be the fairest child that ever nature formed, as thou mayst see me now; and another lady of Fairyland named Transeleyne gave me a gift that I do know all that any man can know or think, good or ill. The third lady, to do more for me, and to please my mother better, granted me that there is no country so far, but that if I will wish myself there, I shall be there at once with what number of men I list, and moreover, if I will have a castle or a palace at my own device, it shall be made at once, and as soon gone again when I list; and what meat or wine I wish for, I have it at once; and also I am King of

F ᶜ Momur,

Momur, which is four hundred leagues from hence, and if I list, I can be there at once. Know for truth thou art arrived at a good port, I know well thou hast great need of meat, for these three days thou hast had but small sustenance, but I shall cause thee to have enough. I demand of thee whether thou wilt have meat and drink here in this meadow, or in a palace, or in a hall; command as thou wilt, and thou shalt have it for thee and thy company."

"Sir," quoth Huon, "I will follow your pleasure, and never do nor think the contrary."

"Huon," quoth he, "as yet I have not shewed thee all the gifts that were given me at my birth. The fourth lady gave me that there is no bird nor beast, be they never so cruel, but if I will have them I may take them in my hand; and also I shall never seem older than thou seest me now, and when I shall depart out of this world my place is prepared in Paradise : well I know that all things created in this mortal world must needs have an end."

"Sir," quoth Huon, "such a gift ought to be well kept."

"Huon," quoth Oberon, "well were you counselled when you spake to me, you had never before so fair an adventure : shew me by thy faith if thou wilt eat, and what meat thou wilt have, and what wine thou wilt drink."

"Sir," quoth Huon, "so that I have meat and
drink

drink I care not what it is, that my company and I may be rid of our famine."

Then Oberon laughed at him and said:

"Sirs, all ye sit down in this meadow and doubt not that what I shall do is done by the might of our Lord God."

Then Oberon began to wish and said to Huon and his company, "Sirs, rise up quickly;" the which they did, and saw before them a fair and rich palace, garnished with chambers and halls, hung with rich cloth of silk beaten with gold, with tables set ready full of meat. When Huon and his company saw the rich palace before them they had great marvel, but Oberon took him by the hand and with him mounted up into the palace. There they found servants ready, bringing to them basins of gold, garnished with precious stones, and they gave water to Huon, and he sat down at the table. Oberon sat at the head of the table on a bench of ivory richly garnished with gold, and that seat had such virtue given it by the fairies, that if any man tried to poison him who was sitting on it, as soon as he came near he fell dead.

Now Huon began to eat at a great pace, but Gerames had small wish to eat for he believed that those who ate would never depart thence. When Oberon saw this, he said:

" Gerames, eat and drink, for as soon as thou hast eaten, thou shalt have leave to go when thou list; "

so

so Gerames was joyful, and began to eat and drink, for he knew that Oberon would not do otherwise than he had said. After the company had well dined, Huon said to King Oberon:

" Sir, when it shall be your pleasure, I pray you give us leave to depart."

" Huon," quoth Oberon, " I am right well content so to do, but first I will shew you some of my jewels;" then he called Clariand, a knight of the fairies, and said:

" Friend, go and fetch me my cup," and he did his commandment. And when Oberon had his cup in his hand he said to Huon, " Sir, behold ye well, see that this cup is empty."

" That is true, Sir," quoth Huon.

Then Oberon set the cup on the table, and said to Huon:

" Behold the great power that God hath given me, and how that I may do my pleasure;" and he made a sign over the cup three times, and at once the cup was full of wine.

" Lo, Sirs," quoth he, " ye may well see that this is done by the grace of God, yet I shall shew you the great virtue that is in this cup, for if all the men in the world were here assembled together, and the cup were in the hands of any man out of deadly sin, he might drink thereof his fill, but whosoever offers his hand to take it when he is in deadly sin, may

84   not

not drink out of it. If thou canst drink therefore of it, I offer thee the cup."

"Sir," quoth Huon, "I thank you, but I fear I am not worthy to drink thereof, nor to touch the cup. Never have I heard of such a noble vessel; yet know for truth I have confessed all my sins, and repented what evil I have done, and I do pardon and forgive all men, whatsoever injury hath been done to me, and I know not that I have done wrong to any creature, and I hate no man:" so saying he took the cup in both his hands and set it to his mouth, and drank of the good wine that was therein at his pleasure.

When Oberon saw that he was right glad, and came and embraced Huon, saying that he was a noble man : "I give thee this cup as it is; for the dignity of the cup be thou ever true and faithful, for if thou wilt work by my counsel I shall aid thee and give thee succour in all thine affairs ; but as soon as thou makest any lie the virtue of the cup will be lost and lose its bounty, and beside that, thou shalt lose my love and aid."

"Sir," quoth Huon, "I shall be right wary thereof, and now I require you suffer us to depart."

"Stay yet," quoth Oberon, "for I have another treasure which I will give thee, because of the truth and nobleness in thee. I will give thee a rich horn of ivory, which thou shalt bear with thee. As soon

as

as thou dost blow this horn I shall hear thee wher-
ever I am, and I will come at once to thee with a
hundred thousand men of arms to succour and aid
thee if need be. One thing I command thee on
pain of losing my love, and on jeopardy of thy life,
sound not this horn without thou hast great need
thereof: if thou do otherwise, I vow I shall leave
thee in as great poverty and misery as ever man was,
so that whosoever shall see thee in that case shall
have pity on thee. Now depart freely, and God be
your guide."

Then Huon took leave of King Oberon, and
trussed up all his baggage, and put his cup in his
bosom, and the horn about his neck, and they all
took their leave of the King, and Oberon weeping
embraced Huon, who marvelled why he wept, and said:

"Sir, why do you weep?"

"Friend," quoth Oberon, "you may well know,
you have two things with you that I love dearly.
God aid you; more I cannot speak to you."

Thus the fourteen knights departed, and rode
forth until they saw before them a great deep river,
and when they could find no guide nor passage at
which to cross, they wist not what to do, until suddenly they saw a servant of King Oberon pass by
them bearing a rod of gold in his hand. Without
speaking of any word he entered into the river, and
took his rod and struck the water therewith three
times, and the water withdrew both sides in such a
86   wise

wise that there was a path where three men might ride abreast : that done, he departed again without speaking of any word. Then Huon and his company entered into the water and so passed through without any danger, and when they were through it they looked behind them and saw the river close again, and run as it was accustomed to do.

"By my faith," quoth Huon, "I think we be enchanted. Surely King Oberon hath done this, but seeing we are thus escaped out of peril, I trust we shall have no fear from henceforth."

Thus they rode together singing, and ofttimes they spake of the great marvels that they had seen King Oberon do ; and as they rode Huon beheld on his right hand and saw a fair meadow well garnished with herbs and flowers, and in the midst thereof a clear fountain. Then Huon rode thither and alighted, and they let their horses pasture while they spread a cloth on the green grass, and set thereon the meat that King Oberon had given them at their parting, and they drank the drink that they found in the cup.

"By my faith," quoth Huon, "it was a fair adventure for us when we met Oberon, and I spoke to him. He hath shewed me great tokens of love when he gave me such a cup. If I may return into France in safety I shall give it to Charlemagne, who shall make great feast therewith : and if he cannot drink from it, the barons of France will have great joy thereof."

Then

Then again he repented him of his own words, and said:

"I am a fool to think or say thus, for as yet I cannot tell what end I shall come to. The cup that I have is worth more than two cities, but as yet I cannot believe that there is such virtue in the horn as Oberon hath said, nor that he may hear it so far off. Whatsoever fortune fall, I will assay if it hath such virtue or no."

"Ah, Sir," quoth Gerames, "beware what you do; you know well what charge he gave you when we departed; certainly you and we both are lost if you trespass his commandment."

"Surely," quoth Huon, "I will assay it whatsoever fortune fall;" so he took the horn and set it to his mouth, and blew it so loud that the wood rang, and Gerames and the others began to sing and make great joy, and Garyn said:

"Fair nephew, blow still;" and Huon blew till Oberon, who was in his wood fifteen miles off, heard him clearly, and said:

"Ah, I hear my friend blow whom I love best in the world; what man is so hardy as to do him any ill? I wish myself with him with a thousand men at arms;" and at once he was near to Huon with his company. When Huon and his friends heard the host, and saw Oberon come riding on before, they were afraid, and it was no marvel, seeing the commandment that Oberon had given them before.

88   Then

Then Huon said:

"Ah, Sirs, I have done ill, now I see well that we cannot escape, but that we be likely to die."

"Certainly," quoth Gerames, "you have well deserved it."

"Hold your peace," quoth Huon, "dismay you not; let me speak to him."

Therewith Oberon came to them and said:

"Huon, accursed be thou, where are they that will do thee any ill? Why hast thou broken my commandment?"

"Ah, Sir," quoth Huon, "I shall shew you the truth. We were sitting right now in the meadow, and did eat of that you gave us: I believe I took too much drink out of the cup that you gave me, the virtue of which we well assayed. Then I thought to assay also the virtue of the rich horn to the intent that if I should have any need of it, I might be sure thereof. Now I know for truth that all you have shewed me is true, therefore, Sir, in the honour of God I require you to pardon my trespass. Sir, here is my sword, strike off my head at your pleasure; for well I know without your aid I shall never achieve mine enterprise."

"Huon," quoth Oberon, "the goodness and great truth that are in thee constrain me to give thee pardon: but beware, from henceforth be not so hardy as to break my commandment."

"Sir," quoth Huon, "I thank you."

"Well,"

"Well," quoth Oberon, "I know surely that thou hast much to suffer as yet; for thou must pass through a city named Tormont, wherein there is a tyrant called Macaire, and yet he is thine own uncle, brother to thy father, Duke Seguin. When he was yet in France he thought to have murdered King Charlemagne, but his treason was known and he would have been slain, if thy father Duke Seguin had not been alive. He was sent to the Holy Sepulchre to do his penance for the ill that he had done, and after he was there he renounced the faith of our Lord God, and took on him the pagan law which he hath kept ever since so sorely that, if he hear any man speak of our Lord God, he will pursue him unto the death. Whatever promise he maketh, he keepeth none, therefore I advise thee trust not in him, for surely he will put thee to death if he may, and thou canst not escape if thou go by that city. I counsel thee, take not that way if thou be wise."

"Sir," quoth Huon, "for your courtesy, love, and good counsel I thank you, but whatsoever fortune fall to me, I will go to mine uncle; and if he be such an one as you say, I shall make him to die an ill death. If need be I shall sound my horn, and I am sure you will aid me at my need."

"Of that you may be sure," quoth Oberon, "but one thing I forbid thee, sound not the horn without thou be hurt, for if thou do the contrary I shall so martyr thee that thy body shall not endure it."

Then

Then Huon took leave of King Oberon, and said:

"Sir, I have marvel why you weep; I pray you shew me the cause why you do it."

"Huon," quoth Oberon, "the great love that I have for thee causeth me to do it, for hereafter thou shalt suffer so much ill and travail that no human tongue can tell it."

"Sir," quoth Huon, "you shew me many things not greatly to my profit."

"Sure," quoth Oberon, "and yet thou shalt suffer more than I have spoken of, and all by thine own folly."

After that Oberon was departed, Huon and his company mounted on their horses, and so rode forth until they came to the city of Tormont. When Gerames, who had been there before, saw the city, he said to Huon:

"Ah, Sir, we be ill arrived here, we are in the way to suffer much trouble."

"Be not dismayed," quoth Huon, "for by the grace of God we shall right well escape; for whom God will aid no man can hurt."

Then they entered into the city, and as they came to the gate, they met a man with a bow in his hand, who had been sporting without the city. Huon rode foremost and saluted him in the name of God.

"Friend, what call you this city?"

The man stood still and had marvel what men they were that spake of God, and said:

"Sirs,

"Sirs, the God in whose name you have saluted me keep and defend thee from evil. Howbeit I desire you, inasmuch as ye love your lives, speak softly that ye be not heard, for if the lord of this city know that ye be Christian men he will slay you all. Sirs, you may trust me, for I am christened, but I dare not be known, I have such fear of the duke."

"Friend," quoth Huon, "I pray you shew me who is lord of this city, and what is his name?"

"Sir," quoth he, "he is a false tyrant, when he was christened he was named Macaire, but he hath renounced God, and now he is so fierce and proud that he hateth nothing so much as them that believe in Jesus Christ: but, Sir, I pray you shew me whither you will go."

"Friend," quoth Huon, "I go to the Red Sea, and from thence to Babylon. I would tarry this day in this city, for I and my company are sore weary."

"Sir," quoth he, "if you will believe me you will not enter into this city to lodge, for if the duke know it none can save your lives ; therefore if it be your pleasure I shall lead you another way beside the town."

"Sir," quoth Gerames, "for God's sake believe him that counselleth you so truly."

"Know for truth," quoth Huon, "I will not do thus. I see well it is almost night, the sun is low,

therefore

therefore I will lodge this night here in this town, for a good town should never be forsaken, whatsoever befall."

" Sir," quoth the strange man, " seeing it is so, for the love of God I shall bring you to a lodging where ye shall be well and honestly lodged in a good man's house, that believeth in God. His name is Gonder, provost of the city, and he is well beloved of the duke."

" Friend," quoth Huon, " God reward thee."

So the man went on before through the town till he came to the provost's house, whom they found sitting at his gate. Huon, who was a fair speaker, saluted him in the name of God and the Virgin Mary. The provost rose up and beheld Huon and his company, and had marvel what they were, seeing they saluted him in the name of God : then he said :

" Sirs, ye be welcome, but in God's name I desire you to speak softly that ye be not heard, for if the duke of this city knew you, ye would be utterly lost : but if it please you to tarry this night here in my house, for the love of God all that I have in my house shall be yours to do therewith at your pleasure: I abandon all to you. I thank God I have in my house food enough, that if ye bide in my house a year, ye shall not need to buy anything without."

" Sir," quoth Huon, " for this fair proffer I thank you;" and so he and his company alighted, and the servants of the house took their horses and set them

93   up,

up, while the host took Huon and Gerames and the others, and brought them to their chambers to dress: thence they came into the hall, where they found the tables set and covered, and so sat down and were richly served with divers meats.

When they were done and risen, Huon called Gerames and said:

"Go in haste into the town and get a crier, and cause it to be cried in every market-place and street, that whosoever would come and sup at the provost's house, as well noble as simple men, women and chidren, rich and poor, and all manner of people of whatever estate or degree they be, should come freely, and nothing pay, neither for meat nor for drink, whereof they should have as they wished."

Also he commanded Gerames that he should buy all the meat he could get in the town, and pay ready money for the same.

"Sir," quoth Gerames, "your pleasure shall be done."

"You know well," quoth the host, "that I have abandoned to you all that is in my house; therefore, Sir, you shall not need to seek for anything further; take of my goods at your pleasure."

"Sir," quoth Huon, " I thank you. I have money enough to furnish what we need, and also, Sir, I have a cup of great virtue; for if all the people that are within this city were here present, they should have drink enough from it, for it was made in Fairyland."

94   When

When the host heard Huon he began to smile, and believed that these words were spoken in jest, so Huon foolishly took the horn of ivory from his neck and took it to his host to keep, saying :

" Host, I take you this to keep, for it is a precious thing, therefore keep it safely, that I may have it again when I ask for it."

"Sir," quoth he, "I shall surely keep it, and when it please you it shall be ready;"and so he took the horn and laid it up in a coffer ; but after there fell such an hour that Huon would rather have had it than all the goods in the world, as ye shall hereafter hear.

Thus when Gerames had this commandment of Huon, he went into the city and caused it to be cried in divers places as he was commanded, and when the cry was made, there was no beggar, vagabond nor ribald, juggler nor minstrel, old nor young, but came to the provost's house ; and they were in number more than four hundred. And Gerames bought up bread, meat, flesh, and other victuals, all that he could find in the city, and paid for it ; thus the supper was dressed and every man seated at the tables. Huon served them with his cup in his hand, pouring out into each man's pot from his own, and yet ever his cup was full. Now when the people had well eaten and drunken, and their brains were warmed with the good wine, some began to sing, and some to sleep at the table, and some beat the boards with their fists so that it was

95   a marvel

a marvel to see the way they behaved, and Huon had thereof much joy. The same time the duke's steward came into the town to buy his master's supper, but he could find neither bread nor flesh, nor any other victuals, whereof he was sore displeased. Then he demanded the cause why he found no victuals as he was accustomed to do.

"Sir," quoth the butchers and bakers, "a young man is lodged in the house of Gonder the provost who hath made to be cried in all the city, that all beggars and ribalds should come to sup at his lodgings, and he hath bought up all the victuals that he could get in the town."

Then the Paynim in great despite went to the palace to the duke and said:

"Sir, I can get nothing in the town for your supper: there is a young man lodged in the provost's house that hath bought up all the victuals to give a supper to all the beggars, vagabonds, and ribalds that can be found in the town."

When the duke understood that he was sore displeased, and swore by Mahound that he would go and see that supper, and commanded all his men to be ready in harness to go with him. As he was going out of his palace, a traitor who had stolen secretly out of the provost's house where he had been at supper said:

"Sir, know for truth there is in your provost's house a knight who hath given a supper to all people that

that would come thither, and, Sir, this knight hath a cup worth more than all this city, for if all the people that live between east and west should lack drink, they should all have enough, for as often as the cup is emptied it fills again at once."

When the duke heard that he had great marvel and said such a cup were good for him, and swore by Mahound that he would have that cup.

"Let us go thither, for my will is to have that cup. All those knights shall lose their horses and baggage, I will leave them nothing."

He went forth with thirty knights and stopped not till he came to the provost's house and found the gates open. When the provost perceived him he came to Huon, and said:

"Ah, Sir, you have done ill; here is come the duke in great displeasure. If God has not pity on you, I cannot see how you can escape from death."

"Dismay you not," quoth Huon, "for I shall speak so fair that he shall be content;" and with a merry cheer he came to the duke, and said:

"Sir, ye be welcome."

"Beware," quoth the duke, "come not near me, for no Christian man may come into my city without my license, wherefore thou must know that ye shall all lose your heads, and all that ye brought hither."

"Sir," quoth Huon, "when you have slain us you shall win but little thereby; it were great wrong for you so to do."

97   G   "I shall

"I shall tell thee," quoth the duke, "why I will do it, that is because ye be Christian men. Show me by thy faith why hast thou assembled all this company here to supper."

Quoth Huon :

"I have done it because I am going to the Red Sea, and these poor men will pray to God for me that I may return in safety. Sir, this is the cause that I have made them to sup with me."

"Well," quoth the duke, "great folly hast thou spoken, for thou shalt never see fair day, you shall all lose your heads."

"Leave all this, Sir," quoth Huon, "I pray you and your company sit down and eat and drink at your pleasure, and I shall serve you as well as I can; and then, if I have done any wrong, I will make you amends in such wise that you shall be content, for if you do me any hurt it shall be but a small conquest for you. Methinks, Sir, if you would do nobly, you should somewhat forbear us, for I have heard say you were once christened."

Then the duke said to Huon :

"Thou hast said well ; I am content to sit, for as yet I have not supped ;" and he commanded every man to be disarmed, and to sit down at the table ; the which they did. So Huon and Gerames served them, and they were well served at that supper, and after Huon took his cup and came to the duke, and said :

98   " Sir,

"Sir, see you not here this cup, the which is void
and empty?"

"I see well," quoth the duke, "there is nothing
therein."

Then Huon made the sign of the cross over the
cup, and straightway it was full of wine; so he took
the cup to the duke, who had great marvel thereof,
but as soon as he took the cup in his hands it was
void again.

"What," quoth the duke, "thou hast enchanted
me."

"Sir," quoth Huon, "I am no enchanter, but this
for the sin that you are in. Set down the cup, for
you are not worthy to hold it; in an evil hour were
you born."

"How art thou so bold," quoth the duke, "to
speak thus to me? Thou art but a proud fool, thou
knowest well it lieth in my power to destroy thee,
and there is no man dare say the contrary. I pray
thee tell me thy name, and where thou wert born,
and whither thou goest, and of what kin thou art."

"Sir," quoth Huon, "for anything that may fall
to me I shall not hide my name nor kindred. I was
born at Bordeaux on the Garonne, son to Duke
Seguin who is dead seven years and more."

When the duke heard how Huon was his nephew,
he said: "Ah, nephew, son of my brother, why hast
thou taken in this city any other lodging than mine?
Shew me whither thou wilt go."

99   "I am

"I am going to Babylon," quoth Huon, "to the Admiral Gaudys, to do to him a message from King Charlemagne of France because I slew his son there." So he shewed his uncle all his adventure, and how the King had taken away his land, nor should he have it again till he had done his message to the admiral.

"Fair nephew," quoth the duke, "in like wise was I banished the realm of France; but since then I have renounced the faith of Jesus Christ, and I have married in this country a great lady, by whom I have lands to govern, whereof I am lord. Nephew, I will that thou come and lodge with me in my castle, and to-morrow you shall have some of my barons to conduct you till you come to Babylon."

"I thank you, Sir," quoth Huon, "since it is your pleasure I will go with you to your palace." Then Gerames came quietly and said to him: "Sir, if you go thither, you may perhaps repent your self." "It may well be," quoth Gonder the provost.

Then Huon ordered to truss all their gear and to make ready their horses, and took with him his cup, but he left still his horn with the provost; so he went with his uncle to his castle, and lay there all night. The next morning Huon came to his uncle to take his leave.

"Fair nephew," quoth the duke, "I pray you tarry till my barons come that shall conduct you on your journey." "Sir," quoth Huon, "since it pleases you I am content to abide." Then they sat down to dinner.

CHAP. VI.

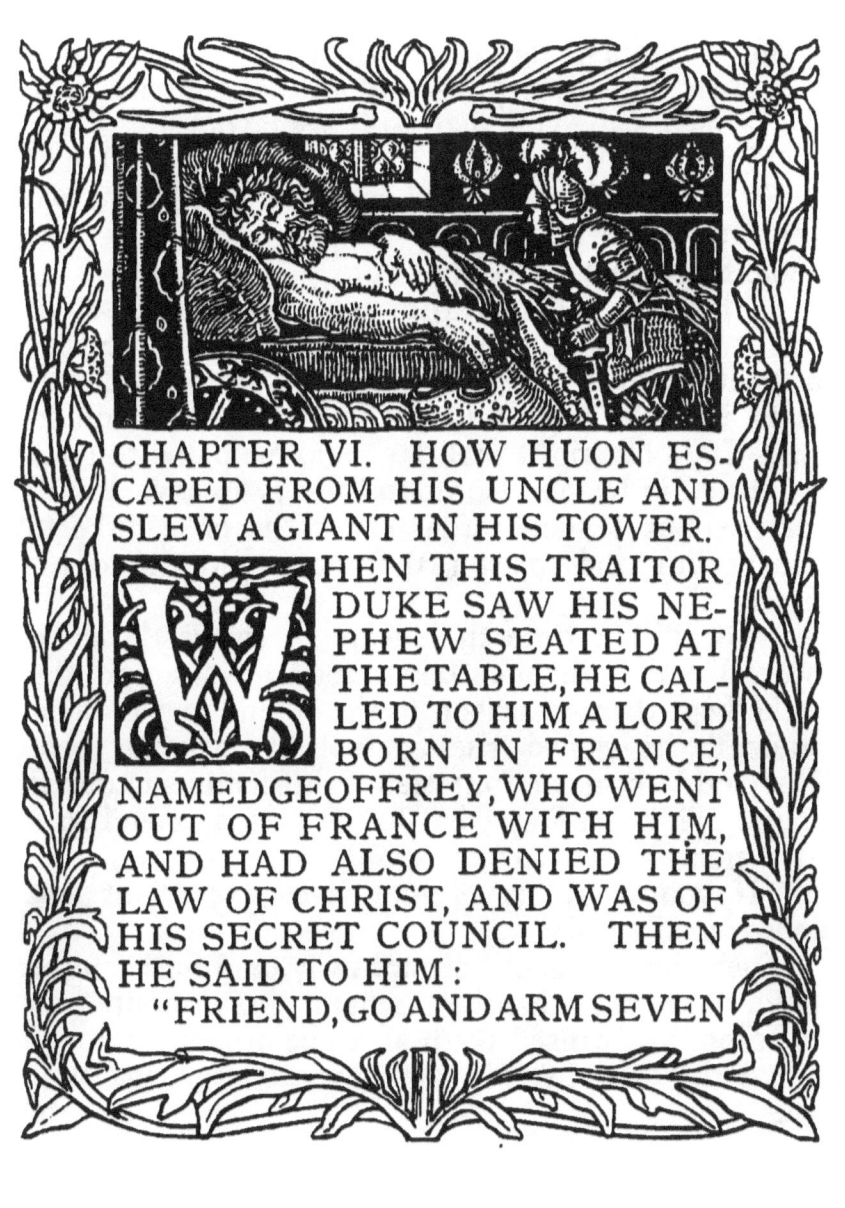

CHAPTER VI. HOW HUON ES-
CAPED FROM HIS UNCLE AND
SLEW A GIANT IN HIS TOWER.

HEN THIS TRAITOR
DUKE SAW HIS NE-
PHEW SEATED AT
THE TABLE, HE CAL-
LED TO HIM A LORD
BORN IN FRANCE,
NAMED GEOFFREY, WHO WENT
OUT OF FRANCE WITH HIM,
AND HAD ALSO DENIED THE
LAW OF CHRIST, AND WAS OF
HIS SECRET COUNCIL. THEN
HE SAID TO HIM:
    "FRIEND, GO AND ARM SEVEN

score Paynims, and cause them to come hither. Let them slay my nephew and all that are with him, for if one escape you shall lose my favour."

"Sir," quoth Geoffrey, "your will shall be done."

So he went into a chamber where there were two hundred suits of armour hanging; but when he came there he said to himself:

"Alas, this villain traitor would slay the son of his brother, who when I was in France did me once a great courtesy, for I should have been dead and slain if Duke Seguin his father had not succoured me. It is but right that I should help his son for what he did to me. Confound me, if he have any ill for me, but I shall rather cause the false duke to dearly buy the treason that he would do to his nephew."

Now at that time there were in the castle seven score French prisoners taken upon the sea, and the duke kept them in prison to the intent to put them to death, he was so cruel against all Christian men. But God, Who never forgetteth His friends, succoured them. This Geoffrey went to the prisoners and said to them:

"If you would save your lives, come out and follow me."

Then they came out straightway, and he brought them into the chamber, where the armour was hanging, and caused them all to be armed.

"Sirs," said he, "if you have courage and will

to issue hence, it is time now to shew your man-hood."

"We shall do your commandment," quoth they, "and die in the quarrel, to come out of bondage into freedom."

When Geoffrey heard them, he was right joyous, and said:

"Know surely that there is here in this palace at dinner the son of Duke Seguin of Bordeaux, nephew to the duke, lord of this house. Once was this lord christened, but he hath denied the faith of our Lord God Jesus Christ, and hath commanded me to arm seven score Paynims to come and slay his nephew and his company."

When they were all armed, and swords by their sides, they followed Geoffrey to the palace, and when they entered, Huon said to his uncle:

"Sir, these men in armour that have come into the hall, are they those you have commanded to come and conduct me on my journey?"

"Huon," quoth the duke, "it is otherwise than thou thinkest, thou shalt surely die, there is no remedy, thou shalt never see fair day again."

Then he said: "Step forth, Sirs, look that no Christian men escape you, but let them all be slain."

When Huon saw the malice of his uncle and his false treason he was sore abashed, and rose up suddenly and set his helm on his head and took his sword in his hand. Then Geoffrey came in and

103   cried:

cried : " Saint Denis, ye noble Frenchmen, take heed that no Paynim escapes alive, but slay them all."

The Frenchmen drew out their swords and fought with the Paynims on all parts so that within a short time they were all slain. The duke saw that these were no Paynims since they slew his men, and was in great fear of his life, and fled away into a secret chamber. When Huon perceived that they were Frenchmen who had thus succoured him he pursued the duke with his sword in his hand, all bloody with the blood of the Paynims he had slain. The traitor duke saw that his nephew followed him, and fled from chamber to chamber till he came to a window opening upon the garden side, and so leapt out thereat and ran away, whereof Huon and Geoffrey and the other Frenchmen were right sorrow-ful. They closed the gates and raised the bridges, to the intent that they should not be surprised, and then they came into the hall to make acquaintance with one another, whereof they had much joy, but if God had not helped them, their joy would have been turned into sorrow. When the duke came into the town he made a cry that all men able to bear arms should come to him, and he with all that he could raise, came before the palace, more than ten thousand persons, and they all swore the death of the Christians. When the duke saw he had such a number he was joyful and commanded his engines and ladders to be raised up on every part,

and

and with picks and mattocks they broke down a corner tower. The Christians within defended them valiantly, but their defence would have availed them little, if our Lord God had not helped them. When Huon knew the danger he was in, he was sore displeased, and said :

"I ought to be sore annoyed when I see that we be thus kept in by my uncle. I fear me we shall never more see good days."

Then Gerames said :

"For the love of God, Sir, blow now your horn."

"It is not in my power to do it," quoth Huon, "for the provost Gonder hath it in keeping."

"Ha, Huon," quoth Gerames, "in an evil hour we came acquainted with you, for now by your folly and pride we are in the way of destruction."

As they were thus devising, Gonder the provost came to the duke and said :

"Sir, I have great marvel that you thus destroy your own palace, great folly you do therein, I would counsel you leave this assault, and let there be a peace made between you and your nephew on the condition to let him and his company go safely away."

"Provost," quoth the duke, "I pray thee go and do the best that thou canst. I will do as thou dost counsel me."

Then the provost came to the palace and said to Huon :

"Sir,

"Sir, for God's sake speak with me."

"Who art thou?" quoth Huon.

"I am your host the provost, and I require you inasmuch as ye love your lives, keep well this palace."

"Sir," quoth Huon, "for your good counsel I thank you, and I desire you, for the love you bear me, and in that you would help to save my life, give me again the horn of ivory that I gave you to keep; for without that I cannot escape death."

"Sir," quoth the provost, "it is not far from me;" and so he took it out of his bosom and delivered it to Huon in at a window on the garden side.

When Huon saw that he had his horn of ivory again he was joyful, and no marvel, for it was the security for his life. He set it to his mouth, and began to blow it, but Gerames said:

"Ah, Sir, you should never discover your secrets so easily, for if this provost had been untrue, he might have told all your secrets to the duke, and you would have been lost. Also, Sir, I beg you not to blow your horn as yet, for you be not yet hurt; King Oberon commanded you so at his parting."

"Why," quoth Huon, "am I to tarry till I be slain? Surely I will blow it without any longer delay."

And so he blew it sore, till the blood came out of his mouth; and all that were in the palace began to sing and dance, and the duke and all those that
were

were at the siege of the palace could not do otherwise. Then King Oberon, who was in his city of Momur, said :

" I hear my friend Huon's horn blow, I know well he hath some business on hand. I wish myself where the horn was blown with a hundred thousand armed men."

He had no sooner made this wish but he was in the city of Tormont, and he and his men fell on the Paynims and slew them till their blood ran down the streets like a river, but first he made it to be cried that as many as would receive baptism their lives should be saved, so that thereby many were christened. When Huon saw King Oberon come to the palace he went and thanked him for his succour at that time of need.

" Friend," quoth Oberon, " as long as you believe and do what I tell you, I shall never fail to succour you in all your affairs."

Thus all that were in the town and would not believe on God were slain, and the duke was taken and brought to the palace to Huon, who was right joyful to see his uncle taken. Then the duke said :

" Fair nephew, I pray you have pity on me."

" Ah, untrue traitor," quoth Huon, " thou shalt never depart hence alive; I shall never respite thy death."

Then with his sword he struck off his uncle's head,
and

and made his body to be hanged over the walls of the town, that his ill deeds might always be had in memory and be an example to all others. Thus that country was delivered from the traitor.

When all was done King Oberon said to Huon:

"My dear friend, I will take my leave of thee. I shall not see thee again till thou hast suffered so much pain and ill and poverty and mis-ease that it will be hard to speak of; and all through thy own folly."

When Huon heard that he was all afraid and said:

"Sir, methinks you say great wrong, for in all things I will observe your commandment to my power."

"Friend," quoth Oberon, "seeing thou wilt do so, remember then thy promises. I charge thee, on pain of thy life and losing for ever my love, be not so hardy as to take the way to the tower of Dunother. It is a marvellous great tower standing on the sea-side. Julius Cæsar caused it to be made: there was I long nourished. Thou never didst see a tower so fair or better garnished with chambers and glass windows and rich tapestry hangings within. At the entry of the gate are two men of brass, each of them holding in their hands a flail of iron, wherewith they beat day and night without cease by such a measure that when the one striketh with his flail the other is lift up ready to strike, and they beat so quickly that

108   a swallow .

a swallow flying cannot pass by unslain.   Within
this tower is a giant named Angolafer ; he took from
me the tower and a noble suit of armour of such
virtue that whosoever hath it on his body cannot be
hurt or weary, nor can he be drowned with water, nor
burned by fire.   Huon, my friend, I charge thee go
not that way, as thou fearest my displeasure, for
against that giant thou canst make no resistance."

" Sir," quoth Huon, " know for truth, that day I
departed out of France I took on me a vow that I
should never eschew any adventure I might hear
of, though it were never so perilous, for any fear of
death.   I had rather die than not fight that giant ;
there is no man shall hinder me, and I will conquer
again your noble armour, it shall do me good service
hereafter, it is a thing not to be forsaken ; and if I
have need of your aid I shall blow my horn, and you
will come and help me."

" Huon," quoth Oberon, " if thou breakest the horn
in blowing it, thou shalt have no aid from me."

" Sir," quoth Huon, " you may do your pleasure,
and I shall do mine."

Then Oberon departed with out more speech, and
Huon abode in the city, which he gave to Geoffrey
and to the provost his host, with all the land that
his uncle held.   Then he made him ready, and took
gold and silver plenty, and took leave of Geoffrey
and of his host, and of all other, and he and his
company departed, riding over hills and dales, night

109   and

and day, without finding any adventure worthy to be had in memory for a certain space. At last he came near the sea-side where the tower of the giant was, and when he saw it, he said to his company:

"Sirs, yonder I see a tower which was forbidden me by Oberon, but, if God helps me, I shall see what is within it before night, whatever happens."

Gerames looked on the tower, and began to weep, saying:

"Ah, Huon he is a fool that agreeth to the counsel of a child. Beware that you break not the commandment of King Oberon, for if you do, great ill is like to come of it."

"If all the men now living," quoth Huon, "should forbid me to go thither, I would not obey them, for you know well I departed out of France for no other reason but to seek out strange adventures, and I demand nothing else. Speak no more to the contrary, for ere it be night I will fight with the giant, though he be harder than iron. I shall slay him or he me, and you, Gerames, and all the others, abide you here in this meadow till I return again."

Then Gerames, all weeping, said:

"I commend you to the safeguard of God."

And Huon armed him, and kissed all his men one after another, and left his company all piteously complaining, and set forth alone and on foot, taking with him his cup and his horn, and rested not till he came to the gate of the castle of Dunother, where
he

he saw two men of brass that without ceasing beat the air with their flails. He beheld them well and thought it was in a manner impossible to enter without death. Then he wondered greatly, and said to himself that King Oberon had shewed him the truth, and he thought that without the grace of God it were impossible to enter. He looked about to see if there were any other entrance, and at last he saw near a marble pillar a basin of gold fastened with a chain, so he approached it, drew out his sword, struck three great blows on the basin so that the sound of it might be heard within the castle. Now there was in the tower a maiden called Sebylle, and when she heard the basin ring she wondered greatly, and went to a window and looked out and saw Huon waiting to enter. Then she went back again and said :

"Alas, what knight is yonder without that would enter? If the giant wakes he will slay him at once, for if there were a thousand knights together they should be destroyed. I desire greatly to know who he is, and where he was born, for meseems he should be of France. I will go to the window to see if I may have any knowledge of him."

Then she went out of her chamber, and went to a window near the gate, and looked out and saw Huon all armed abiding at the gate, and looked on the blazon of his shield, whereon was portrayed three crosses gules, whereby she knew well he was of France.

"Alas,"

"Alas," quoth she, "I am but lost if the giant knows that I have been here;" and she ran back in haste, and went to the room-door where the giant lay and slept, and perceived that he was asleep, for he snored so that it was a wonder to hear him. Then she ran back again quickly to the gate and opened a wicket, out of which there issued such a wind that it caused the two men with their flails to stand still at rest, and she returned hastily into her chamber. When Huon saw the little wicket open he came forward and entered, for the two men with their flails were at rest, thinking forthwith to find them that had opened the wicket, but he was sore abashed when he could find no creature. There were so many chambers that he wist not whither to go to find that which he sought for, and he looked about, till he saw a pillar; near it fourteen men lay dead, and he marvelled and sought to return. So he went out of the hall and came to the gate weening to have found it open, but it had closed by itself and the men were beating again with their flails.

"Alas," quoth Huon, "now I see well I cannot escape from hence."

Then he returned into the castle and hearkened, and as he went about he heard the voice of a damsel piteously weeping. He came to where she was, humbly saluted her, and said:

"Fair damsel, I cannot tell if you can understand

my

my language or not, I would know of you why you make this great sorrow."

" Sir," quoth she, "I weep because I have great pity on you, for if the giant within who is asleep, hap to wake, you are but dead."

" Fair lady," quoth Huon, "I pray you shew me what you be, and where you were born."

" Sir," quoth she, "I am daughter to Guinemer, who in his time was earl of Saint Omers, and kinsman to Duke Seguin of Bordeaux."

When Huon heard that, right humbly he kissed her, and said: "Dame, know for truth you are my near kinswoman, for I am son to Duke Seguin: I pray you tell me what adventure hath brought you into this castle."

" Sir," quoth she, "my father had devotion to see the Holy Sepulchre, and he loved me so well that he would not leave me behind him. As we were on the sea near to the city of Ascalon in Syria, there rose a great tempest in the sea, so that the wind brought us near this castle, and the giant being in his tower, saw us driven into his port in great danger of drowning, and came down out of his palace and slew my father and all them that were with him except myself, and so brought me into this tower where I have been these seven years and never heard a Mass. Now, cousin, I pray you, what adventure hath brought you hither into this strange country?"

" Cousin," quoth he, " seeing you will know of

113   H   mine

mine adventure, I shall shew you the truth. King Charlemagne hath sent me with a message to the Admiral Gaudys in Babylon by mouth and by letters. As my way lay I came by this tower, and I asked of a Paynim who was within it. He answered me and said there was a great and horrible giant who hath done much ill to them that passed this way, and I thought to fight with him and to destroy him, and deliver the country from him. I have left my company here in a valley to tarry for me."

"Dear cousin," quoth she, "I wonder greatly you should take such folly on you; if there were five hundred men together, all well armed, they durst not abide him when he is armed, for none can endure against him: therefore, cousin, I counsel you to return ere he wakes, and I will open you the wicket so that you may pass out without danger."

When Huon understood the damsel, he said:

"Cousin, know for truth I will see what man he is ere I depart hence; it shall never be said to my reproach in the court of any prince that for fear of a miscreant I was of so faint a courage that I durst not abide him. Certainly I had rather die than such a fault should come on me."

"Ah, cousin," quoth she, "then I see well both you and I are destroyed; but seeing it is thus I shall shew you the chamber where he sleepeth, and when you have seen him you may yet return. First go into this chamber that you see here before you,

114   wherein

wherein you shall find bread and wine and other victual; in the next you shall find clothes of silk and many rich jewels; then, in the third chamber you shall find the four gods of the Paynims, they be all of fine massy gold; and in the fourth you shall find the giant lying asleep on a rich bed: then, Sir, if you believe me, I counsel you to strike off his head sleeping, for if he awake you cannot escape death."

"Dame," quoth Huon, "if God will, it shall never be laid to my reproach that I should strike a man without his knowledge."

Then Huon departed from the lady, his sword in his hand, and his helm on his head, and his shield about his neck, and so he entered into the chambers till he came to the third where he saw the four gods. When he had well regarded them he gave each of them a stroke with his sword, and entered into the chamber where the giant lay sleeping. The bed that he lay on was so rich that the value of it could not be appraised; the coverings, curtains, and pillows, were of such beauty that one could not but wonder at them. The chamber was hung with rich cloth and the floor covered with carpets. When Huon had seen all this he looked on the giant who was seventeen feet long, and his body of corresponding width; but a fouler and more hideous creature was never seen, a great head and ears, camuse nose and eyes burning like a candle.

"Ah," quoth Huon, "I would King Charlemagne

was

was here to see us two fight, for I am sure then my peace should be made with him ere I departed. Ah, Lord God, I humbly require Thee to be my succour against this enemy, for if it be not Thy pleasure I cannot endure against him."

Then Huon advanced and made the sign of the cross, casting in his mind what he should do, for he thought that if he slew him sleeping it should be a great reproach to him, and it would be said that he had slain a man unarmed, and then he said to himself, "Shame have I if I touch him ere I have defied him."

So Huon cried out aloud, and said : "Arise, thou heathen hound, or I shall strike off thy head."

When the giant heard Huon speak he awoke fiercely and beheld Huon, and rose up so quickly that he broke the bedstead he lay on, and said :

"Friend, they that sent thee hither loved thee but little, and feared not me."

When Huon heard the giant speak French he had great marvel, and said : " I am come hither to see thee, and it may be that I have done foolishly."

The giant said :

" Thou sayest truth, for if I were armed as thou art, five hundred men like thee could not endure, they should all die. But thou seest I am without sword or weapon, yet for all that I fear thee not."

Then Huon thought in himself it would be great shame to him to assail a man without armour or

weapon ;

weapon; and said: "Go and arm thee straightway or I shall slay thee."

"Friend," quoth the giant, "this that thou sayest proceedeth of a good heart and of courtesy."

Then he armed him and took in his hand a great falchion, and without tarrying sought for Huon, who had withdrawn into the palace to wait for him.

"What art thou?" quoth he, "behold me here ready to destroy thee without thou make good defence. Yet I pray thee tell me who thou art to the extent that I may, when I have slain thee, tell how I slew such a one that by his folly came to assail me in my own palace. Great pride it was in thee that thou wouldst not strike me till I was armed; whosoever thou art, thou seemest son to a noble man. I pray thee shew me whither thou wouldst go, and what moved thee to come hither, that I may know the truth of thine enterprise, and when I have slain thee, I may make my vaunt to my men that I have slain a man who thought scorn and disdain to strike me till I was armed."

"Paynim," quoth Huon, "thou art in great folly when thou thinkest me but dead. Seeing thou wilt know the truth I tell thee I am a poor knight, from whom King Charlemagne hath taken his lands, and he has banished me out of the realm of France, and hath sent me to do a message to the Admiral Gaudys at Babylon; my name is Huon, son of Duke Seguin of Bordeaux. Now have I shewed

thee

thee all the truth of mine enterprise, I pray thee tel me where thou wert born, and who was thy father, to the extent that when I have slain thee I may make my boast in King Charles's Court, before all my friends that I have slain such a great marvellous giant as thou art."

"If thou slayest me, thou mayest well make thy avaunt that thou hast slain Angolafer the giant, who hath seventeen brethren, of whom I am the youngest. Also thou mayst say that unto the Dry Tree and the Red Sea there is no man but is tributary to me. I have chased the Admiral Gaudys, to whom thou wouldst go, and have taken from him divers of his cities, and he doth me yearly service of a ring of gold to buy his head withal. Also I took from Oberon this mighty castle, for he could not resist me with all his enchantments, and I took from him a suit of rich armour; thou never didst hear of such a one, for it hath such virtue that whosoever can put it on him can never be weary nor discomfited. But there is therein another virtue for he that must wear that armour must be without spot of deadly sin, and his mother must be blameless: I believe there cannot be found any man that can wear this armour. And it is so rich that whosoever hath it on his body cannot be harmed by fire or water. By Mahound, I have proved it, and because I have found such courtesy in thee that thou gavest me leave to arm me, I

118   give

give thee leave to try if thou canst put on that armour."

Then the giant went to a coffer and took it out, and came to Huon, saying: "Lo, here is the good armour, I give thee leave to put it on thy body."

Then Huon took the armour and went back a little, and put off his own arms, and took it, and straightway put it on his body. Then he did on his helm, and took his shield and his sword in his hands, and devoutly thanked our Lord God for His grace.

Then the giant said: "By Mahound, I little thought thou hadst been such a man, the armour befitteth thee well. Now I have requited thy courtesy, I pray thee put off my armour and deliver it me again."

"Hold thy tongue," quoth Huon, "God punish thee, I need such armour. Know for truth I will not give it up for fourteen of the best cities between this and Paris."

"Friend," quoth the giant, "seeing thou wilt not render me again the armour, I am content to let thee depart freely without hurt or damage: and also I will give thee my ring of gold which the Admiral Gaudys gave me, for I know well it shall stand thee in good stead if thou dost thy message. When thou comest to the gate of his palace thou shalt find four gates, and at every gate four porters, so that at the first gate when they know thou art a Frenchman, one of thy hands shall be cut off, and at the second gate thy other hand, and at the third gate one of thy

thy

thy feet, and at the fourth the other foot, and then shalt thou be brought before the admiral, and thy head stricken off. Therefore to escape these perils and deliver thy message and surely return, give me again my armour, and I will give thee my ring of gold. When thou shewest it thou shalt be received with great honour at every gate, and thou mayest go and return in the palace at thy pleasure, and no man shall be so hardy as to stay thee, if thou hadst slain five hundred men. When I have need of men or money I lack not if I send this ring for a token, therefore I pray thee let me have my armour again."

Then Huon said: "Ah, thou fell and false deceiver, know that if all the preachers between the East and the West preached to me a whole year, and thou wouldst give me all that thou hast and thy ring therewith, I would not give back the good armour that is now on my body. First I shall slay thee, and then I will have the ring thou praisest so greatly, whether thou wilt or no."

When the giant had heard Huon and saw that he could in no wise get again his armour, he was sorrowful and so sore displeased that his eyes seemed like two burning candles. Yet he demanded of Huon if he would not do otherwise.

"No, truly," quoth Huon, "though thou be great and strong, I have no fear of thee, seeing I have on this good armour, therefore in the name of God and of His divine power I defy thee."

"And

"And I thee," quoth the giant, "for all thy armour thou canst not endure before me." Then he approached Huon and lifted up his falchion, thinking to have stricken him, but he failed, for the stroke glanced off the armour, and the falchion struck a pillar and entered more than two feet into it. When Huon, who was quick and light, beheld that marvellous stroke, he stepped forward with his good sword in his hand, seeing how the giant had his falchion stuck in the pillar, and struck him so on the arms that he cut off both his hands and they with the falchion fell down to the earth. The giant gave so marvellous a cry, for the pain of his wound, that it seemed as if the tower had fallen to the ground, and the damsel Sebylle in her chamber was sore afraid, and came out, snatching up a staff she found on her way. As she came to the place where she heard the cry she met the giant fleeing away to save himself, but she cast the staff between his legs so that he fell to the earth, and Huon hasted him, and gave the giant many a great stroke, and the giant cried out so loud that it was very terrible to hear him, but Huon lifted up his sword and gave him such a stroke on the neck that his head flew to the earth. Then Huon wiped his sword and put it up in its sheath, and came to the head thinking to have taken it up and set it on the height of the tower, but the head was so great and heavy that he could not remove it or turn the body. So he smiled

and

and said : " Good Lord, I thank Thee for Thy grace
that Thou hast given me the might to slay such a
creature. Would to God that this body and head
were now in the palace of Paris before Charlemagne,
King of France, so that he knew that I have slain
him."

Then Huon went to a window and looked out
to see where his companions were and said to them :
" Ahi, Sirs, come up hither, you may do it safely, for
the palace is won and the giant is slain."

When Gerames and Garyn and the others heard
that, they were joyful and thanked our Lord God,
and came to the gate where Sebylle the damsel
went and opened the wicket so that the brazen men
stayed, and they entered and followed her till they
came to Huon. They all wept for joy when they
saw him ; they embraced and kissed him, and asked
if he had had any hurt.

" Sirs," quoth Huon, " I thank God I feel no
hurt," and he brought them to where the giant lay
dead. When they saw him they marvelled how
Huon could have slain him, for they were afraid to
see him lie dead ; afterward Gerames asked of Huon
who the damsel was that was there, and Huon told
how she was his cousin and all the story of how she
came thither, whereof they had great joy and embraced her. Then they all unarmed them and
went to supper and ate and drank at their pleasure ;
but their joy endured not long, as ye shall after hear.

CHAP. VII.

CHAPTER VII. HOW HUON SET
OUT FOR BABYLON, AND WHAT
THINGS THERE BEFEL HIM.

E HAVE WELL SEEN
BEFORE HOW HUON
CONQUERED THE
GIANT WITH THE
GREAT JOY OF HIS
COMPANY; BUT ON
THE NEXT DAY HE CALLED
THEM ALL TOGETHER AND
SAID: "SIRS, YE KNOW WELL
THE BURDEN THAT I HAVE

taken on me touching the Admiral Gaudys. It is therefore convenient that I do the message I am charged with by King Charlemagne as quickly as I can. Wherefore I desire you all to keep good and true company with this noble damsel, and to tarry for me here the space of fifteen days. If I return not then, go you all into France, and take this noble lady with you, and salute from me King Charlemagne and all the peers of France, and shew them the hard adventures I have had and how I am gone to perform his message."

When his companions heard that they were sorrowful and said :

"Sir, you desire us to tarry here fifteen days; know for truth we shall tarry here for you a whole year."

Then Huon made him ready to depart and armed himself, and took his cup and horn, and the giant's ring which he put on his arm, and kissed his cousin and all the others, and they all made great lamentation for his departing, and went up and looked out of the windows after him as long as they might see him. Huon went on till he came to the seashore, where there was a little haven in which there was always some kind of ship or vessel by which to pass over the sea, and found none there. Then was he in great wonder and said :

"What shall I do since I can find no boat here to pass in? Alas, in an ill hour I slew Charlot, whereby I am thus in danger; howbeit I did it in

my

my own defence: great wrong hath King Charles done to banish me out of my country."

Suddenly he saw on his right hand a great beast like a bear come swimming towards him, so he made on his head the sign of the cross, and drew out his sword to defend himself with, thinking the beast would have assailed him. But he did not, for he went a little way off from Huon, and shook himself in such wise that his skin fell off, and then he was as fair a man and as well formed as could be seen. Huon had great fear and wonder when he saw this beast become a man, so he approached him and asked what he was, whether he was a human being or an evil spirit come thither to tempt him: "Right now, thou didst swim in the sea, and crossed great waters in the guise of a marvellous beast: I charge thee, in the name of God, do me no hurt and show me what thou art. I believe thou art one of King Oberon's companions."

"Huon," quoth he, "dismay thee not, I know thee well, thou art son to Duke Seguin of Bordeaux; noble King Oberon hath sent me unto thee. Once I broke his commandment, wherefore he hath commanded me to be for thirty years a beast in the sea."

"Friend," quoth Huon, "I will trust thee till I am past the Red Sea."

"Huon," quoth Malabron, "I am sent hither for no other thing but to bear thee whither thou wilt, therefore make you ready and recommend yourself

to

to the safeguard of our Lord, and then let one alone."

Then Malabron entered again into the beast's skin, and said to Huon : " Sir, mount on my back."

Huon made the sign of the cross when he saw the beast enter again into his skin, and prayed God to save and conduct him, and so leaped upon him ; the beast entered into the sea and swam as fast as a bird could fly, so that within a very short space of time he traversed the great river Nile, the which cometh from Paradise, a very dangerous river for the great multitude of serpents and crocodiles that be therein, howbeit there were none that did him any trouble. When they came to land Huon was quite joyful, but Malabron said :

"Right dearly shall I buy the time that ever I knew thee, for to do you this pleasure I shall remain yet ten years more in the sea as a beast. I have great pity on thee, for there is no man born of woman that knoweth the ill and poverty that shall fall hereafter on thee ; I shall suffer much for the love I have to thee, but I shall bear it in patience. Yonder thou mayest see the city whither thou wouldst go : thou knowest what has been commanded thee and what thou hast to do. Yet whatever befalls break not the commandment of King Oberon, and always say the truth, for as soon as thou makest any lie thou shalt lose the love of King Oberon. Thus God be with thee, for I may no longer tarry."

So

So he went again into the sea, and Huon tarried there alone, and presently took the way to the city, and entered therein without hindrance of any man. As soon as he entered he met a thousand Paynims going a hawking, and another thousand coming homeward; a thousand horses going to be new-shod, and another thousand coming from shoeing; then he saw a thousand men playing at chess, and another thousand that had just been mated; and another thousand talking and devising with the damsels; and a thousand coming from drinking the admiral's wine, and another thousand going thither. When he had gone a great way into the city, and seen much people, he had great marvel, and studied thereon so much that he forgot the giant's ring upon his arm, and the men that met him had also wonder when they saw one go afoot all armed. At last Huon came into a great place before the first gate of the palace, where there stood a vine growing on brick pillars of divers colours, under which the Admiral Gaudys would sit one day in each week, and give audience to all suitors. When he had looked at all this he came to the first gate of the palace and cried to the porter: "Friend, I pray thee, open the gate." Then the porter said with a good-will: "If thou be a Saracen thou shalt enter."

Alas, poor unadvised Huon, thinking not on King Oberon's commandment, nor on the giant's ring on his arm! If he had but showed it, he needed

needed not have made any lie. When Huon heard the Paynim demand whether he were a Saracen, he said: "Yea." The porter said: "Then may you securely enter."

So Huon passed the first bridge and gate, and ere he came to the second, he remembered how he had broken King Oberon's commandment, whereat he was so sorrowful that he wist not what to do, and sware that he would never lie more: then he took the ring in his hand, and came to the second gate, and said to the porter:

"Thou Paynim villain, open this gate, for I must enter."

When the porter heard him speak so fiercely, he said:

"How is it that the first porter was so hardy as to let thee enter in at the other gate?"

"I shall shew thee," quoth Huon; "seest thou not this ring, which is a token that I may go where I list."

When the porter heard him and saw the ring, he knew it well and said:

"Sir, ye be welcome: how fareth the lord that you come from?"

Huon, who would not lie, passed the bridge and gave no answer, and so he came to the third gate. The porter came to him and Huon shewed him the ring, so he let down the bridge and opened the gate, and with great reverence saluted Huon and suffered

him

him to pass. When he was thus past the three bridges, he said to himself:

"Alas, what shall become of me, seeing I have so quickly broken my promise to him that hath done so much for me? Alas, I forgot the ring that was about my arm. Howbeit, I trust that Oberon will not be displeased for it, seeing I did it not wilfully, but that I forgat it: I trust he will pay no more regard to this deed than he did when I blew the horn without any cause."

When Huon saw that he was past the three gates, he went on to the fourth gate with the ring in his hand, and met with no man but they did him honour when they saw the ring. Then he said to the fourth porter:

"Thou villain porter, open the gate."

When the porter heard him, he had great marvel, and said:

"Who art thou, that art armed, and speakest so fiercely to me? Lay away thine armour, and shew me who thou art, and whither thou wilt go; for armed as thou art, it is not possible for thee to enter. Shew me, by thy faith, how hast thou passed the other three bridges."

Then Huon said:

"Hold thy peace, Paynim. I am a messenger sent from the noble King Charlemagne, and whether thou wilt or no, I will pass this way and go to the palace to the Admiral Gaudys; neither thou nor

129   I   any

any other can stop me. Behold this token that I shew thee."

The Paynim knew it at once, and let down the bridge, opened the gate, kneeled down, kissed and embraced Huon's legs, desiring pardon that he had made him tarry so long.

"Paynim," quoth Huon, "good day."

"Sir," quoth the porter, "you may go to the admiral who will make you good cheer and great honour, nor is there anything you can desire but it shall be granted to you, yea, though it be his only daughter, for love of the lord from whom you bring this ring as a token: and, Sir, tell me how doth the Lord Angolafer? Comes he hither or not?"

"Porter," quoth Huon, "if he come hither, all the fiends of hell must bring him," and therewith he passed on without any more words. But he said to himself:

"Ah, Lord Jesus Christ, help and aid me in all my works. I was tempted by an evil spirit when I made a lie at the first gate; I did it in carelessness of heart and lack of remembrance, whereof I am now right sorry."

Thus Huon went forth till he came to the palace and entered into a fair garden wherein the admiral took his pleasure ofttimes. No fruit nor tree nor flower could be wished for, summer or winter, that was not there, and in the midst of the garden there was a fair fountain coming out of the river Nile,

130   that

that cometh from Paradise, which fountain was then of such might, that if any sick man did drink thereof, or washed his hands or face therein, at once he was made whole; if a man was of great age he returned to the age of thirty years, and a woman became fresh and fair as a maid of fifteen. Sixty years was that fountain of great fame, but ten years after Huon came, it was destroyed by the Egyptians, who made war on the admiral that was then Lord of Babylon. When Huon had washed his hands and face in the fountain he looked on the palace and thought it wondrous fair, and as he looked further he saw near by a great serpent who kept the fountain, to the extent that no traitor should touch it and escape without death; but when the serpent saw Huon, it bowed down without seeking to do him ill. Huon sat down by the well, and began piteously to weep, and said :

"Lord, without thy succour it is impossible for me to depart hence alive. Ah, noble King Oberon, forsake me not now in this need for the trespass that I have done should be forgiven me, seeing I did it negligently, for lack of remembrance. I will know certainly whether you will leave me for so small a cause; whatsoever fall, I shall assay it to know the truth;" then he took his horn and blew it fiercely.

When King Oberon in his forest heard it, he said: "Ah, I hear the false knight blow his horn. Little he cares for me, for at the first gate of the

palace

palace of Babylon he made a false lie. If he blow till the veins in his neck burst asunder he shall have no succour from me, whatever mischief may fall to him."

Then Huon in the garden blew so sore that the admiral who was seated at his dinner, rose from the board with all his lords and ladies and damsels, knights and squires, boys and scullions of the kitchen came into the hall to the admiral, and began to dance and sing, and made great joy; the sorer that Huon blew his horn, the more they danced and sang. When Huon left off blowing, the admiral called his barons, and ordered them to arm, and said :

"Sirs, go into this garden, for surely some enchanter is there. Take heed he escape not and bring him to me alive, for I will know of him why he hath done this. If he escape he will do us, be-like, more ill."

Now Huon had blown a long time, and had seen no one come to him, so he was sore cast down, and said :

"Sure my end draws near, when King Oberon forsakes me, in whom I had my trust. Ah, dear lady mother, and brother Gerardin, I shall never see you more. Ah, noble King Charlemagne, great wrong have you done me to banish me thus without cause, for what I did was in my own defence, God forgive it you. Ah, King Oberon, well may I call

thee

thee unnatural, thus to leave me for one small fault. Certainly if thou be noble I hope thou wilt pardon me ; at least, I put all before God, and to Him I submit me. But, whatsoever fall, I will enter into the palace and do my message that King Charlemagne hath commanded me to do."

So he made him ready and departed from the fountain, thinking to find the admiral at dinner at that hour.

Now as he mounted up the steps of the palace he came before two of the admiral's principal gods which were set in the middle of the palace, richly adorned, before them, two great torches burning, so that no Saracen came before them that did not do them reverence; but Huon passed by them and would not once look on them, nor would he speak to any man that he met, so that the folk had great marvel and said one to another :

" I believe this man that has come into the palace all armed is some messenger from some great prince to the admiral."

Now a Paynim king was speaking to the admiral, and was but new come, for that same day the Admiral Gaudys was to deliver to him his daughter, the fair Claramond, in marriage. Huon said to himself :

" If I acquit myself truly to King Charlemagne I must slay this Paynim king, since he sitteth so near the admiral. I must straightway strike off his head,

and

and then shall God do with me at His pleasure;" so he came near the table, and drew out his sword, and therewith gave the king such a stroke that his head fell on the table, and the admiral was covered with his blood. Then Huon said with a loud voice:

"Ah, what a good beginning is this! The rest I remit to the aid of God, whom I pray to help me in the rest of my enterprise. On this point I have now quit myself before King Charlemagne."

But the admiral said to his barons:

"Take this man that hath done me this offence, and murdered the king sitting at my table: if he escape, look me never in the face."

Then the Paynims assailed Huon on all sides, and cast darts and swords at him to slay him, but his good armour saved him from death, and with his sword he slew many a fell Paynim, so that none durst approach him. When he saw that he was like to be sore oppressed, he took off his ring from his arm and cast it on the table before the admiral, saying:

"Sir Admiral, beware on pain of thy life of doing me any hurt or damage, by this token that I shew thee."

When the admiral saw the ring, he knew it well and began to cry that no man should be so hardy as to touch him that had slain the Paynim king, so every man left Huon alone, whereof he was right glad. Then he said to the admiral:

"I will

" I will that from henceforth thou do as I command thee."

" Friend," quoth the admiral, "thou mayst do in my palace what thou wilt; whatsoever thou commandest shall be done, no man shall say the contrary."

Then Huon saw where his daughter, the fair Claramond, sat by her father, and he went to her and kissed her three times before her father, whereof the damsel was abashed; but she saw him so fair, and felt his mouth so sweet, that she thought she should die for sorrow without she might have him for her lover, and therewith she changed colour and blushed as ruddy as a rose.

When Huon had kissed the lady, he turned to the admiral and said:

" Sir Admiral, know for truth I am christened, and am a messenger sent from noble King Charlemagne to thee, because there is no prince, Christian or heathen, but obeyeth his commandments, except thyself. Therefore by me he sendeth thee word, that since the dolorous day of Roncesvalles, where he lost his two nephews, Roland and Oliver, he has never assembled so much people as he will do this next summer to fall upon thee, by water and by land, unless thou wilt believe in the law of Jesus Christ. If thou wilt believe me, be christened ere this mischief fall upon thee."

" Speak no more of that," quoth the admiral, " for

I had

I had rather be hewn to pieces and slain than leave my law to believe on another god."

"Moreover, Sir Admiral," quoth Huon, "King Charles commandeth thee to send a thousand sparrowhawks, a thousand goshawks, a thousand bears and a thousand boarhounds chained together, a thousand young varlets and a thousand damsels, a handful of thy beard and four of thy greatest teeth."

"Ha," quoth the admiral, "I see thou art hardy and outrageous to bid me do this thou hast said, and great marvel have I at thy master that he is so foolish as to command me to send him my beard and teeth. He hath sent me more than fifteen messengers and asked but part of this thou speakest of, but all fifteen have been hanged, and thou, by thy folly, shouldst make sixteen, but that by reason of the ring thou bearest we dare not touch thee. I pray thee, by the faith and law thou dost believe in, shew me who hath given thee that ring."

Then Huon, sore abashed that he dare not make a lie for fear of King Oberon, said:

"Sir, I will not hide the truth for fear of thee or of any Paynim here. Know that with this good sword I have slain your lord, Angolafer the giant."

When the admiral heard that, he said to his lords:

"Look that this ribald escape not, for by all the gods I believe in, I shall have no joy in my heart till I see him taken."

136   Then

Then Paynims and Saracens on all sides assailed
Huon, and he recommended himself to God, and
thought he should never see fair day more, and so
with his sword in both his hands he defended himself nobly, slaying, cutting off heads, arms and feet
of the Saracens, and of many he made the brains fly
abroad on the pavement. Great horror was it to
behold him, for by reason of that noble armour, no
Paynim could do him any damage, but gave way
before him, nor durst approach. Then Huon, full
of wrath, as he fought saw on one side of the palace,
an arch in the wall, and still fighting, he made his
way there, and set his back to the arch that none
should come behind him. There he raged like a
wild boar in a wood, and defended himself in such
wise, that whosoever he touched with a full stroke,
had thereafter no need of any surgeon. Thus for a
long space Huon endured, and had no great harm.
But at last the force of the Paynims was so great
that it was not possible for him to sustain it, and he
waxed weary and his strokes grew feeble; ofttimes
he called upon God and the Virgin, whiles on the
other part the admiral cried to his men and said :
"Ha, faint-hearted knaves, great shame it is to
you all that one man so long endures against you
all, and you can neither take him nor slay him."
Then the Paynims, when they heard their admiral
so belittle them, came in a great rage all at once
upon Huon, alone under the arch, and the admiral's
nephew

nephew came upon him, and when Huon saw him
approach, he lifted up his sword and gave the
Paynim such a stroke on the helm that he clave his
head to the breast; and therewith his sword fell out
of his hands, and a Saracen took it up, and all the
Saracens at once ran upon Huon, and took him, and
did off his armour, and took his cup and his horn
from him. Now when he was disarmed the
Saracens beheld him well, and one said to another
how they never saw so fair a man before, affirming
that if all Frenchmen were such as he was, there
was no king able to resist them.

So Huon was taken and brought before the
admiral, who was right joyful to see him. Then he
called his barons and asked what should be done to
the caitiff who had done them such harm as to slay
one of his most powerful kings, and his nephew as
well, besides many others; they all answered with
one voice that he should be slain straightway.
Then stepped forth an old ancient admiral of six
score years of age, one of the admiral's privy council,
and said:

" Sir Admiral, you may not do thus for the love of
this good day, the which is the feast of Saint John:
according to our law no man shall die on that day:
but, Sir, respite his life for a whole year, till the day
of the feast of your gods, since on that day you
must offer two champions to do with them your
sacrifice; let this man be one, the other will come by

138   that

that time; which of the two champions is overcome, make you sacrifice to the gods of him, for so you vowed to the gods the first day you took on you the lordship of Babylon. Sir, if it were not that this man had slain your nephew, you ought not to slay him, but rather to thank him, for by him the man you ought to hate most in the world is slain, that is the great giant Angolafer, for by his death you are out of all servitude and bondage, and by this man set at liberty."

When the Admiral Gaudys had well heard the Paynim, he said:

"Seeing it is so that you give me this counsel, and that mine ancestors have made this custom, I will not do the contrary, but it shall be as you have said."

Then was Huon led away by four Paynims, and the jailer was bidden to give him meat and drink sufficient: and when Huon saw how he was in prison he was right sorrowful, and began to remember the noble duchess his mother, and Gerard his brother, and said:

"Ah, Oberon, how is it that thou art so unnatural to me as to suffer me to endure so great misery for so small an offence: it is not unknown to thee that my offence was but only by forgetfulness."

Now leave we speaking of Huon, and say somewhat of the fair Claramond, daughter to the admiral.

139   When

When it was night and she was all alone in her
bed, she remembered the French knight who had
kissed her three times in the presence of her father,
and she was in great sorrow because he was put in
prison, and said to herself: " If he were not a knight
of great valour he would never have been so bold as
to have done as he hath done this day."

Then she thought that he was well worthy to be
beloved and succoured, so straightway she rose and
made her ready, and secretly took a torch of wax in
her hand and lighted it, and came from her room as
secretly as she could: it was about midnight and
every man was asleep in the palace. She went
straight to the prison, and came at so good a time
that she found the jailer asleep and stole away his
keys and opened the prison door. When Huon saw
the candle-light and the open door of the prison, he
was in great fear lest they would take him out to
put him to death, or to do him some displeasure,
and began to make pitiful complaints. The lady
who could well speak French, understood all Huon's
complaints, and said:

" Huon, dismay thee not; I am Claramond,
daughter to the admiral, whom thou didst kiss
three times this day in presence of my father.
If you love me and will do my will, I will deliver
thee out of prison, for I have had no other thought
or imagination since then but to deliver thee out
of the danger that thou art in."

140   " Lady,"

"Lady," quoth Huon, "God reward you for the great courtesy you would shew me; but, fair lady Claramond, you are a Saracen and I am christened. When I did kiss you it was by the command of King Charlemagne, who sent me hither, or else I had rather be in perpetual prison here than touch any part of your body as long as you are a Saracen."

"Huon," quoth the lady, "since you are of that mind, you shall end your days here in prison miserably; trust me, if I can, you shall suffer for the refusal you have made of me:"

Then she departed from the prison, and came to the jailer and awoke him, saying:

"Friend, I charge thee, on pain of thy life, that thou give neither meat nor drink these three days or nights to the French prisoner who is in thy keeping."

"Madam," quoth the jailer, "your order shall be obeyed."

Then the lady went again to her bed right pensive and full of fantasy. Huon was three days and nights without meat or drink, and on the fourth day he said, all weeping:

"I see well I must die for hunger; I humbly pray God to aid and succour me, and grant me the grace that I may not do anything against His pleasure or His holy law, for any evil that may come to me."

Thus this noble Huon complained all weeping;
there

there is no creature that might hear him, that would not be partaker of his great sorrows.

But the lady Claramond, who caused them, came every morning and evening to the prison to hear what Huon would say, and each time she asked Huon if he would answer her or not, and ever she found him at one point. At the last when she saw that, she asked of him whether he would promise to take her with him into France, and there take her to be his wife, if she delivered him out of prison.

"If thou wilt promise me this," quoth she, "thou shalt have meat and drink sufficient at thy pleasure."

"Dame," quoth Huon, "I promise you faithfully I shall do your pleasure, whatsoever may hap to me thereby."

"Then know for truth," quoth the lady, "that for the love of thee I will become christened and believe in the law of our Lord, as soon as we come into any place where it may be."

Then Huon thanked her, and she caused him to have meat and drink, whereof he was right joyful. So she called the jailer and said :

"Go thy way in haste to the admiral my father, and tell him that the French knight is dead three days ago for feebleness and hunger."

"Lady," quoth the jailer, "I am ready to do thy bidding."

So he went to the admiral and said :

142   "Sir,

"Sir, the French knight that was in my keeping is three days dead for famine."

"Ha," quoth the admiral, "I am sorry for it, seeing it cannot be mended, I will pass over it, but I had rather that he were alive."

Thus as you have heard was Huon respited from death, and it is a common saying that one day of respite is worth a hundred years. So the jailer returned to the prison unto the lady, and told her what he had said to the admiral.

"Well, friend," quoth the lady, "if thou wilt be secret, and aid me in such things as I wish to have, I shall make thee rich for ever."

"Lady," quoth he, "I am ready to die in thy quarrel. I shall do you service as you command, the fear of death shall not hinder me."

Now let us leave speaking of Huon, who was ofttimes visited, and had all things as he desired, and was well lodged at his pleasure, and let us speak of Gerames and of those that were with him in the castle of the giant.

CHAP. VIII.

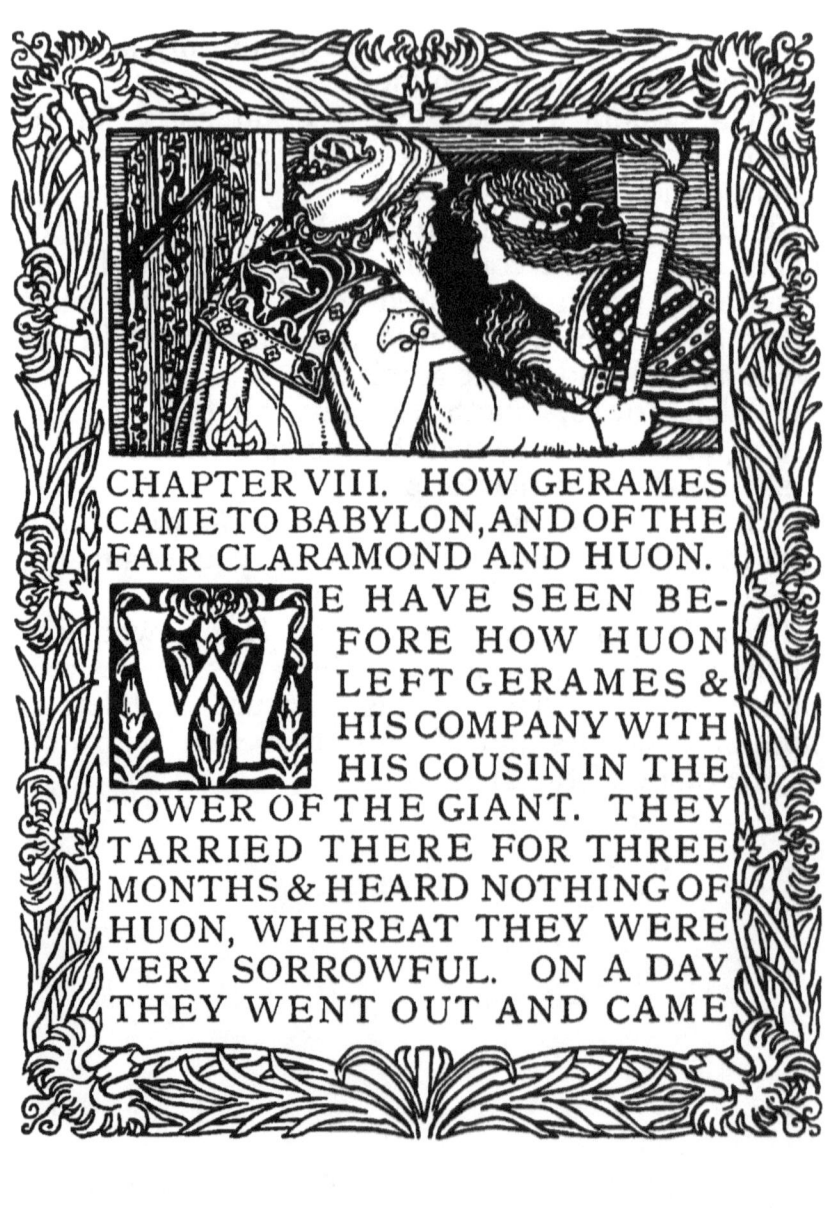

CHAPTER VIII. HOW GERAMES CAME TO BABYLON, AND OF THE FAIR CLARAMOND AND HUON.

E HAVE SEEN BEFORE HOW HUON LEFT GERAMES & HIS COMPANY WITH HIS COUSIN IN THE TOWER OF THE GIANT. THEY TARRIED THERE FOR THREE MONTHS & HEARD NOTHING OF HUON, WHEREAT THEY WERE VERY SORROWFUL. ON A DAY THEY WENT OUT AND CAME to the seaside, if there might be there any word of Huon, and as they looked on the sea they saw a ship with thirty Paynims in it, loaded with great riches. So Gerames said to his companions when he saw how the ship was coming to that port:

"Let us go and see if we can learn any tidings of Huon from them."

By the time the mariners had cast their anchor Gerames had come to them, and asked of them whence they came, and whither they would go.

"Sir," quoth they, "we would go to this town to pay to Angolafer the giant the tribute we are bound to pay every year; therefore, Sir, we desire you to shew us where we may find him."

Then Gerames waited until they were all landed out of the ship, and then he said:

"Ah, ye unhappy Paynims, ye shall never depart hence, for he that ye ask for is dead, and all ye shall bear him good company."

So saying, Gerames called to his companions:

"Sirs, let all these Paynims be slain," and then they set upon them straightway, so that all were slain, not one escaped alive, since the Christians were armed and the Paynims had neither weapon nor armour, otherwise they durst not land in the giant's country. Then Gerames and his friends entered into the ship and took all they found there, and bare it into the tower, and afterward they went to dinner and made great joy of their adventure.

K   After

After dinner Gerames said: "Sirs, if we were now in France, and King Charlemagne asked of us what is become of Huon, none of us could tell whether he is alive or dead. If we should say that he is dead and he should afterward return home, we should be reputed false men for ever after, both we and our children: a man may be a prisoner fourteen or fifteen years, and yet come home again at the last safe and sound. If you will believe me, we shall do like true men. We have now in this port a good ship well furnished with every thing, we have here gold and silver in plenty, we can soon victual our ship, and then let us take the sea and never cease sailing till we hear some news of our lord Huon. If we do thus we do as true men ought to do. I desire every man of you to shew his counsel."

Without taking any longer respite they all answered with one voice that they were ready to accomplish what he had devised, and they took gold and silver and all their riches, and bore them into the ship, and furnished it with wine, biscuit, salt meat, and artillery. When their ship was garnished they put into it their horses and their armour, and all thirteen companions entered it, the damsel being with them. They weighed the anchor and hauled up the sail, leaving the tower of the giant empty, and no man therein, and sailed along the coast till they came to the high sea, and till they came to Damietta,

146   and

and entered into the river Nile, and at last they arrived at Babylon, and came into the port, and took out their horses. Gerames, knowing well the language and the manner of entering the four gates, said to his companions: " Let us leap on our horses and enter into the city to see if we may hear any news of our master Huon."

Thus they rode forth and entered the city, and they agreed with one another that they would go to the palace, but when they were come thither they should all hold their peace and suffer only Gerames to speak.

"Ah, good Lord," quoth Gerames, as they rode through the town, " I beseech Thee of Thy grace grant us that we may hear some good tidings of our master Huon of Bordeaux, for whom we be in jeopardy of death."

They passed all the four bridges and gates, Gerames shewing forth such reasons that the porters were content, came before the great hall, there they alighted and mounted up, all thirteen, the damsel being with them. When they were in the hall they saw the Admiral Gaudys sitting on a rich chair garnished with gold and precious stones, and Gerames came before him and said in the Saracen tongue :

"The same Mahound that causeth the vine and the corn to grow, save and keep the Admiral Gaudys, whom I see sitting among his barons."

" Friend,"

"Friend," quoth the admiral, "thou art welcome. I pray thee shew me who thou art and whither thou wouldst go."

"Sir," quoth Gerames, "I am come from the good city of Montbraunt, and I am son to King Ivoryn."

When the admiral heard that he rose to his feet and said:

"Thou art welcome, son of my brother. Fair nephew, I pray you, how is my brother Ivoryn?"

"Sir," quoth Gerames, "when I departed from him I left him in good health, and he saluted you by me, and hath sent you twelve Frenchmen by me, which were taken upon the sea, as they were going a pilgrimage to the holy sepulchre of God in Jerusalem. He desireth you to put them in prison until the day of Saint John the Baptist, at which day ye must make the feast of your God: then bring them into the meadow here without, bind them to stakes, and let your archers shoot at them that you may know who shoots best. This damsel that is here with me is to be put to your daughter to teach her to speak the French language."

"Fair nephew," quoth the admiral, "it shall be done as you have said: I give you power to command everything in this house at your pleasure. I pray you shew me what is your name."

"Sir," quoth he, "I am called Jeracle."

"Well," quoth the admiral, "from henceforth you
shall

shall be my chief chamberlain and have the key of the prison in your keeping, to put these caitiffs therein and do with them at your pleasure. Love them but a little, yet let them have meat and drink sufficient that they die not for famine, as but lately died a Frenchman sent me by King Charles of France who was called Huon of Bordeaux, a right fair young man in truth."

When Gerames heard that he had never before so great sorrow of heart. His displeasure was so great that he had near hand run on the admiral; he took up a staff that lay by him and gave each of the Frenchmen such strokes on their heads that the blood ran down, but they suffered it and durst not stir, they were in such fear of the admiral, but they cursed Gerames in their hearts for his strokes.

When the admiral saw how he had well beaten the Frenchmen, he said: " Fair nephew, it seemeth well you love but little these Christians."

" Sir," quoth he " I hate these Christian men more than any men in the world: all the way that I have come I have thus beaten them three times every day in honour of my god Mahound, and in despite of the law of Jesus Christ on whom they believe."

Thus then Gerames departed from the admiral, and led with him the twelve French prisoners, beating them till he came to the prison, and none of them durst speak one word, but they cursed Gerames to themselves.

149   As

As they went prisonwards they met the lady Claramond, and she said :

"Cousin, I am right joyous of your coming, but I would shew you a secret matter, if I dare trust in you, so that you promise not to discover me."

"Cousin," quoth Gerames, "by my faith that I owe to my god Mahound, you may well shew me your will and pleasure ; I shall not discover you were my eyes to be drawn out."

When the damsel heard that promise she said :

"Fair cousin, five months past there came to my father the admiral a French knight with a message from King Charlemagne, who called himself Huon of Bordeaux. When he had done his message, he slew a Paynim king as he sat at the table by my father, and after came and kissed me three times and after slew many Saracens : wherefore at last he was taken prisoner and set in prison, where he is yet. Howbeit, I made my father believe that he died of famine ; yet cousin, he is alive, as well served of meat and drink as my father is."

When Gerames heard the damsel thus speak he was both sorrowful and angry, for he thought she did it to deceive him, so he passed forth and made her no manner of answer, but came to the prison and put in the prisoners rudely ; while Claramond went away right sorrowful that she had shewed so much of her mind to Gerames, whom she took to be her cousin. Huon being in the prison had great

marvel

marvel what prisoners they were that were let down into the prison, but he could not see them, the prison was so dark, so he drew near them to hear them speak. At last one of them began to make his complaint and said:

"Ah, Lord Jesus, succour us, for Thou knowest well that we have not deserved this we suffer, but it is for the love of our young lord Huon of Bordeaux whom we have loved so well that now we be lost for ever. Dear Lord Christ, have mercy on our souls."

When Huon heard what he said, he knew well they were Christians and Frenchmen, so he approached them and said:

"Sirs, ye that be here, I pray you shew me what ye be and how ye be come hither."

"Sir," quoth one of them, "five months past there departed from us a young knight, with whom we departed out of the realm of France, son of a noble Duke Seguin of Bordeaux. This knight slew Charlot, son to King Charlemagne, by misadventure, wherefore he was banished out of the realm of France and sent to do a message to the Admiral Gaudys. Now is he dead in prison, as it is shewed us, and, Sir, we went to seek him, and are betrayed by one of our company."

When Huon heard him speak he knew him well and said:

"Be of good comfort and make good cheer, for I am here, Huon, safe and in good health, thanked be

God

God and the admiral's daughter, who loves me and hath saved my life: soon shall ye see how she will come and visit us. But I pray you, Sirs, what is become of old Gerames, is he left behind to keep the tower with the damsel my cousin, whom I left in your keeping?"

"Sir," quoth they, "a worse creature or more untrue traitor was never born: he hath betrayed and beaten us and put us in this prison: as for the damsel she is with the admiral's daughter."

When Huon perceived that they all were of his company he went and kissed them and said: "Sirs, know of a surety that all that Gerames hath done is to the intent to deliver us: I know so well the truth of Gerames. Make good cheer, for as soon as night cometh we shall be visited with great joy."

"Surely," quoth they, "we believed that Gerames had forsaken the faith of Jesus Christ and become a Saracen, for he hath made the admiral believe he is son to his brother King Ivoryn of Montbraunt."

When Huon heard that he had great joy at his heart and said:

"The truth of Gerames and the love that he hath always shewed me shall be right profitable in spite of Oberon, who hath forsaken me for a small offence."

Now leaveth this story to speak of Huon and his company being in prison, and speaketh of old Gerames who studied for the deliverance of Huon and his company.

Now

Now sheweth the story when that Gerames was returned to the admiral he said :

"Sir, the Frenchmen that I brought are fast in prison, and well beaten."

"Fair nephew," quoth the admiral, "they have had but an evil neighbour of you."

Then Gerames went into his chamber and studied how he might furnish the prisoners with victual, and at last he got together sufficient for them. When night came he went with his food to the prison, for he might do what he list since every man was ready to do him service : so he sent the men away and tarried there alone a while. He had not been there long when the admiral's daughter came thither, and when Gerames saw her he wist not what to think.

"Fair cousin," quoth he, "I pray you shew me what you do here at this hour."

"Dear cousin," quoth she, "the great trust I have in you hath made me to come hither, because to-day I discovered all my secrets to you, and that which I am about to do. I would you would leave the law of Mahound, and receive the Christian faith, and go with me into France with these prisoners. We shall find the manner how to depart, and to have with us all the prisoners that you have put in prison."

When Gerames heard the lady he was joyful, for then he knew she went not about to deceive him, but that she did it of the good will she bore to Huon ;

howbeit

howbeit he thought he would not discover himself to her till he knew the truth from Huon, so he answered the damsel fiercely:

"Oh thou false wench, how art thou so bold as to speak or think thus? Surely the admiral thy father shall know it as soon as he cometh out of his chamber, and then shalt thou be burnt and the Frenchman hanged."

"Ah, Sir," quoth she, "I pray you let me go into the prison with you that I may see Huon once yet ere I die: I am content to lose my life for love of him, nor will I live one day after him: therefore let me once take leave of him."

"For this once," quoth Gerames, "I am content that you go with me."

Then he took a torch in his hands, opened the door, and entered.

No sooner was he in the prison than Huon knew him, and came up and embraced him, saying:

"Ha, my true lover, blessed be the hour that I found you;" and all came and kissed him.

When Claramond saw their manner she was joyful, for she saw well that her purpose should surely be carried out, and she came up to Huon and asked if they were his servants that made so great cheer together.

"Lady," quoth Huon, "surely all these that be here are my men: you may trust them in safety, for there is none of them but shall do your commandment."

154   "Huon,"

" Huon," quoth the damsel, " their coming pleaseth me right well."

Then Huon said to his company:

" I pray you make good cheer to this noble lady; by her we shall be delivered, for it is she that hath saved my life : " and they all together thanked her.

" Sirs," quoth she, " if you will work by my counsel, I shall shew you how I may aid you to deliver yourselves hence. Know all of you that I believe firmly in Jesus Christ, and at this day I leave the Admiral Gaudys my father because he believeth not in our Lord Jesus, and hateth so Christian men, he cannot abide to hear men speak of them, but believeth only in Mahound and in his idols, therefore my heart cannot love him : if he did otherwise I would bring no evil on him for all the good things in the world. I shall bring you all into my chamber at the hour of midnight, where I shall provide armour for you all, and then I shall shew you my father's room, and ye shall find him sleeping and bind him, and when he is bound then shall we depart in safety."

When Huon heard her he said :

" Madam, if God will, your father shall not be hurt, the day shall come that you shall otherwise deliver us; I thank you that you desire our deliverance so much. Now depart hence with Gerames, for it is near hand day, that our business be not perceived."

Then

Then the lady and Gerames closed again the prison doors, and went into the palace, and every day Gerames and the lady went to visit the prisoners, and bore them all things needful for them, and Gerames was always with the admiral and did what he would, for there was no Paynim that durst do contrary to his commandment. Now leave we to speak of the Admiral, of Gerames, and of Huon, until the time that we return to them again.

As you have before heard, Huon slew the giant Angolafer, which giant had seventeen brethren all elder than himself; and when the death of Angolafer was known, and his elder brother, named Agrapart, was advertised of it, he took thereof great sorrow. He was as great as his brother was, seventeen feet long, and big thereafter; he was a foot between the brows, his eyes redder and more burning than a brand of fire, the gristle of his nose as great as the muzzle of an ox, and with two teeth issuing out of his mouth more than a foot long each of them: if I should describe his foul figure at length it should annoy all the hearers thereof: ye may well believe that when he was in displeasure he had a fearful cheer, for then his eyes seemed two burning torches. When he knew of the death of his brother he sent all over his country that every man should come to him in harness, and so they did: and after they were come, he declared to them the death of his brother Angolafer, and said how it was in his mind to go to

Babylon

Babylon to the Admiral Gaudys, to take possession
of the lands and seigniories that were his brother's,
and also to have the tribute that was due by the
admiral. Then all his lords said :

" Sir, command at your pleasure, and we shall
obey it."

" Well, Sirs," quoth he, " then I will that every
man leap on his horse to go toward Babylon : " and
so they all obeyed and leaped on their horses, and
rode so long that they came into a plain near to the
city of Babylon : ten thousand men together. Then
Agrapart said :

" Sirs, tarry ye all here till I come again, for I will
go all alone and speak with the Admiral Gaudys : "
he armed him and took a great falchion in his hands
and departed all alone, and so went and entered into
the city of Babylon and passed the four gates, there
was no Paynim that durst say him nay. He rested
not till he came to the palace where the admiral
was sitting at dinner, and Gerames sitting before
him : then he came to the table and said :

" The same god Mahound under whom we live,
who causeth the wine and corn to grow, confound
the Admiral Gaudys as an ill caitiff and an untrue
traitor."

When the admiral saw how he was thus dispraised,
he said :

" Agrapart, in this that thou hast said thou liest
falsely, thus shamefully to rebuke me in my own

court

court before all my lords; shew me the cause why you do me this injury."

"Admiral," quoth he, "it is because there is come into thy court he that slew my brother, whom thou oughtest straightway to have slain : wherefore, if it were not for my honour I would strike thee on the nose with my fists, thou set him in prison without any more hurt doing to him. Therefore, thou traitor thief, by Mahound be thou cursed; thou art not worthy to sit in a royal seat : arise up, it is not meet for thee to sit there."

Therefore he drew the admiral so rudely out of his chair that his hat and crown fell down to the earth, and he was sore abashed; but Agrapart sat down in his chair and said :

"Thou false traitor, my brother is dead, therefore from henceforth thou shalt be my subject, for it pertaineth to me to have the lands my brother had, and the tribute they wert wont to pay him, or else I shall strike off thy head. Howbeit, I will not act against right, for if thou wilt prove the contrary, or find two champions so bold as for thy love to fight with me in open battle, I shall fight with them or more, if thou wilt send them to me. If it be so that I am overcome and discomfited with two of them, I am content that from henceforth thou shalt hold my lands frank and free, without any tribute-paying; and if it so be that I conquer them both, then thou shalt be my subject, and pay me tribute for ever, and
158   also

also pay me every year four drachms of gold for thy head-money."

"Agrapart," quoth the admiral, " I am content thus to do, and to match two of my men to fight with thee."

When he had said this, the admiral cried aloud :

" Where be the two gentle knights that will be ever my friends? Now is the time come that all the goodness and great gifts that I have given among you should be rewarded. If there be any among you that will fight against this giant, I shall give him my daughter Claramond in marriage, and after my death he shall have all my heritage, no man shall say nay thereto."

But for any fair words or promises that the admiral could make there was no Paynim so hardy as to come forward, whereupon the admiral made great sorrow and began to weep.

When Agrapart the giant saw him he said :

" Thy weeping cannot avail thee, for whether thou wilt or not, it behoves thee to pay these four pieces of gold yearly : I am sure there is no Paynim dare fight against me."

It sore grieved the heart of the lady Claramond to see her father weep, and she said :

" Oh, my father, if I knew it should not displease you, I would shew you one thing which should bring you out of this doubt."

" Daughter," quoth he, " I swear by Mahound I will not be displeased whatsoever thou sayest."

159   " Sir,"

"Sir," quoth she, "I have told you once that the Frenchman that brought you the message from King Charlemagne was dead in prison; but surely he is yet alive. If it please you I shall fetch him to you, and I warrant you he will take on him this battle against the giant, for he shewed you how he slew Angolafer; I have hope by the aid of Mahound he will in like wise slay his brother, this giant Agrapart."

"Daughter," quoth the admiral, "it is my pleasure that you fetch the prisoner to me; for if he may discomfit this giant, I am content that he and all his company shall depart frank and free at their pleasure:" so the lady and Gerames went to the prison and took out Huon and all his company and brought them before the admiral. Then the admiral looked hard at Huon, and marvelled that he was in so good case, though his colour was somewhat pale by reason of lying so long in prison; and he said:

"Friend, it seemeth by thy looks that thou hast had a good prison."

"Sir," quoth Huon, "I thank your daughter for it, and I pray you shew me for what cause you have as now sent for me."

"Friend," quoth the admiral, "I shall shew thee. Behold yonder armed Saracen who hath challenged me to fight with him hand to hand, or against two of the best men I have, and I can find none so bold

as

as to dare fight against this Paynim. If it be so
that thou wilt take on thee this enterprise for me, I
shall deliver thee and all thy company free to go
into thy own country at thy pleasure, and conduct
thee in safety to the city of Acre. Also I will give
thee a sompner mule laden with gold which thou
shalt present from me to King Charlemagne, and
every year from henceforth I will send him a like
present for my head-money, and will make him such
writings thereon as his council can devise. If he
have any war I will send him two thousand men
paid for a year, and if he desire me in person, I shall
pass the sea with a hundred thousand Paynims to
serve him, for I had rather been in servitude there
than pay four drachms to this giant. Moreover,
if thou wilt abide with me, I will give thee my
daughter Claramond in marriage, and the half of my
realm to maintain thine estate."

"Sir," quoth Huon, "I am content to do this if I
may have my own armour, and my rich horn of ivory
and my cup which were taken from me when I was
made prisoner."

"Friend," quoth the admiral, "all shall be
delivered to thee: thou shalt not lose the value of
one penny:" and he sent for the horn and cup and
the armour, and delivered them to Huon, whereof
he had great joy.

When Agrapart saw and knew that the admiral
had found a champion to fight with him, he said to

L the

the admiral : " Sir, I will go out and speak with my knights, and in the meantime let thy champion be ready apparelled, for I shall not tarry long. I shall have no joy till I have torn his heart from his body ; " and therewith he departed and went to his men.

Huon did on his coat of mail, and gave his horn of ivory to Gerames, saying :

" Friend, I pray you keep my horn till I return again ; " then he prayed our Lord to forgive him his sins, to succour and aid him to discomfit that foul giant. When he had made his prayers he put on his harness as quickly as though he had never been in prison, whereby he knew well that God was pleased with him. Then he said :

" Oh, noble King Oberon, I pray thee, seeing God is pleased with me, put away thy displeasure and pardon me : for the breaking of thy commands I have been sore punished ; be not displeased if I spake any hasty words in my prison, famine caused me to do it. I confess I did ill in breaking thy commandment, yet it was only by negligence and forgetting. Ah, Sir, what courtesy you shewed me when you found me in the wood and gave me your rich horn and cup, by the which I have been ofttimes succoured. Now, Sir, I require thee to pardon me all my trespasses and help me at my need, for I see well that without the grace of God and your help there is nothing can save my life."

Thus Huon besought God for pardon and grace

to

to destroy his enemy: and when he had made his prayer there came a Saracen to Huon, and said:

"Sir, here is your own sword that you lost when you were taken."

"Friend," quoth Huon, "you do me great courtesy, God give me grace to reward thee," and he did on his helm, and girt on his sword: and the admiral sent him a good horse, the best in all his court. Huon was right joyful thereat, and thanked the admiral, for the saddle, harness, and bridle of the horse were so rich that the value of it could not be counted: then he made the sign of the cross, and mounted on his horse, armed at all points, and so rode out of the palace into a fair meadow, and there made a course to assay his horse. Afterward he stopped him before the admiral, who was sitting in a window of his palace, and he looked on Huon and said to his lords:

"These Frenchmen are to be feared and dreaded, for Huon is a goodly young man: and it had been a great pity if he had been slain."

So he commanded the field to be kept by a thousand Saracens, that no treason should be done, and said to Huon: "Mahound be thy guide."

When Agrapart saw Huon he said:

"Thou that art of so great courage as to fight against me, how near akin art thou to the admiral, seeing thou wilt put thyself in adventure of death for the love of him?"

163   "Paynim,"

"Paynim," quoth Huon, "know for truth I am nothing akin to the admiral, but I was born in the realm of France; and if thou desire to know what I am, I say unto thee that I am he who slew thy brother."

"For that," quoth the Paynim, "I am the more sorrowful; and yet again joyous, since Mahound hath done me the grace to have power to revenge his death : yet if thou wilt believe and worship my god Mahound, forsake thy belief, and go with me into my country, I shall make thee so great a lord that none of thy kin was ever such, and I shall give thee my sister in marriage, who is a foot greater than I am, and black as a coal."

"Paynim," quoth Huon, "I care neither for thy land nor for thy sister, keep them both; beware thou of me, for I shall never have joy in my heart till I have slain thee, as I did thy brother. I defy thee in the name of God and of the Virgin."

"And I thee," quoth the giant, "in the name of Mahound."

So they went asunder to take their courses, and ran at each other, and met so fiercely that their spears broke in pieces, and both their horses fell to the earth ; but the champions quickly sprang up, and came each at the other. Agrapart took up his falchion to strike Huon, but he stepped a little on one side, whereby the Paynim missed his stroke and Huon lifted up his sword and struck the giant so

marvellous

marvellous a stroke on the helm, that he struck off a quarter thereof and wounded him sore, and the stroke descended and cut off his ear, so that the bright blood ran down to the ground. Then Huon said:

"Paynim, thou art unhappy, for thou mightest have been content with the death of thy brother, and not have come hither to suffer as much thyself: never more shalt thou see fair day."

When the giant saw himself hurt he had great fear and said:

"Cursed be he of Mahound that forged thy sword: I yield me to thee; take here my sword; I pray thee do me no hurt."

"Paynim," quoth Huon, "have no doubt, seeing thou dost yield thee to me there is none so hardy as to do thee any displeasure:" and he took him by the arm and brought him into the city, whereof the admiral and all his lords had great joy; but the great joy that Claramond had passed all other.

CHAP. IX.

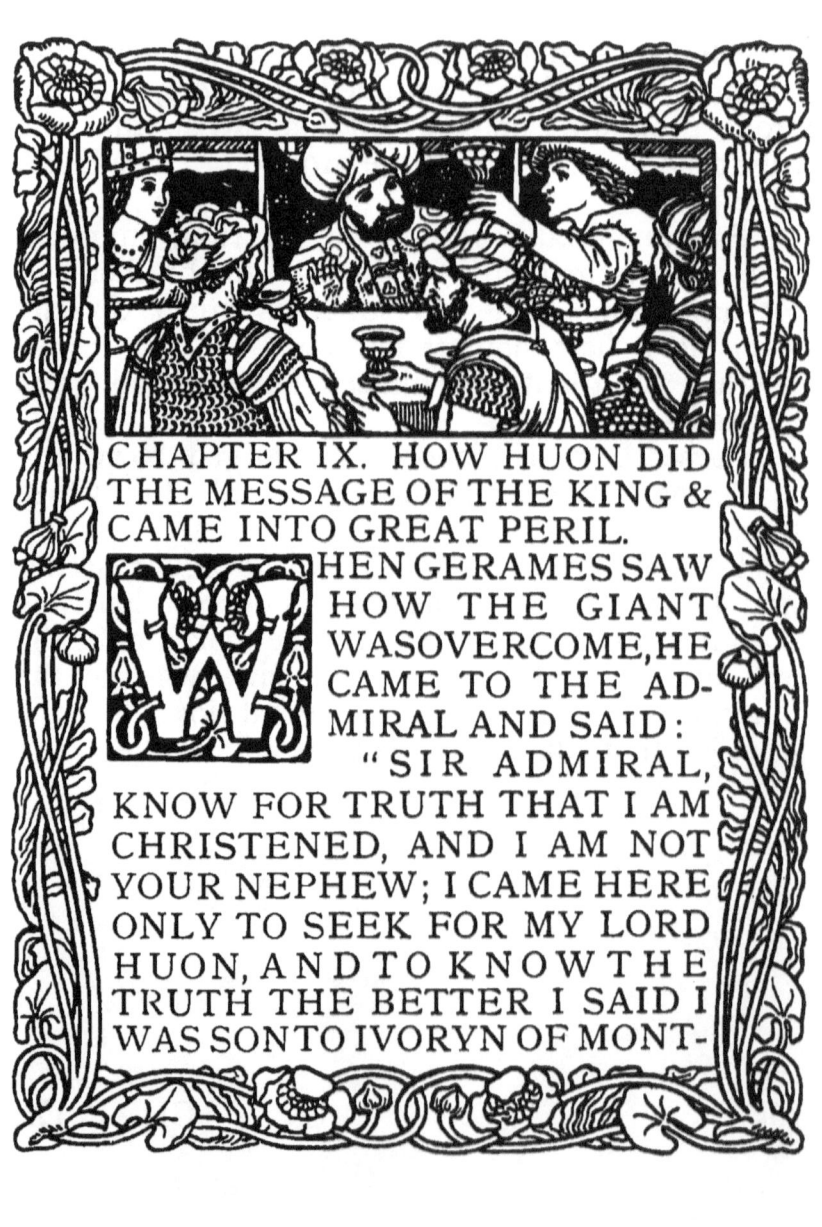

CHAPTER IX. HOW HUON DID
THE MESSAGE OF THE KING &
CAME INTO GREAT PERIL.

WHEN GERAMES SAW
HOW THE GIANT
WAS OVERCOME, HE
CAME TO THE AD-
MIRAL AND SAID:
"SIR ADMIRAL,
KNOW FOR TRUTH THAT I AM
CHRISTENED, AND I AM NOT
YOUR NEPHEW; I CAME HERE
ONLY TO SEEK FOR MY LORD
HUON, AND TO KNOW THE
TRUTH THE BETTER I SAID I
WAS SON TO IVORYN OF MONT-

braunt, your brother, thereby to know the certainty of what was become of Huon, for I knew well he was sent to you on a message from King Charlemagne."

When the admiral heard Gerames he had great marvel and said :

" It is hard for any man to know the craft and subtlety that is in a Frenchman."

Then he turned and saw Huon coming up the steps, bringing with him the giant, so he went and met him, and Gerames and his friends followed him, right joyful that they had seen the victory. When Huon saw the admiral he took Agrapart by the hand, and said to the admiral :

" Sir, I deliver him into your hands, who this day did you the injury to draw you out of your chair; I deliver him to you to do with him at your pleasure."

When Agrapart heard that he kneeled down and said :

" Sir Admiral, he hath much to do that thinketh foolishly; this I say of myself, for to-day when I came to you I thought myself the most puissant man that reigned on the earth, and that you were not sufficient nor worthy to serve me. But ofttimes believing deceiveth his master, for I thought that I would not have turned from my path for ten men, but otherwise is fallen to me, for I am discomfited by one man alone, and am taken and brought into your hands, so that you may do with me at your

167   pleasure.

pleasure. Yet, Sire, I beg you have pity on me, and pardon the outrage I have done on you."

The admiral answered and said how he would pardon him on the condition that he should never after do wrong to him, or any man in his country, and beside that, said he, "you shall become my man, and do me homage before all them that are here present."

"Sir," quoth Agrapart, "I am ready to fulfil your pleasure," and he did homage to the admiral in the presence of all them that were there, and in great joy they all sat down to dinner. The admiral did great honour to Huon and made him sit by him, with Agrapart and Gerames and the other Frenchmen, and for their service and many dishes of sundry sorts of meats, I speak not of them. Huon, who had great desire to finish his enterprise, drew out his cup which Gerames had given to him with his horn of ivory, and said to the admiral :

"Sir, you may see here this rich cup in my hand, all empty."

"Sir," quoth the admiral, "I see well there is nothing therein."

"Sir," quoth Huon, "I shall shew you how our law is holy and divine." Then he made the sign of the cross three times over the cup, which was straightway full of wine, whereat the admiral had great marvel.

"Sir," quoth Huon, "I present you this cup, that

you

you may drink thereof, then shall you see the goodness of the wine."

The admiral took it in his hand, and straightway the cup was empty, and the wine vanished. Then the admiral had great marvel and said:

"Huon, you have enchanted me."

"Sir," quoth Huon, "I am no enchanter, but it is because you are sinful, since your law is of no worth. You may perceive that my saying is true by the great virtue that God hath put into this cup."

"Huon," quoth the admiral, "trouble not yourself to speak to me of changing my belief and taking yours: but tell me whether you will abide here with me or go into France, for I will perform what I have promised."

"Ah, Sir Admiral," quoth Huon, "I know you will keep covenant with me in what you have promised me; but I pray you have pity on your own soul, and leave your faith since it is neither good nor just. If you do not I swear by my faith I shall call here so many men-at-arms that all the houses in your palace and city shall be full."

When the admiral heard Huon say this, he turned to his own men and said:

"Sirs, well may you hear the pride that is in this Frenchman, who hath been more than half a year in my prison, and now threateneth to slay me because I will not take on me his law and leave my own. I have great marvel where he should find so many

men

men as he hath said, or what hinders me to slay him at my pleasure."

"Sir," quoth Huon, "I ask of you once more if you will do as I have said."

"Huon," quoth the admiral, "beware, on pain of your eyes, and as you love your life, that you speak no more to me of this matter, for by the faith that I owe to Mahound, if all King Charlemagne's host were here assembled, it should not save thy life."

"Admiral," quoth Huon, "I fear that too late you will repent."

When Huon saw that the admiral would not leave his law to receive Christendom, he set his horn to his mouth and blew it with such force that the blood burst out of his mouth. The admiral and men put the tables from them and rose, and all that were in the palace began to sing and dance. Now King Oberon was in his wood and heard the horn blow, and said:

"Ah, I know surely that my friend Huon hath great need of me, I pardon him his trespass for he hath been sufficiently punished: there is not in all the world so noble a man as Huon is, it is pity that his heart is so light and mutable: I wish myself with him, with a hundred thousand men well armed."

Straightway he and all his company were in the city of Babylon, and they began to slay all such as would not believe on Jesus Christ, but Oberon went

to

to the palace with all his chivalry, every man with his sword naked in his hand. When Huon saw Oberon he embraced him and said:

"I ought greatly to thank God and you that you have come so far to aid me in my needs."

"Huon," quoth Oberon, "while you believe me and work by my counsel, I shall not fail you."

On all sides they slew Paynims, men, women, and children, except such as would be christened, and Oberon took the admiral and delivered him into the hands of Huon, who had thereof great joy, and asked of him whether he was minded to leave the law of Mahound and to take Christendom.

"Huon," quoth the admiral, "I had rather be hewn all to pieces than take your law and forsake my own."

Oberon then said to Huon:

"Why do you tarry to put him to death?" and he lifted up his sword and struck the admiral that his head flew off from his shoulders.

"It lieth well in thy power now," quoth Oberon, "to be quit with Charlemagne:" so Huon took the admiral's head and opened his mouth and took out his four greatest teeth, and cut off his beard, and took thereof as much as pleased him.

Then said Oberon:

"Now thou hast in thy hands the admiral's teeth and beard, look as thou lovest thy life, that thou keep them well."

"Ah,

"Ah, Sir," quoth Huon, "I beg you put them in such a place that they may be well kept, so that I may have them in time of need, for I feel that my heart is so light again that I shall otherwise forget them or lose them."

"In this thing," quoth Oberon, "I think thou speakest wisely. I wish them in Gerames' side in such manner that they shall do him no hurt."

No sooner had he spoken the word, than by the will of God, and the power he had from the fairies, they were closed in Gerames' side in such wise that no man could see them. Then he said to Huon:

"Friend, I must go to my castle of Momure; I desire you to do well, and you shall take with you Claramond, daughter to the admiral. I charge you, on pain of your life, and inasmuch as you fear to displease me, embrace her not till ye be married together in the city of Rome, for if you do the contrary you shall find such poverty and misery, that though you had double the mischief you have had since you came out of France, it should be nothing in regard to what shall come on you hereafter if you break my commandment."

"Sir," quoth Huon, "by the pleasure of our Lord I shall well beware of doing anything against your pleasure."

Then Oberon made ready a rich ship, well garnished with cabins, and so richly hung that it was incredible to be heard tell of or seen : there was

no

no cord, but it was of gold and silk. If I should shew you the beauty and riches of this ship, it would be over long to recite. When the ship was furnished with victuals, Huon put therein his horses, and Oberon took leave of him, and kissed and embraced him, sore weeping. When Huon saw him weep he had great marvel and said:

" Dear Sir, for what cause do you weep?"

" Huon," quoth he, "the thing that moveth me thus to do is because I have great pity on thee. If you knew the poverty and misery you shall endure, every member thou hast should tremble for fear. I know for certain thou hast so much to suffer that no human tongue can rehearse it:" and Oberon departed without more speaking. When Huon saw Oberon depart he was right pensive, but his youth put him out of his sorrow, and he set him to make his ordinance in the city. The fair lady Claramond he caused to be christened, and after he married his cousin Sebylle to an admiral of the country who was newly christened, and Huon gave them the city of Babylon and all that belonged thereto. Further, he made a little ship to go with his own ship, that he might send ashore for victuals when need was, and he and all his company went into his great ship after he had taken leave of his newly married cousin that was right sorrowful at his departure. Then they lifted up their sails and had a good fresh wind, and so sailed till they were out of the river Nile; and

passed

passed by Damietta and came into the high sea where they had wind at will.

On a day they sat at dinner and made good cheer, for by reason of the cup they had wine at their pleasure.

"Ah," quoth Huon, "greatly am I bound to thank King Oberon that I have such a cup and horn and armour, and whenever I blow my horn I can have men enough to aid me. Also I have the admiral's beard and teeth, but specially I have the fair lady Claramond whom I love so perfectly that I can no longer endure it. Howbeit the dwarf Oberon to mock me hath forbidden me in any wise to embrace her. Yet I will that he should know that in this case I will not obey him, for she is my own, and I will do with her at my pleasure." When Gerames heard him, he said: "Alas, Sir, what will you do? You know well Oberon never as yet made any lie to you, but you have always found him true. If he had not been so both you and we would have been lost before this time, and now you would break his commandment. If you embrace this lady before the time come that he hath set you, great misfortune shall fall thereby on us."

"Gerames," quoth Huon, "I will not forbear for you or any other, but straightway I will embrace her; and if any of you be afraid, I am content he depart in the little ship and go where he list and he may take victual into it for his provision."

"Sir,"

"Sir," quoth Gerames, "since you will do no otherwise I am right sorrowful; I will depart and so will all our company."

Then Gerames departed out of the great ship and entered into the little one, and the thirteen in his company, and Huon tarried still with the lady. When he saw that all his company was departed, he said to Claramond:

"Dame, surely I must embrace you."

When she heard Huon, she fell down sore weeping, and humbly desired him that he would forbear until they were married together in the city of Rome, according to the promise that he had made to King Oberon.

"Fair lady," quoth Huon, "no excuse can avail, for it must be thus."

Then he came near and took her in his arms and embraced her, and no sooner had he done his will than there rose such a marvellous tempest that the waves of the sea seemed as great and high as mountains. Therewith it blew and thundered and lightened that the sea was fearful to behold, and the ship was so tormented that it burst all to pieces, so that there remained but one piece of timber whereupon Huon and the lady were, but it happened so well for them that they were near to an island, and the wind drove them thither. When they saw that they were arrived safe on the land, they both kneeled down and thanked God that they had escaped the peril of drowning.

The

The other company that were in the little ship drove
at adventure in the sea, crying to our Lord to save
them from drowning, for they had seen how the ship
with Huon and the lady was broken by the sea, and
thought surely that they were perished. But leave
we speaking of them, returning again to Huon of
Bordeaux and the fair lady Claramond.

When they saw that they were driven ashore all
naked they entered into the island and found there
neither man nor woman. The earth was fair and
green and the weather fair and hot, so they hid
themselves in the green bushes that they should not
be perceived, and the lady wept piteously. Then
said Huon :

" Fair lady, be not cast down, for if we die for
love we shall not be the first : Tristran died for the
love of the fair Iseult, and she for him :" and all
weeping, they kissed each other again. As they lay
wrapped in the green grass, ten Saracens arrived in
a little boat who entered into the island to take fresh
water and other things that they needed. When
they had obtained it they said to each other :

" Let us go forth into this island, and see if we
can find any adventure."

Now they were pirates of the sea, and had served
before the Admiral Gaudys, father to the fair Claramond. Huon, who was with his lover in the green
herbage heard the people coming near and thought
he would go to them to see if he could get any food.

" Dear

"Dear lover," quoth Huon, "I pray you go not hence till I return."

"Sir," quoth she, "God be your guide, but I beg you to return again shortly."

So he departed, naked as he was born, and came to them ere they had dined, and saluted them, desiring them humbly for the love of God to give him some bread. One of them answered and said:

"Friend, thou shalt have enough, but we pray thee shew us what adventure hath brought thee hither."

"Sir," quoth Huon, "the tempest of the sea hath brought me hither, for the ship that I was in perished, and all my company."

When they heard him they had great pity and gave him two loaves of bread, Huon took them and departed thanking them, and went to his lover and gave her part of the bread, whereof she was glad.

In the meanwhile the pirates that had given Huon the bread said one to another:

"This man that is just gone from us hath surely some companion: let us go privily after him and we may find out his company, for if he were alone he would not have come to us."

"Let us go and see," quoth all the others, "and not return till we know the truth."

Then they went in a body and followed Huon as privily as they could till they came near him and saw him and the lady near by, eating of the bread they had given him ; and there they stood still to find out if any one knew him or the lady. Now among them there was one that said :

"Sirs, never believe me, if this lady is not the fair Claramond, daughter to the Admiral Gaudys, and he that is with her is the same Frenchman that fought with Angolafer and slew him, and also the admiral. It is happy that we have found them, and especially that he is naked without armour, for if he were armed, our lives were but short."

When they knew for truth that it was Claramond, daughter to the Admiral Gaudys, they drew near them, crying aloud :

"Ah, dame Claramond, your flight availeth you nothing, for by you and by your means your father hath been slain by the thief that sitteth there by you; therefore we shall bring you to your uncle Ivoryn of Montbraunt, who shall make of you an example to all other, and the traitor that is by you shall be flayed alive before your face."

When the lady saw these Paynims she was right sorrowful and sore discomfited, so she kneeled down and held up her hands and prayed them humbly that they would have pity on the Frenchman, and as for her own life, she would leave it to their pleasure to slay her, or drown her, or to bring her to her uncle.

"And, Sirs, I swear by Mahound, that if you will grant my request, if I can be agreed with my uncle

178   Ivoryn,

Ivoryn, I shall do you all such pleasure that you and all yours shall be rich for ever after. And little shall ye win by the death of one poor man."

"Dame," quoth they, "we are well content to leave him here, but we shall do him all the shame and rebuke we can, that he may remember it ever after."

So they took Huon and laid him on the grass and bound his eyes, hands, and feet, so that the blood ran out at his nails, and he was in great distress. Then he swooned three times, and called on our Lord for to have pity on him and forgive his sins. It were impossible to shew the pitiful complaints that the sweet Claramond made when she saw her lover Huon so handled, and that she must depart from him : or to tell the complaints of Huon when his lover Claramond was gone. But now we leave speaking of him and tell of the fair Claramond.

When these thieves had brought the fair Claramond into their ship they gave her a gown and a mantle furred with ermine, for they were robbers of the sea, and had much goods in their ship, and sailed forth night and day, till a wind took them whether they would or not, into the port of Anfalerne. At that time they entered the admiral was newly risen from his dinner, and was standing leaning out of a window in his palace when he perceived the ship at anchor in his haven and saw the banners and streamers waving in the wind whereby he knew that

the

the ship was going to King Ivoryn of Montbraunt. Thereupon he with his lords went down to the haven, and cried out aloud, saying:

"Sirs, what merchandise have you brought?"

"Sir," quoth they, "we have brought spices and clothes of silk, wherefore, Sir, if we should pay any tribute or custom, we are ready to pay it at your pleasure."

Then Galaffer the admiral said:

"I know well enough if ye should pay any tribute, you should not choose but do it. But, Sirs, I pray you tell me what damsel is that I see in your ship sore weeping?"

"Sir," quoth they, "it is a slave, a Christian woman, whom we bought at Damietta."

The lady heard well the admiral's question, and what answer the mariners had made, so she cried out:

"Ah, Sir Admiral, for the love and honour of Mahound, have pity on me for I am no slave, but I am daughter to the Admiral Gaudys of Babylon who is dead, slain by a Frenchman. These mariners here have taken me and would carry me to my uncle, King Ivoryn of Montbraunt, and I know surely if he had me he would burn me in a fire."

"Fair lady," quoth the admiral, "dismay you not, for you shall abide with me whether they will or not." Thereon he commanded the mariners to bring the lady to him, but they answered they would

180   not

not do so. Then the admiral bade his men take her by force, and they of the ship began to make defence ; but soon were they all slain, and the lady brought to him. Yet by chance one of them that were in the ship escaped and fled to Montbraunt, howbeit, the admiral cared not greatly for it since he had the lady, whom he brought into his palace. When he looked on her and saw her so exceeding fair, he was taken in love, so that straightway he would have married her after the Saracen law, but she was right sorrowful, and said :

" Sir, reason it is that I do your pleasure since you have rid me out of the hands of these pirates of the sea. But I pray you for the love that you bear me that you will forbear your pleasure at this time, for I have made a faithful vow and promise that for a year and a day from henceforth I will not marry. Indeed, Sir, I am now sorry for that vow for love of you, seeing I am right joyful that you do me so much honour as to have me for your wife : our great god Mahound reward you. For the love of him I pray you be content till my vow is accomplished."

" Fair lady," quoth he, " know for truth that for the honour of my god Mahound, and for the love of you, I am content to tarry this year, yea, this twenty years, to be sure of your love then."

" Sir," quoth she, " Mahound reward you " : then she said to herself :

" Ah, dear Lord Jesus Christ, humbly I pray Thee

to

to give me grace to keep my truth to my lover Huon, for before I shall do the contrary I will suffer as much pain and grief as ever woman did, and I will never break my troth for fear of death." Now leave we to speak of her, and speak of the thief that escaped out of the ship.

Ye have heard how one of the mariners escaped and fled away by land, and at last he came to the city of Montbraunt where he found Ivoryn, to whom he shewed the whole matter, how his brother the Admiral Gaudys was slain by a young French knight, and how he and his company found the said knight and your niece the fair Claramond whom we thought to have brought to you. But the Admiral Galaffer hath taken them from us by force, and hath taken our ship and slain all your men that were within, so that none escaped but I alone."

When King Ivoryn heard the mariner he said :

"Ah, Mahound, how have you suffered my brother Gaudys thus piteously to be slain, and my niece his daughter to consent thereto. Certainly the grief that I feel at my heart constrains me rather to desire death than life, especially when I see him that is my own subject and holds his lands of me, keep my niece and slay my men. Alas, I cannot well say what I should do therein, a little thing would cause me to slay myself."

Then he called his lords in great displeasure, and caused the mariner to come before them, and shew

the

the whole matter to them, how his brother was slain, and how the Admiral Galaffer held his niece by force, and had slain his men. When the lords heard this they said to Ivoryn :

" Sir, our advice is that you should send one of your secret messengers to the Admiral Galaffer, and command him to send you your niece straightway, and to make amends for slaying your men, and send you word by writing what cause hath moved him thus to do. If it be that pride doth so stand in him that he will not obey your commandments, you may go and make war on him in a just quarrel, and take from him all the lands he holds of you."

When Ivoryn heard his lords he said :

" Sirs, I perceive your opinion is good."

A messenger was appointed, and his charges given him, and so he departed and rode until he came to Anfalerne, where he found the Admiral Galaffer, saluted him in the name of Mahound, and declared his message at length. As soon as Galaffer heard his message, he said :

" Friend, go and say to King Ivoryn that as for the delivery of his niece I will not do it, and as for his men that be slain it was their own folly, and as touching my coming to him I will not, let him do what he can : if he come and assail me I shall defend myself as well as I can."

When the messenger heard that he said :

" Sir Admiral, since you will do no otherwise, in

the

the name of our god Mahound, and in the name of King Ivoryn, I defy you. He sendeth you word by me that he will leave you neither city, town nor castle, but he will put them all to flame and fire, nor leave you one foot of land, and, if he may take you, you shall die a shameful death."

When the admiral saw how he was defied, he was more inflamed than a burning fire-brand and said to the messenger :

" Go, and say to thy lord that I set nothing by his threats, and if I may know when he cometh, I will do him so much honour that I will not wait for him to come into my country, but I will come to meet him. Say further, that if I can take him, I shall soon rid his soul from his body."

So the messenger departed and came to Montbraunt.

When Ivoryn saw him he said :

" Friend, what saith Galaffer ? Will he send me my niece ?"

" Sir," quoth the messenger, "he will not do it. He saith he fears you not, and if you be so bold as to assail him he will come to meet you and fight with you, moreover I heard him swear that if he may take you he would slay you without mercy."

When Ivoryn heard that he shook for anger, and was so that he could not speak a word for a long while, but when he had somewhat assuaged his ire he swore by his god Mahound that he should never
184   have

have joy nor mirth at his heart till he had destroyed the town of Anfalerne and slain the Admiral Galaffer. In haste he sent for his lords, and with them concluded to summon his men of war, giving them a day to be with him within fifteen days before Monbraunt, the which thing was done for at that day they were all assembled, as ye shall hereafter hear. Now leaveth the story to speak of them and returneth to speak of King Oberon.

Now sheweth the story that while Huon was left bound in the island, King Oberon was in the wood where he was accustomed to be, because the place was delectable and far from people. Suddenly he sat him down under a fair oak and began to weep and complain. When Gloriant, a knight of Fairyland saw him, he had great marvel and asked him why he grieved so much.

"Gloriant," quoth the King Oberon, "the perjured Huon of Bordeaux causeth me thus to do; I have perfectly loved him, and yet he hath trespassed my commandments. When I departed from him I caused him to have the Admiral Gaudys at his pleasure, and the fair Claramond his daughter, and I gave him my rich horn of ivory and my good cup, which he hath lost by his pride and folly. Therefore he has been punished, and lies all naked, bound hands and feet and blindfolded in an island, where I will let him die miserably."

"Ah, Sir," quoth Gloriant, "for the honour of our

Lord

Lord Jesus Christ, call to your remembrance that by God's own mouth Adam and Eve were forbidden to eat the fruit that was in Paradise, and they broke God's commandment: yet He had great pity on them, and therefore, Sir, I pray you have pity on Huon."

Then Malabron stepped forth and said:

"Ah, Sir, for the honour and reverence of God I desire you grant me this once that I may go and aid him."

When Oberon saw how earnestly he was prayed by Gloriant and Malabron he was sore displeased and said:

"Malabron, it pleaseth me well that this caitiff Huon who endureth much pain be visited by thee, for the which I condemn thee to be twenty-eight years a monster in the sea, beside the years thou art already condemned to. I will that thou give him no counsel nor aid but to bear him out of the isle that he is in and set him on the mainland, then let him go whither he will, for I desire never more to see him. Also I will thee to bring again my rich horn of ivory and cup, and my harness; fetch them from where he lost them."

"Ah, Sir," quoth Malabron, "great pain you put him to when for as small an offence you are displeased with Huon. As for the armour that you would have again, you know well that Huon conquered it, great ill you shall do if you cause him not to have it again.

186   But

But since I have licence to bring him out of the island, I pray you shew me in what place it is."

Then Gloriant said:

"Brother Malabron, this isle is near to hell, and it is called the Isle Noisant."

So Malabron departed and came to the seaside, leaped into the sea and began to swim as fast as a bird flies in the air till he arrived in the Isle Noisant and came to Huon, whom he found sore weeping.

"Sir Huon," quoth he, "I pray our Lord to succour and aid thee."

"Ah," quoth Huon, "who is it that speaketh to me?"

"Huon," quoth he, "I am a man who loveth thee, and am called Malabron; I am a beast of the sea who hath before this borne thee over the salt water to Babylon."

"Ah, Malabron, dear brother," quoth Huon, "I pray thee unbind me and bring me out of this dolorous pain."

"With a right good will," quoth Malabron, and he unbound him and opened his eyes.

When Huon saw him he was right joyful, and asked who sent him thither.

"Huon," quoth he, "know for truth it was King Oberon, and whereas I was condemned before to be a beast of the sea thirty years, now for thy sake I must endure twenty-eight years more; yet I care not for the pain for the love I bear thee, there is no pain

187   impossible

impossible for me to bear ; but I must carry again to Oberon the rich horn and cup and armour, for so I have promised him to do."

"Ah," quoth Huon, "I pray our Lord to punish the dwarf who hath caused me to endure all these pains for so small an occasion."

"Huon," quoth Malabron, "you do ill to say such things, for you have no sooner spoken than King Oberon doth know it."

"Certainly," quoth Huon, "I care not what he can do, he hath done me so much ill that I can never love him ; but, Sir, I pray thee tell me if thou wilt bear me hence, or else whether I shall bide here for ever."

"Friend," quoth Malabron, "I will bear thee out of this island and set thee on the mainland, other aid may I not give thee."

Then Malabron took on him again his beast's skin and said :

"Leap upon me," so Huon leaped up on his croup as naked as he was born, and Malabron went into the sea and began to swim till he came to the mainland.

"Friend Huon," quoth he, "more service may I not do thee at this time, but I recommend thee to the keeping of God. Now must I go and seek for the horn, cup, and armour which thou wert wont to enjoy, and bear them to King Oberon as I have promised to do."

Huon

Huon was there alone and naked, piteously complaining, and saying :

"Good Lord, I pray Thee to aid me : I know not
where I am, or whither I may go, yet if I had clothes
to cover my naked skin, I should have some comfort,
for I might go and seek some adventure. Greatly
should I hate the crooked dwarf Oberon, who hath
brought me into all this pain ; but by the faith I
owe since he hath left me thus, to do him the more
spite I shall tell lies enough from henceforth, I shall
not stop for him."

When he had been there a certain space all alone,
he arose and looked about him, to see if he might
perceive any man pass by from whom he might have
succour, for he was near famished for lack of food.
Howbeit he went on his way and went so far that
he found an adventure such as ye shall hear, for our
Lord never forgets His friends.

CHAP. X

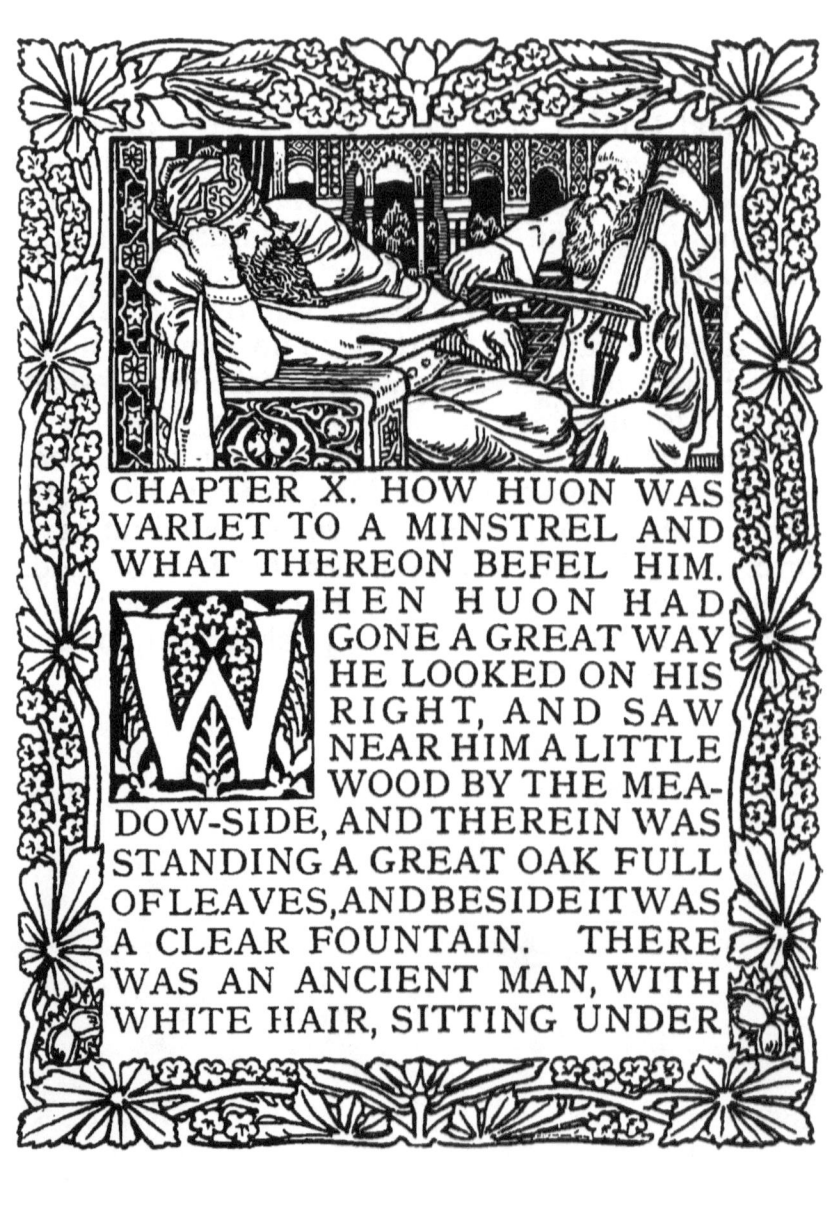

CHAPTER X. HOW HUON WAS
VARLET TO A MINSTREL AND
WHAT THEREON BEFEL HIM.
WHEN HUON HAD
GONE A GREAT WAY
HE LOOKED ON HIS
RIGHT, AND SAW
NEAR HIM A LITTLE
WOOD BY THE MEA-
DOW-SIDE, AND THEREIN WAS
STANDING A GREAT OAK FULL
OF LEAVES, AND BESIDE IT WAS
A CLEAR FOUNTAIN. THERE
WAS AN ANCIENT MAN, WITH
WHITE HAIR, SITTING UNDER

the oak and before him was a little cloth spread abroad on the grass, and on it was flesh, bread, and wine in a bottle. When Huon saw the old man he came to him, and the ancient man said :

" Ah, thou wild man, I pray thee for the love of Mahound do me no hurt, but take meat and drink at thy pleasure."

And as he turned Huon spied lying beside him a harp and a viol whereon he could well play, for in all paganland there was no minstrel like him.

" Friend," quoth Huon, " thou hast named me right, for there is no more unhappy man than I living."

" Friend," quoth the minstrel, "go to yonder bag and open it, and take what you like best to cover your naked skin, then come to me and eat at your pleasure."

" Sir," quoth Huon, "good adventure is come to me thus to find you ; Mahound reward you."

" Sir," quoth the minstrel, " I pray thee come and eat with me and keep me company, for thou shalt not find a more sorrowful man than I am."

" By my faith," quoth Huon, "a companion of your own sort have you found, for there was never man that hath suffered so much poverty as I, praise be to Him that formed me. But since I have found meat to eat, blessed be the hour that I found you, for you seem to be a good man."

Then Huon went to the bag, took clothes, came

back

back to the minstrel and sat down by him and ate
and drank as much as pleased him. The minstrel
looked on Huon and saw that he was a fair young
man and courteous, and then he asked of him where
he was born and by what chance he arrived there in
such evil case. When Huon heard how the minstrel
asked concerning his estate he began to study in
himself whether he should shew the truth or else to
lie, then he thought within himself :

"If I shew this man the truth of my adventure I
am but dead. Ah, Oberon, for a small offence thou
hast left me in this case, for if I shew the truth of
my life to this man I am but dead, I shall never
trust thee more. For the love that I have to my
lover thou hast me in hate, but seeing it is so, as
often as I have need I shall lie, nor shall I stop for
fear of thee, but rather do it in thy despite." Then
Huon said to the minstrel :

"Sir, you have asked of mine estate, and as yet I
have made you no answer, the truth is I find myself
so well at mine ease that I forgot to answer you, but
I shall now shew you, since you would know it. I
was born in the country of Africa, and fell in
company with divers merchants by the sea in a ship,
thinking to have sailed to Damietta, but a great
misfortune fell upon us : there arose such a horrible
tempest that our ship perished, and of all that were
within it, none escaped but I, and I thank Mahound
that I am escaped alive, therefore I desire you now
192   to

to shew me your adventure as I have shewed you mine."

"Friend," quoth the minstrel, "since you will know it, know for truth I am named Mouflet, I am a minstrel as thou seest here by my instruments, and from here to the Red Sea there is no one so cunning on all instruments as I am, and I can do many other things. The dolour that thou seest me make is because of late I have lost my good lord and master, the Admiral Gaudys who was slain miserably by a vagabond of France called Huon, Mahound shame him and bring him to an ill death, for by him I am fallen into poverty and misery. I pray thee tell me thy name."

"Sir," quoth Huon, "my name is Salater."

"Well," quoth the minstrel, "Salater, dismay thee not for the great poverty thou hast suffered, thou seest what adventure Mahound hath sent thee, thou art now better arrayed than thou wert and if thou wilt follow my counsel thou shalt have no need. Thou art fair and young and oughtest not to be dismayed, but I that am old and ancient have cause to be discomfited, seeing in my old days I have lost my lord and master the Admiral Gaudys who did me so much good and profit. I would it pleased Mahound that he that slew him were in my power."

When Huon heard that he spake no word, but cast down his head.

"Salater," quoth the minstrel, "seeing my lord is

dead I will go to Montbraunt to King Ivoryn to shew him the death of his brother the Admiral Gaudys. If thou wilt abide with me and bear my fardell and harp afoot, before half a year passes I warrant thou shalt have a horse, for whensoever thou shalt hear me play upon my instruments all the hearers shall take therein such pleasure that they shall give me both gowns and mantles, so that thou shalt have much ado to truss them in my bag."

"Ah," quoth Huon, "I am content to serve you and to do all your commandments."

Then Huon took the bag on his shoulders and the harp in his hands and Mouflet his master bore the viol, and thus the master and the servant went on their way to go to Montbraunt.

"Ah," quoth Huon, "my heart ought to be sorrowful when I see myself in this case, that now I must become a minstrel's varlet. It is Oberon the dwarf that has done me all this annoyance. If I had now my good armour, my horn and my cup, I would reckon all the trouble I have endured as nothing. How is the chance now turned that I must serve a poor minstrel when I had thirteen knights to serve me."

When Mouflet heard Huon make such sorrow within himself he said :

"Dear brother Salater, take good comfort, for before to-morrow at night thou shalt see the good cheer that shall be made to me, whereof thou shalt

194   have

have part, and half of all the goods that I can
get."

"Master," quoth Huon, "Mahound reward you
for the goodness that you have shewed me, and
shall do": thus the master and the servant went
forth together talking. At last Huon spied coming
behind them certain men of arms holding the way
to Montbraunt.

"Master," quoth Huon, "here behind us are
coming men in armour; I know not if they will
do us any harm or not."

"Salater," quoth Mouflet, "be not abashed, we
will abide here and know whither they will go."

Within a while the men of war came to them, in
number five hundred persons; the minstrel saluted
them and said:

"Sirs, I pray you shew me whither you will go."

"Friend," quoth one of them, "because we see
that you be a gentle minstrel I shall shew you. We
are going to King Ivoryn of Montbraunt, who is
making war upon the Admiral Galaffer because that
of late the damsel Claramond, daughter to the
Admiral Gaudys, passed by Anfalerne, who should
have been brought to her uncle, King Ivoryn of
Montbraunt. The Admiral Galaffer took her by
force, and slew all them that led her, and married
the fair Claramond; whereof King Ivoryn is as
sorrowful as may be. For that cause we be sent for
by King Ivoryn, who assembleth all his power to
195   destroy

destroy the Admiral Galaffer. Now have I showed
you the cause of our going to the city of Montbraunt."

When Huon of Bordeaux understood the Paynims were going where the lady Claramond was, he
was surprised and said to his master :

"Sir, let us go to war with them."

"Salater," quoth Mouflet, "beware what thou
sayest, for I would not come where war was for anything."

Thus they went forth until they came to Montbraunt, and went straight to the palace where they
found King Ivoryn and all his barons. When the
minstrel saw him he saluted him in the name of
Mahound and said :

"Sir, I am right dolorous for the news I bring
you, for, Sir, your brother, my lord and master the
Admiral Gaudys, is piteously slain."

"Mouflet," quoth Ivoryn, "these news have been
brought to me before this time, whereof I am sorry,
and also I am sorry for my niece the fair Claramond,
who is kept from me by the Admiral Galaffer, and
for any message that I can send to him he will not
send her to me. By the faith I owe to my god
Mahound, I shall make him such war that the
memory of it shall be for a hundred years hereafter,
for I shall not leave him a foot of land, but bring it
all into fire and flame and clean destroy him ; and
in despite of his teeth I will see my niece Claramond,
196   and

and if I may get her I shall cause her to be stricken to pieces and burn her into ashes, for my brother is dead by a villain of France whom she loved."

When Huon heard him speak of his lady, his heart rose and he made a promise in himself that before the month was past he would go and see her or find a means to speak with her. Then King Ivoryn called Mouflet the minstrel, and said :

" Friend, I pray thee do some thing to make me merry, for by reason of this displeasure that I have had my joy is lost, therefore it were better for me to take some mirth than to be long in sorrow."

"Sir," quoth Mouflet, " I am ready to do your pleasure": and took his viol and played on it in such wise that it was great melody to hear it, and all the Paynims there had great joy and mirth, and made great feast. Huon heard it and said :

" May this great joy turn to me, that I may hear some good news of her whom I sore desire to see."

When the minstrel had finished his song, the Paynims did off their clothes, and some gave him their gowns, and some their mantles ; each thought himself right happy that could give the minstrel anything. Huon had enough to do to gather together the clothes that were given him, and put them into his bag, whereof Huon was joyful because he should have the half. King Ivoryn beheld Huon, and said to them that were about him: "Great pity it is that so fair a young man should serve a minstrel."

" Sir

"Sir King," quoth Mouflet, "be not abashed though this young man doth serve me, he hath cause so to do, for when your brother was dead I departed from thence to come hither, and by the way I found a great oak, under the which I sat me down to rest, and thereby was a great fountain, fair and clear. There I spread abroad a towel on the green grass, and set thereon bread and drink and such meat as I had. The same time this young man arrived and came to me all naked, and prayed me for the love of Mahound to give him some of my bread, and as I did, and clothed him as you see, I did so much for him that he promised to serve me and to bear my fardell and my harp, and moreover, when I came to any ford of water he would set me on his shoulder as easily as though I had been nothing, he is so strong, and bear me over."

"Ah, poor caitiff," quoth King Ivoryn, "hast thou lived so long and canst not perceive why he doth it? He abideth till thou hast gotten some riches and then he will cut thy throat and cast thee into the river, and then go away with all thy riches. Cause him to come and speak with me."

"Sir," quoth Mouflet, "he shall come to you," and so called Huon and brought him to King Ivoryn.

"Ah, friend," quoth the King, "I pray thee show me where thou wert born, for I have pity of thee to see thee in so low estate as to be varlet to a minstrel,

it

it were better for thee to serve some prince or help
to keep a town or a castle, rather than thus to lose
thy time; I wot not what I should think of thee,
but that it seemeth to me that thou art of a faint
courage. What hath moved thee thus to do? Thou
seest thy master has nothing but what he getteth
with his viol, canst thou find no other craft to live
by more honestly?"

"Sir," quoth Huon, "I know crafts enough,
which I shall name to you if you will hear me."

"Say on," quoth Ivoryn, "for I have great
desire to know what thou canst do, but one thing
I warn thee: make no vaunt of anything without
thou canst do it indeed, for in everything I will
prove thee."

"Sir," quoth Huon, "I can mew a sparrowhawk,
and I can chase the hart, and the wild boar, and
blow the prise, and serve the hounds their rights,
and I can serve at table before a great prince, and
I can play at chess and tables as well as any other
can do, nor did I ever meet man who could win off
me unless I choose."

When King Ivoryn heard Huon, he said: "Hold
thee to this, for I shall prove whether what thou
sayest be true or not."

"Yet, Sir, I pray you let me show further what
I can do, and then assay me at your pleasure."

"By Mahound," quoth the King, "I am content
thou shewest all that thou canst do."

"Sir,"

"Sir," quoth Huon, "I can write well, arm me, and set the helm on my head, and bear a shield and spear, and ride and gallop a horse, and when it cometh to the point where strokes should be given, you may well send forth a worse than I. Also, Sir, I can right well enter into ladies' chambers to embrace and kiss them, and to do them any service."

"Friend," quoth Ivoryn, "by what I hear from thee, thou canst do more things than should turn to good, but to prove thee, I shall cause thee to be essayed at the play of chess. I have a fair daughter, with whom thou must play, on the condition that if she win, thou shalt lose thy head, and if thou canst mate her, I promise that thou shalt have her to wife for one day, and a hundred marks of gold beside."

"Sir," said Huon, "I would be glad to forbear that enterprise."

"By Mahound," quoth the King, "it shall not be otherwise, come thereof what will." While the King was making this bargain, a Paynim went into the ladies' chamber, and told her how there was with the King, her father, a young man, whom he would make to play at chess with her on the condition that if the young man lost the game he should lose his head, and if he won he should have to wife for one day, and a hundred marks of money: "and, dame," quoth he, "I assure you
that

that he that shall play against you is the fairest man that ever I saw, pity it is that he should be a varlet to a minstrel as he is."

"By Mahound," quoth the lady, "I hold my father wrong when he thinketh that I should suffer a man to die for winning a game of chess." Then Ivoryn sent two kings for his daughter, who brought her to the King, her father, and Ivoryn said: "Daughter, thou must play at chess with this young varlet that thou seest here, so that if thou win he shall lose his head, and if he win, I will that he shall have thee to wife for a day."

"Father," quoth the lady, "seeing it is your pleasure, it is right that I do it whether I will or no." Then she looked on Huon, whom she found right fair, and she said to herself, "By Mahound, for the great beauty that I see in this young man, I would this game were at an end, so that I were his wife this day."

When the lady was come, their places were made ready, and she and Huon sat down, while the King Ivoryn and his barons sat down about him to see them play. Huon said to the king: "Sir, I require you that no man should speak in our game, neither for one party nor the other."

"Friend," quoth the King, "have no doubt thereof," and for more security he caused it to be cried through all the palace that no man should be so bold as to speak one word, on pain of death.

Then

Then the chess men were made ready, and Huon said: "Lady, what game will you play at?"

"Friend," quoth she, "at the usual game, to be mated in a corner." Then they both began to study their first moves. There were Paynims looking over Huon, but he cared not for any of them, and studied only his game, which he began so that he lost some of his pawns. In this he changed colour, and blushed as red as a rose. The damsel perceived him and said: "Friend, what are you thinking of; you are nigh mated. Soon my father will strike off your head."

"Dame," quoth he, "as yet the game is not done; great shame shall your father have, when you are my wife, and I am but a varlet to a poor minstrel." When the barons heard Huon say this they all began to laugh, but the lady was so taken with the love of Huon for the great beauty that she saw in him, that she forgot all her play in thinking of him, and so she lost the game. Huon was joyful, and called the King and said: "Sir, now may you see how I can play, for if I studied a little I could mate your daughter when I wished."

When the King heard him, he said to his daughter: "Arise, cursed be the hour that you were born; great dishonour hast thou done to me, when thou hast mated so many great men, and now I see that a miserable varlet hath mated thee."

"Sir," quoth Huon, "trouble not yourself for

that

that cause. As for the wager that I have won, I am content to release it freely; let your daughter go into her chamber and sport with her damsels, and I shall go serve my master, the minstrel."

"Friend," quoth the King, "if thou wilt shew me this courtesy, I shall give thee a hundred marks of money."

"Sir," quoth Huon, "I am content with your pleasure." The lady went her way sorrowful, and said to herself: "Ah, false, faint heart, Mahound confound thee: if I had known that thou wouldst thus have refused my company, I would have mated thee, and then thou hadst lost thy head."

The next day King Ivoryn made a cry through all the city that every man should be armed and mounted on their horses, since it was his mind to set forward toward his enemies. Then every man armed him, many helmets glittered in the sun, many trumpets and drums began to sound, and it was marvel to hear the noise that filled the city.

When Huon saw that he had not wherewith to arm him his heart mourned right sore, for he would gladly have gone forth with other men if he had had any horse to ride on. He came to King Ivoryn, and said: "Sir, I beg of you let me have a horse and harness that I may go with you to the battle, and then shall you see how I can aid you."

"Friend," quoth Ivoryn, "I am content that you come with me: "and he bade one of his chamber-

lains

lains deliver him horse and harness. The chamber-
lain said: "Sir, beware what you do, for often such vagabonds are fickle-hearted; if he has horse and armour he may as soon join your enemies as keep with you. Never trust me, but he is some counterfeit varlet."

"When the King heard him, he said: "It may well be, yet, let him have a good suit of armour and helmet and shield, and let his horse be of small value, so that he shall not go far off, though he would." At the same time a Paynim was near by who heard the King grant that Huon should have armour; he went to his house and took out of his coffer an old rusty sword and brought it to Huon, saying: "Friend, I see well you have no sword to aid yourself with, and therefore I give you this which I have long kept in my coffer."

Huon took the sword which the Paynim had given him in mockery, for he thought it of small value, and drew it out of the sheath, and saw letters written thereon in French, telling how this sword was forged by Galans, who in his day forged three swords. This sword was one of the three, one was Durandel which Roland had, and the other was Courtain. When Huon had read the letters he was right joyful, and said to the Paynim: "Friend, for this good sword that you have given me I thank you: if I may live long enough, I promise you I shall reward you the double value of it."

After

After the sword there was brought him good armour, a helmet, a shield, and a spear with a rusty head, but Huon cared little for it, by reason of the great desire that he had to come to the place where he might shew his strength and manhood. Then there was brought to him a lean bald horse, with a long neck and a great head, and when Huon saw him he took him by the bridle and leaped upon him without any foot in the stirrup, in the sight of a thousand Paynims there present, and some said it was not well done to give him a horse which could not serve or aid him in time of need.

When Huon was mounted on his lean feeble horse he was sorrowful, for he perceived how they mocked him and said softly to himself: "Ah, ye false Paynims, if I may live a year, I shall return your mockery." Then he rode forth with the others, but for all he could do with his spurs the horse would go his own soft pace. So King Ivoryn departed from Montbraunt with his great army, and tarried in the fields for his men, and when they were all assembled together he departed and took the way to Anfalerne, which was but four leagues off. When they came there they ran before the city and drove away all the beasts, cattle and sheep, and sent them to Montbraunt.

When the Admiral Galaffer saw that King Ivoryn was before his gates, and that he had driven away all this prey from about the town, he was so

sorrowful

sorrowful that he was near hand out of his wits. Then he came to the fair Claramond and said: "Dame, the great love I have set on you has this day cost me dear, for on account of you I see my country destroyed and my men slain or led into servitude."

"Sir," quoth she, "I am sorry thereof; it lieth in you to amend it, seeing this evil is come to you by me, for it is in your power to render me to King Ivoryn, and thereby you and your country shall be in rest and peace."

"Fair lady," quoth Galaffer, "by the grace of Mahound I will not render you into the hands of Ivoryn your uncle for any fear I have of him, if you will marry me."

"Sir," quoth she, "you may do with me as you please after the years are past for accomplishing my vow."

"Dame," quoth Galaffer, "before I render you to your uncle I shall not have a foot of land; first it shall be clean destroyed."

When Sorbryn, nephew to the Admiral Galaffer, heard his uncle make such sorrow, he said: "Fair uncle, be not dismayed, though Ivoryn hath taken and slain some of your men and driven away your beasts. If I live I shall give you four for each of yours. I will go and arm me and issue out to Ivoryn; then I will bid him set one or two of his boldest men to fight with me. If it be so that I
be

be overcome, then his niece Claramond shall be rendered to him to do with her at his pleasure, and if I discomfit his men, then he shall depart and render you again the double of all the damage he hath done you in this war. Better it were that the war should be ended by two men than that so many people should be destroyed."

" Fair nephew," quoth Galaffer, " I never heard a better word, I am well content if you will have it thus:" and Sorbryn went and armed him. He was a goodly knight, in all the land of the Paynims there was not his peer, nor one approaching him in valour. When he was armed, his good horse Blanchardine was brought to him, a horse as white as snow, and so beautiful that there was none like him, nor could any one esteem the value of the riches on his bridle, saddle and armour. So Sorbryn leaped on his horse without any stirrup, and took a great spear and rode out of the city. When he saw King Ivoryn afar off, he cried aloud and said: "Ah, thou Ivoryn of Montbraunt, the Admiral Galaffer hath sent me to thee that thou mayst arm one of the most valiant men of thy court and let him come against me. If he can vanquish me, then he shall deliver to thee thy niece Claramond, and if I overcome thy man, then thou shalt return to thy city and suffer thy niece to remain still with him, and also restore all the harm thou hast done him and his in the war."

When

When Ivoryn heard the Paynim he looked about him to see if any of his men would take upon him this enterprise and fight with Sorbryn, but there was no one that durst speak a word for fear of him, and men said that whoever did was like to miserably finish his days. While Ivoryn was speaking with Sorbryn, Huon was among the Paynims and heard what Sorbryn said, and saw that no man durst go against him. Then as well as he might he got himself out of the press on his lean horse; he struck him with his spurs, but the horse would neither trot nor gallop for anything he could do, but went still his own pace.

The old minstrel beheld his varlet Huon making ready to fight against the Paynim, and when he saw that he was so ill horsed he cried out: "Sir King Ivoryn, it is great dishonour to you that you have given a horse worth nothing to my varlet, who goeth for your sake to fight with Sorbryn, where none of your own men dare adventure: great sin it is that he hath not a better horse."

Huon said to Sorbryn: "Saracen, I pray thee speak with me."

"Friend," quoth Sorbryn, "what wilt thou with me?"

"Paynim," quoth Huon, "I require thee prove thy manhood against me."

"Then," quoth Sorbryn, "tell me art thou a Paynim or a Saracen?"

"Friend,"

"Friend," quoth Huon, "I am neither Paynim nor Saracen, but Christian; and though thou seest me but poorly apparelled despise me not, for I am come of noble extraction, wherefore I require thee by thy law that thou believest in, let me not go without battle."

"Friend," quoth Sorbryn, "in this request thou shewest great folly, for thou dost desire thy death. I have pity of thee, and therefore I counsel thee to return."

"Paynim," quoth Huon, "I had rather die than return before I have jousted with thee."

Then they went from each other to take their course, but for all that Huon could do his horse would not advance, whereof he was sore displeased and said: "I would I might win the horse that this Paynim doth ride on." With this, he set his shield against his enemy, and Sorbryn came running like the tempest, and with his spear struck Huon's shield such a stroke that the buckles could not resist the stroke, but the shield was pierced through and through and carried away, but the good harness saved Huon from all hurt, and he moved no more for the stroke than if he had been a strong wall: whereof Ivoryn and all other had great marvel.

They said to one another how they had never seen before so great a stroke, nor a goodlier accept of it without falling to the earth, and every man praised Huon greatly for holding himself so firmly.

o   " By

"By Mahound," quoth Ivoryn, "our man is fierce and of great boldness; I would he were mounted now on my horse."

Then Huon who had received the stroke cast down his spear in great wrath, took his sword with both his hands and gave the Paynim a great stroke therewith on his helm as he passed. The stroke was so mighty that neither the helm nor coat of steel could resist it, but his head was cloven to the shoulders, and he fell down dead in the field. Then Huon, who was quick and light, took the good horse Blanchardine by the rein, alighted from his own horse, and without foot in stirrup leaped up on the Paynim's horse, leaving his own in the field. When he saw himself on Blanchardine he smote him with his spurs to prove him, and the horse began to leap and corvet and gallop as it had been the thunder, so that the Paynims marvelled that he did not fall to the earth. Huon proved him well, turned him in and out, and thought he would not give him for the value of a kingdom, and at last came to King Ivoryn with twenty gambades.

"By Mahound," quoth Ivoryn, "this youth seems rather son of a king than varlet to a minstrel:" and he came to Huon, embraced him, and made him great cheer.

Galaffer and the Paynims within Anfalerne were by this time issued out of the city, and when the
admiral

admiral saw his nephew slain, he rode about him three times, making a piteous complaint and said : "Ah, right dear nephew, I may well deplore your youth, when I see you thus piteously slain. If I live long your death shall be dearly bought." So the dead body was carried into the city with great lamentation, and he and his men entered into the battle. Great was the slaughter on both sides, and Huon did marvels ; he slew and beat down all that came within his stroke, and no Paynim durst abide him, but all fled like sheep do from the wolves, and within short space he brought the enemy to open discomfiture, so that the Admiral Galaffer with much pain fled and entered into the city, right sorrowful for the loss that he had received that day, since the third part of his men were slain in the battle.

The valour of Huon was so great that King Ivoryn and his men stood still to behold his valiant deeds. As Huon fought, he spied out the Paynim that had given him the sword and remembered the promise he had made him, so he lifted up his sword and struck a Paynim such a blow that he clave his head to the breast, and he fell dead ; then Huon took his horse and gave it to him that had given him the good sword, saying : "Take the gift of this horse for a reward of the good sword you gave me."

Shortly to tell, Huon did so much that there was no Paynim that durst abide him, but they all fled
211   into

into the city of Anfalerne, closed the gates, and raised the bridges, while King Ivoryn's men departed with the booty they had won. So Huon was conveyed with great triumph, riding side by side with King Ivoryn, to Montbraunt where they were received with great joy. But the Admiral Galaffer entered into Anfalerne in great sorrow for Sorbryn his nephew who was dead, and for the men he had lost in battle, and when he was disarmed he caused his nephew to be buried with sore weeping and lamentation.

So Ivoryn entered into Montbraunt and went and disarmed him, and his daughter came to him to wish him joy, and when he saw her he said : " Dear daughter, in a good hour wert thou mated by the minstrel's varlet, for to-day in the battle against the Admiral Galaffer he was discomfited by the prowess of the varlet by whom thou wert beaten : thanked be my god Mahound, for by him I have overcome my enemies. Beside that, he fought hand to hand against Sorbryn, nephew to the Admiral Galaffer, and slew him. If I may live a year, the service he hath done me shall be right well rewarded."

Then King Ivoryn went up into his palace and his daughter with him, and Huon went to the lodging where the minstrel was, and there he disarmed him and went with his master to the palace.

When King Ivoryn saw them he stepped forth
and

and took Huon by the hand and said : " Friend, you shall go with me and sit at my table, for I cannot do you too much honour for the good service you have done me. I abandon to you all my house to do therein at your pleasure, take all my gold and silver and jewels, and give thereof at your pleasure : I ordain and will that all that you command shall be done, and when I go out you shall go with me." "Sir," quoth Huon, "for the great honour that you have done me I thank you."

Then they sat down at the table, and when they had dined the King and Huon sat together on rich carpets, and Mouflet the minstrel tuned his viol and played so melodiously that the Paynims who heard him wondered greatly ; and the viol made so sweet a sound that it seemed to be the singing of the mermaids of the sea. King Ivoryn and his lords had thereof such great pleasure that it seemed to them that they were in the glory of Paradise, and there was no Paynim but gave him gowns and mantles and other jewels. The minstrel saw Huon sitting by the King, and said : " Friend, yesterday I was your master and now I am your minstrel : I think you have now little care for me. I pray you come to me and gather together these clothes, and put them in my bag as you have done before this." And when the King and his lords heard that, they began to laugh. Now let us leave speaking of them and tell of the old Gerames.

213   CHAP. XI.

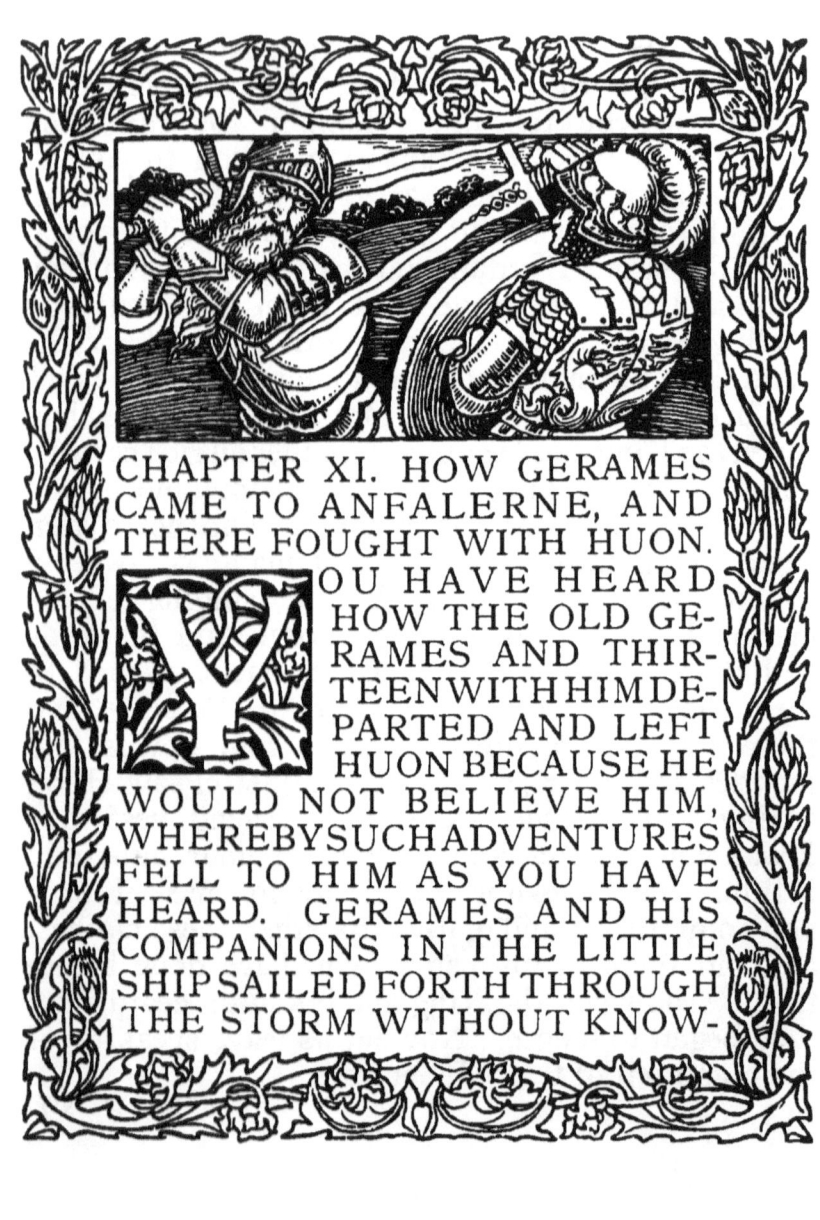

CHAPTER XI. HOW GERAMES
CAME TO ANFALERNE, AND
THERE FOUGHT WITH HUON.
YOU HAVE HEARD
HOW THE OLD GE-
RAMES AND THIR-
TEEN WITH HIM DE-
PARTED AND LEFT
HUON BECAUSE HE
WOULD NOT BELIEVE HIM,
WHEREBY SUCH ADVENTURES
FELL TO HIM AS YOU HAVE
HEARD. GERAMES AND HIS
COMPANIONS IN THE LITTLE
SHIP SAILED FORTH THROUGH
THE STORM WITHOUT KNOW-

ledge of what was become of Huon, though they thought he was dead rather than alive. Within a month they were driven by another tempest to the port of Anfalerne, and when Gerames saw they were arrived there, he said to his company : " Sirs, we be not arrived at a good port, in this city dwelleth a Paynim king who believes neither in God nor in Saints. A fiercer Paynim cannot be found from here to the Red Sea, he is called the Admiral Galaffer. Without God has pity on us, I cannot see but we are like to die ; and we cannot turn back."

Now the admiral was risen from dinner, and looking out at a window, he beheld the seaside, and perceived the little ship in which were Gerames and his companions. When he saw it he went down with some of his men, desiring to know who they were that arrived. As he approached the ship, he said : "Sirs, what men be you that are thus arrived at my port ? "

" Sir," quoth Gerames, " we be Frenchmen, pilgrims, we are going to the Holy Sepulchre, and fortune of the sea hath brought us hither. If there be any tribute that we ought to pay, we are ready to do your pleasure."

" Sirs," quoth the admiral, " have no fear that I or any of mine shall do you any displeasure, for if you will abide with me you are welcome."

" Sir," quoth Gerames, " if it please you, tell us the cause why."

215   " Sir,"

"Sir," quoth the admiral, "I shall shew you. True it is that near me dwelleth King Ivoryn of Montbraunt, who maketh great war upon me ; he slayeth my men, and destroyeth my country, whereof I have great sorrow in my heart."

"Sir," quoth Gerames, "if your quarrel be just and rightful, we shall all be ready to aid you truly, but without your quarrel be good, we will not abide with you."

"Sirs," quoth the admiral, "I shall shew you the truth. On a day I stood in a window and looked down on the seaside, as I did now when you arrived at the port, and I saw a ship coming which took anchor where you are now. In the ship there was a damsel and ten mariners, who thought to have led her to King Ivoryn of Montbraunt : I cannot tell where they took her, she was daughter to the Admiral Gaudys, Mahound take his soul. I know for certain that if King Ivoryn had the damsel, he would burn her, because it hath been shewn him that she was the cause of the death of her father the Admiral Gaudys, who was brother to Ivoryn. When I was advertised that the ten mariners would have delivered her into the hands of her uncle Ivoryn, I took her from them and slew them all because they would not deliver her up with fair treatment, and thus I have wedded the damsel. When Ivoryn heard this he made war on me, and came before my city with all his power, and he hath
216   slain

slain my men, and led away all my cattle and provision, and hath burnt and destroyed my country. He hath with him a young man of I know not what country, and this last day he slew a nephew of mine called Sorbryn, whom I right dearly loved, for he was son to my sister. I have such sorrow at my heart for him that it cannot be appeased. Moreover he hath led away his horse called Blanchardine, the which is the best horse in ten realms, his like is not in all the world. Wherefore I desire you, as I may desire your service, to abide with me, and to do so much that I may have the said young man taken prisoner, and the horse restored to me again. If you can do this I shall so reward you that you shall always be rich, and all those in your company."

"Sir," quoth Gerames, "if he come any more hither, and you shew me him, I shall do my best to bring him and the horse too to you."

"Friend," quoth the admiral, "if you will shew me this courtesy I shall abandon all my realm to be at your pleasure and commandment." With these words the old Gerames issued out of the ship and all his company with him, and entered into the city of Anfalerne with the Admiral Galaffer.

When they came to the palace Gerames said: "Sir, I and my company beg you to shew us the damsel for whose sake you maintain this war."

"Friend," quoth the admiral, "if you were a young man I would not shew her to you, but I see
217   well

well you be old and ancient, wherefore no young lady will set anything by you." Then the admiral took Gerames by the hand and led him into the chamber where Claramond was.

As soon as the lady saw Gerames, she knew him, and began to change colour, and fell down in a swoon in the chamber, making a great cry. When the admiral saw that he was right sorrowful and said: "Fair lady, why are you so moved? Are you troubled at the sight of this old man that I have brought hither?"

"Nay, surely, Sir," quoth she, "it is but a pain that hath taken me in the right side, from which I often suffer great annoyance. If it were your pleasure, Sir, I would gladly speak with this French knight, since they usually know many things, and perchance he may shew me such things that shall be good for my health, since Frenchmen are right subtle in giving good counsel."

"Dame," quoth the admiral, "it pleases me well, you may speak to him in private for a while." Then the lady called Gerames, and said: "Friend, I pray thee give me some good counsel that I may be eased of the pain that I endure."

"Dame," quoth Gerames, "for the honour of you and the admiral here present, I shall aid you in such wise that you shall be eased of the pain you suffer from:" for Gerames, who was subtle, well perceived the mind of the lady. Then he

218   approached

approached her, and sat down with her on a couch.

"Gerames," quoth the lady, "what adventure hath brought you hither, I pray thee?"

"Dame," quoth he, "we be come hither by reason of a tempest of the sea, but I pray you what is become of Huon?"

"By my faith," quoth she, "I believe he is dead, for when you departed from us such a marvellous tempest arose on the sea that all in our ship perished, and the ship itself was broken into small pieces. Huon and I saved ourselves on a plank of wood, whereby we arrived at an isle that was near us; but when we were on land ten mariners came on us and took me from thence, leaving Huon there blindfold, with hands and feet fast bound, so that he could not release himself. The ten mariners brought me hither, and the Admiral Galaffer hath slain them all. I think of a surety Huon is dead, and thus I am here, engaged to wed with this admiral. As yet I am not married, for I have made him believe that I had made a vow to Mahound for two years to come, for the love of Huon whom I cannot forget. As long as I live, I shall never forget him, and shall always be ready to die in pain to keep me from marrying any man alive. Ah, Gerames! if you could help me to escape from hence with you, you would do me a great courtesy, for if I might escape hence and come into a Christian realm, I
would

would go into some abbey of nuns, that I might pray for my lover Huon."

"Dame," quoth Gerames, "be not dismayed, for if I can escape from hence, I shall carry you with me whatever happens."

Then the admiral came to them, and said: "Friend, you hold over much speech with this damsel. Come away, you have tarried here long enough." So Gerames strained the hand of Claramond, and departed, and the Admiral Galaffer took him by the arm and brought him into the hall to supper, and after supper they consulted of deeds of war. Now let us leave speaking of them, and tell of King Ivoryn of Montbraunt, and of Huon who was with him."

Two days after King Ivoryn had fought at Anfalerne, Huon came to him, and said: "Sir, cause your men to be armed, and let us visit the Admiral Galaffer: a man that is at war ought never to rest till he hath brought his enemy to utter ruin. It seemeth that he setteth little by you when he still keeps your niece against your will, though he is your subject and holds his lands from you.

"Friend," quoth Ivoryn, "you say the truth, I shall follow your counsel."

Then he made it to be cried through the city that every man should make ready to go with the King to Anfalerne. So Huon armed him, and took Blanchardine his good horse, mounted on him

without

without any stirrup, and took a great spear with a
good sharp head in his hand, so desirous was he
of battle. The same time as Huon came to the
palace, Ivoryn's daughter was sitting in a window
in her chamber, accompanied by her ladies and
damsels, and she beheld Huon, and said : " By
Mahound, yonder young man is goodly to behold
sitting on his horse Blanchardine; his armour
becomes him right well, a goodlier man nor a
bolder cannot be found, for in the last fight he
slew Sorbryn the most valiant knight in the land,
and won his good horse. Yet am I displeased
with him that when he played with me at chess
he was not so bold as to claim me for his wife, for
if he had I would have loved him so much that I
would never have left him, though my father had
done his utmost." Thus the ladies talked together
of Huon, who set little store by their praise.

King Ivoryn and his men issued out of the city
and rode forth to Anfalerne, and at the last came
to the gates of the town and there drew up their
line of battle, while Huon, who had great desire to
attain to good renown, came forward with his spear
in his hand and cried aloud to them that were on
the walls ; " Where is Galaffer, your lord ? Go and
shew him that he ought to come and joust against
him that hath slain his nephew. I will serve him
likewise if I meet him in battle, unless he deliver
to me the fair Claramond."

Galaffer

Galaffer was near by and heard what Huon said, knowing well it was he by reason of the horse Blanchardine, whereof his heart was right sorrowful ; so he said to Gerames : " Friend, I shall shew you he that hath done me all this evil, now shall I see if you will keep promise with me."

" Sir," quoth Gerames, " take no heed of him, for by the faith I owe, I shall render both horse and man to you, to do with them at your pleasure."

Gerames rode out all armed, well horsed, and took a good spear in his hand. He was a goodly knight for his age, powerful of body, and greatly feared in his time, and when he was on his horse he stretched himself in the saddle in such wise that his stirrups stretched out a handful or more, and greatly was he praised of the Paynims that saw him.

The Admiral Galaffer made every man to arm himself, and he himself was richly armed, the gate was opened, and Gerames was the first to issue out with his company. When he was without the city he struck his horse with the spurs so that he was a great space before his companions, his spear in his hand, his shield about his neck, and his white beard hanging down on his breast under his helm. Huon on the other side saw Gerames coming and spurred Blanchardine against him, so they met without speaking a word, and struck each other on their shields and broke them ; their harness was

good

good and they took no harm, but their spears broke in their hands so that the shivers flew up into the air, and the stroke was so rude that both knights and horses fell to the earth, but they quickly arose and gave each other great strokes. Gerames, who was expert in deeds of arms, took his sword with both his hands, and gave Huon such a stroke on the helm that he was perforce fain to bend one of his knees to the earth, the stroke was so heavy, and if it had not been by the grace of God, he had been slain. Huon was so stunned with the stroke that he had much ado to rise again, and said: "Lord, succour me and give me grace that I may see the fair Claramond before I die." These words he spoke openly for he thought not that he would be understood, for little thought he that it was Gerames who fought with him. So he came to Gerames with his sword in his hand to be revenged, for never before had he received such a stroke as Gerames had given him, but Gerames knew him by his words, and therewith cast down his sword to the earth, and sorrowed so that he could not speak a word.

When Huon saw it he marvelled greatly why he cast his sword to the earth, and Huon would not then touch him, but said: "Paynim, what is thy mind to do? Wilt thou have peace, or else fight with me?"

"Ah, Sir," quoth Gerames, "come and strike off

223   my

my head, for well have I deserved it seeing I struck you so rudely, but I am sorry for it, for I knew you not." When Huon heard him speak he knew at once that it was Gerames, and joyed greatly in his heart at finding him. The Paynims that looked on wondered greatly what thing the two champions thought to do.

"Sir," quoth Gerames, "we must make up our minds quickly, for I see Paynims assembling on all sides to behold us. I shall shew you what is best for us two to do. Leap on your horse and I will leap on mine and take you and lead you by force my prisoner to the city of Anfalerne. There you shall see your lover Claramond, who will have great joy of your coming and she will tell you her news."

"Friend," quoth Huon, "I shall do as you advise." Then they leaped on their horses and Gerames came to Huon and laid hands on him as though he took him prisoner, and so led him toward the city of Anfalerne, and his companions followed him.

When King Ivoryn saw how Gerames was leading Huon away as his prisoner, he began to cry out, saying: "On forth, ye Saracens, how suffer you this young man to be led away a prisoner to the city of Anfalerne? I shall never have joy at my heart if you let him thus be led away." Then the Saracens dashed into the press to rescue Huon, and on the other hand Galaffer came and met

Gerames

Gerames, and he said to the admiral: "Sir, go and fight with your enemies; behold here the young man that slew your nephew Sorbryn! I shall lead him into the city and set him in some sure prison, and then I will return to you and fight against King Ivoryn."

"Friend," quoth Galaffer, "I beg of you so to do, and return again as soon as you have set him in prison." Gerames departed from the admiral, and went to the city with Huon and his thirteen companions, and when they entered into the city they lifted up the bridges and closed the gates. Now, there were no men of war in the city, for all were in the field with the admiral against Ivoryn, and there were none but women and children and old folks left. When Gerames and Huon saw that they were strong enough for them that were in the city, they went into the streets crying, "Saint Denis," and slew all the men at arms they met, so that within a short space they had clean won the town, for the Paynims on the walls fled and leaped down into the ditches, breaking arms, legs, or necks; and at the last they came to the palace, and there they found the fair Claramond.

When Huon saw her he took off his helm and ran and embraced her, and when she saw that it was Huon her joy was so great that it was marvellous to see, and such joy they made at their meeting that it cannot be recounted. Huon and the lady embraced each other many times, and she said : " Ah, Huon, you be right heartily welcome, for I weened that I should never have seen you."

" Lady," quoth Huon, " I ought greatly to love and cherish you, and I am right joyful that I have now found you in good estate, for there is none living truer than thou."

When all the company had made their salutations to one another, they went to dinner, and were richly served, for there was great plenty in the city. Without the walls, the Saracens fought and slew each other, and such bloodshed was there on both sides that the field was covered with men, dead or sore wounded, and many a horse ran about the field, whose master was lying dead, and the two kings fought one against the other, power against power.

Then two Saracens that were escaped out of the city of Anfalerne came to the Admiral Galaffer, and said : " Ah, Sir, your city is lost to the Frenchmen, who have entered into it ; there is neither man nor woman left, but all are slain. The old knight that came to you and his companions are all servants to the young man who slew your nephew, and when the two Frenchmen were fighting they recognised each other. They are all subjects to the young man that was with King Ivoryn, and it was he that slew the Admiral Gaudys, and discomfited the giant Agrapart. We knew him

well

well when he entered into the city, and would have shewed you thereof, but we durst not till you were returned from the battle. Now they are in your palace at their pleasure, for there is neither man, woman, nor child here, but all were slain, except thirty ladies and damsels who were with her that should have been your wife, and they are put out of the city; you may see them sitting at the gate weeping piteously."

When the Admiral Galaffer heard that he was heavy and sorrowful, and said to his men around him: "Sirs, I pray you give me some counsel at once what I should do, for it is needful." " Sir," quoth they, " of necessity you must go to King Ivoryn and kneel down at his feet, and pray him to have mercy on you : other counsel we cannot give you now."

" Sirs, quoth Galaffer, " I shall do as you have said." Then the admiral, with his sword in his hand, rode through the press and came to King Ivoryn ; then he alighted from his horse and kneeled down before him, saying : " Sir King, I yield to you my sword, with the which, if you please, strike off my head, for I have well deserved your wrath. But, Sir, I pray you, for the love of Mahound, have mercy on me. I offer to make you such amends as you and your lords shall judge, so that you will aid me to take the French-men that are in my city, who have taken away my wife, your niece, Claramond. Sir, the young man

that

that you loved so well, who came but late to your coast with a minstrel, is the same Frenchman that slew your brother the Admiral Gaudys. These tidings I have just heard by two messengers that knew him in his Court, and now there are with him thirteen other Frenchmen, whom I had retained to maintain my war, but they are all subjects to the young man, and now all fourteen are in my palace, and my wife with them."

When Ivoryn heard Galaffer he said: "Alas! I was unhappy that I knew not that this young man had slain my brother: if I had, it should have been dearly bought. Sir Galaffer, cause your men to withdraw from the battle, and I will withdraw mine, and know of my barons what counsel they can give me."

So both parties blew the retreat. Then King Ivoryn said to his lords: "Sirs, what counsel will you give me as touching the Admiral Galaffer?"

"Sir," quoth they, "give him again his lands, seeing he asketh mercy: if he hath done ill, he offereth to make amends."

Then Ivoryn called Galaffer, and said: "Sir Admiral, I render again to you all your lands, and pardon you of all my ill-will, and beside that, I will help you to destroy the Frenchmen that are in your city of Anfalerne."

Galaffer kneeled down and thanked King Ivoryn for the courtesy that he shewed him and offered to

228   do

do, and would have kissed his feet, but Ivoryn would not suffer it, and lifted him up. Thus these two kings agreed together, and swore to have the death of Huon and of his knights.

That day Huon and his companions abandoned the city of Anfalerne, because they were too few to guard it, and retired into the castle, which was very strong. It stood on a rock on the seashore, and was impregnable if it was well victualled : at the corner of it was a strong tower, and underneath the tower was the port where ships came to their anchor. When Ivoryn and Galaffer saw that the Frenchmen had given up the town, they entered it with all their power, and took up their lodgings in the town, but Huon and Gerames and their companions shot out darts and quarrels in such wise that no Paynim was so bold as to show himself near the castle, for if he did he was slain or hurt. Ivoryn and Galaffer were so wroth with the deeds of the Frenchmen, that they raised up a gibbet before the castle to make them afraid. The Paynims took Mouflet the minstrel, bound his hands behind him so tight that the blood ran out of his finger-tips, and hung his viol about his neck. Then he was brought before Ivoryn, who said to him : " Ah, thou false traitor, ill rest thou; remember the goodness that my brother Gaudys hath shewn to thee, when thou hast brought him that slew him to my Court to do me shame. I shall neither eat nor

drink

drink till thou hast thy desert, and that is to be hanged."

"Ah, Sir," quoth Mouflet, "never in all my life have I thought nor done any treason. I knew not that I was bringing to your Court him that slew your brother, the Admiral Gaudys, who was my lord and master. Great sin it were for you to put me to death for what I am not guilty of."

"Thou liest, false traitor," quoth Ivoryn ; and so commanded thirty men to lead him to the gallows. When they were come thither, they caused the minstrel to mount up on the ladder, and the Frenchmen in the castle wondered greatly who it should be that they were going to hang there. Mouflet turned him towards the castle when he was up on the ladder, and cried with a loud voice : "Ah, Huon, how can you suffer me to die here. Remember the courtesy and the goodness I shewed you when you came to me all naked. I gave you then clothing and meat and drink, and abandoned all that I had to you. Ill was it employed if you reward me not better."

When Huon heard the minstrel, he knew that they were hanging Mouflet, who had been his master, and said to his companions : "Sirs, I beg you arm yourselves quickly, for the Paynims here without have raised up a gibbet, and are going to hang thereon a minstrel who hath done me great good. I would be right sorry he should suffer harm."

Then

Then Gerames and his companions made them ready, and issued out of the castle with Huon by a secret postern gate, so that the Paynims about the gibbet knew not of their coming till Huon and his knights were among them; and Huon ran at the soldier who was hanging the minstrel, and struck him clean through with his spear, that he fell down dead; then he took down the minstrel and made him fly away to the postern, his viol about his neck. He that had seen him fly away could not have kept himself from laughing; he ran so fast, that he did not seem to be an old man, but rather of the age of twenty years. While he fled, Huon and his companions slew and beat down the Paynims, so that none of them escaped. King Ivoryn and Galaffer perceived the great stir round the gibbet, and said: "Sirs, the Frenchmen are come out of the castle; see, that none of them enter it again."

The Paynims issued from their lodgings on all sides, and ran together as best they might, without keeping any good order, and Huon and Gerames, when they saw them coming, made as if they were returning to the castle slowly, while the Paynims came after them, crying and howling like dogs. When they came near, Huon suddenly turned, and with his spear met so the first that he ran him clean through the body, so that he fell down dead; and Gerames and the rest struck around them, so that the place ran like a river with the blood of

the

the dead Paynims.   Huon struck with his sword with both hands, and he touched no man without cleaving his head to the teeth ; yet at last the force of their enemies was so great that they could no longer withstand it, and Huon, who was expert in deeds of arms, perceived that it was time to depart, and called his men together.   They drew towards the postern, and with much trouble got in thereat, but yet they were so hurried and pursued that Garyn, of Saint Omer, remained without and defended himself valiantly, till at last he was slain by the Paynims.

Huon was right sorrowful when he saw that Garyn was not entered into the castle, and piteously complained for him, saying : " Ah, dear cousin, who for love of me hast left your wife and children and land and seigniories, I am sorry for your death."

" Sir," quoth Gerames, " leave your sorrow, and think to make good cheer, and keep well our fortress. God hath always aided you, and shall still.   Go we up and make good cheer, for with this sorrow we can win nothing."

Then as they came into the hall, they met Clara-mond, and when Huon saw her, he said : " My fair lover, this day I have lost one of my good friends, wherefore I am sorrowful."

" Sir," quoth she, " I am sorry thereof, but what cannot be recovered must be left ; we be all made to die ; God shall have mercy on him."

With

With such like words Claramond and Gerames appeased Huon, and they came into the hall and disarmed themselves and went to dinner, and after meat they looked out at the windows to see the countenance of the Paynims. Gerames said to the minstrel Mouflet: " My friend, I pray thee take thy viol, and give us a song to make us merry."

Then the minstrel took his instrument, and gave them a sweet song, which was so melodious that they thought they were in Paradise, and they made joy with such an exceeding noise, that the Paynims without did hear it and said among themselves: "These Frenchmen are people to be feared and dreaded;" and they were right sorrowful for the men they had lost by the prowess of these fourteen persons.

When King Ivoryn fully knew the great loss he had suffered, he was right sorrowful, but the Admiral Galaffer said: "Sir, for the honour of Mahound, be not sore troubled about a thing you shall well achieve, and bring to an end. You know well these Frenchmen are but as birds in a cage, for they cannot escape either by land or water, and they have no hope of a rescue. To-day they were fourteen, and now there are but thirteen. You are lodged in a good town, and have the fields and the sea at your pleasure, while it is not possible for them to escape, seeing they have neither ship nor galley to flee in. Appease yourself then, Sir, and suffer them to waste their victuals."

By

By these words, King Ivoryn was somewhat comforted. In the meantime, the Frenchmen in the castle took counsel together, and Huon said to Gerames: "Friend, you see well that we be enclosed here, so that we can neither depart by land nor sea. We look for no succour from any man living, and here before us are lodged the Paynims who have sworn our deaths."

"Sir," quoth Gerames, "true it is; yet I hope that God will send us some good deliverance. If it please you, Sir, let us two go down and amuse ourselves by the waterside, near the gate, till night come." "I am content," quoth Huon; "we may go there and not be seen by the Paynims."

So they went thither, and when it was near hand night Huon looked over the sea and saw a ship coming towards them, and said to Gerames: "Friend, behold yonder comes a ship with full sail. They will arrive at this port. They are Christians I see by the tokens that the ship doth bear, for on the mast there is a red cross." "Sir," quoth Gerames, "by all that I can see the ship comes from France; as I told you before, God will send us a good deliverance." Thereupon, from fear of a tempest, the ship came into the haven and cast anchor.

Then Huon approached the ship and asked for the captain, and for the master of them that were in the ship. The mariners looked round at the place where they were, and knew clearly by the great

tower

tower that they were in the port of Anfalerne, so they feared greatly and said to one another: "We are but dead, seeing we be here in this port, for the lord of this place is the most cruel Paynim between this and the Red Sea:" thus they complained to one another.

Huon, who was near them, understood them well, and said: "Sirs, have no fear of death, for you have arrived at a good port. Shew me, I pray you, whence you came and what you be." They answered and said: "Sir, seeing you can speak French, we shall shew you if you will assure our lives to us."

"Sir," quoth Huon, "have no fear of death or of any hurt to come to you, for we that have this place in keeping are Frenchmen, therefore shew us boldly your desires." "Sir," quoth they, "seeing you would know what we be, we are all born in the country of France, and one of us is of St. Omers, and some of the city of Paris and of divers other parts of the realm of France."

"Friends," quoth Huon, "I pray you shew me if there be any among you born in Bordeaux."

"Sir," quoth one of them, "there is one in this ship that was born in Bordeaux, an old ancient man, I think he is a hundred years of age; his name is Guyer. We are going a pilgrimage for the love of our Lord, to visit the Holy Sepulchre; but fortune by force of the tempest of the sea hath caused us to arrive here, and this tempest hath

235   endured

endured these three days and nights past, wherefore we are so weary and so sore travailed that we can do no more."

"Friends," quoth Huon, "I pray you shew me him you speak of." Then the captain of the ship commanded that the old man of Bordeaux should come forth. Then Guyer the provost came to Huon, and said: "Sir, behold me here. What pleaseth it you to say?"

When Huon saw him he knew at once that it was Guyer the provost, and said: "Friend," I pray you show me where you were born and what hath moved you to come hither, seeing the great age you be of, and further what is your name."

"Sir," quoth he, "I shall shew you the truth. I had a lord whom I entirely loved, he was son to Duke Seguin of Bordeaux, and his name was Huon. It fell about seven years after the death of his father, King Charlemagne sent for him to do his homage, and to receive his land from him. The young man with his brother Gerard, by the commandment of his mother, took the way towards Paris. By the way, King Charlemagne's son, called Charlot, was lying hid in a wood by the counsel of certain traitors, and lay in wait to slay Huon and his brother Gerard, but the case fell otherwise, for Huon slew Charlot, not knowing who it was. Thereon King Charlemagne banished him the realm of France, and charged him before he returned

236   to

to go to Babylon to do a message to the Admiral Gaudys, while his brother Gerard abode at Bordeaux to keep the heritage. The duchess his mother was so full of sorrow that her son was thus banished without a cause, that she took thereof a malady and died of it this five years past, and so thereby Gerard is lord and governor of all the land. He is married to the daughter of the fellest tyrant from thence to Spain, and hath learned of him many ill customs. He has left all the good ways that were of custom in the days of Duke Seguin and of the duchess his mother, and hath raised new taxes and impositions in all his lands. He has chased and put from him all noble men: he destroyeth the burgesses and the merchants, the widows and orphans: no man can shew the evil that he hath done and does every day: and he hath disinherited me. On a day the barons of the country desired me to take the pain on me to go and search by land and water if I could find the young Huon, who is our rightful lord. It is now two years that I have searched for him in divers countries, but I could never hear one word of him, whereof I am right sorrowful, and in seeking him I have spent all my gold and silver. Howbeit these good merchants have taken me into their ship for the love of God. They thought to have brought me into France, but by fortune we be here arrived."

CHAP. XII.

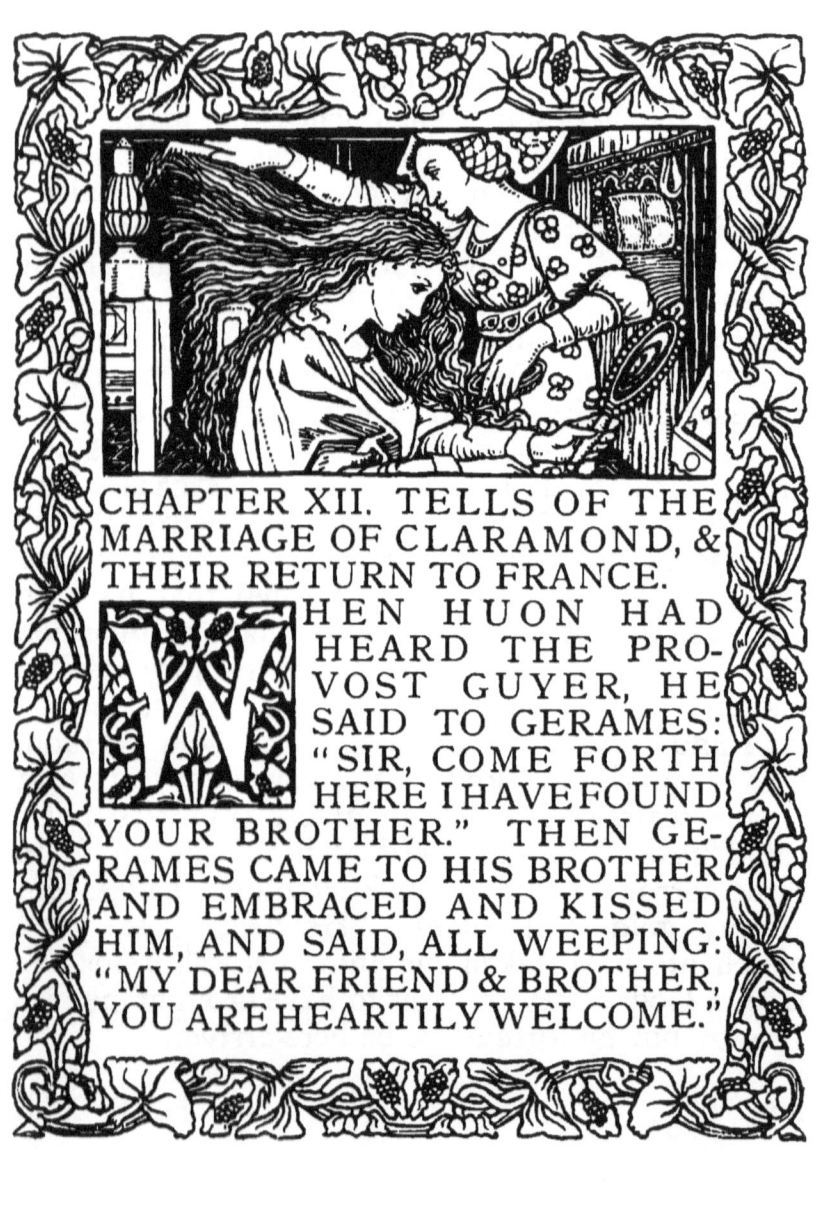

CHAPTER XII. TELLS OF THE
MARRIAGE OF CLARAMOND, &
THEIR RETURN TO FRANCE.
WHEN HUON HAD
HEARD THE PRO-
VOST GUYER, HE
SAID TO GERAMES:
"SIR, COME FORTH
HERE I HAVE FOUND
YOUR BROTHER." THEN GE-
RAMES CAME TO HIS BROTHER
AND EMBRACED AND KISSED
HIM, AND SAID, ALL WEEPING:
"MY DEAR FRIEND & BROTHER,
YOU ARE HEARTILY WELCOME."

"Ah, brother," quoth Guyer, "now I care not whether I live or die, seeing I have found you: and if it were so that I might see my lord Huon once before I died, then I care not how soon it may be."

"Ah, dear brother," quoth Gerames, "you shall not die so soon, and yet you shall see Huon, whose presence you so sore desire. It is Huon to whom you have been speaking all this while."

Then Huon, weeping, came and embraced Guyer, and said:

"My dear friend, your coming is a joy to my heart, for a truer knight cannot be found."

"Sir," quoth Guyer, "do you know me?"

"Yea, truly," quoth Huon, "and do you know me?"

"Yea, Sir," quoth Guyer, "you are sore desired in France. Brother Gerames, I desire you to tell me where you have been since I saw you, for it is sixty years since you departed out of France."

Then Gerames shewed him all his life, and how he found Huon; long were they talking together, whereof they of the ship were right joyful, for then they saw well they were arrived at a good port.

After these things, Huon said to the mariners: "Sirs, I pray you this night make no great noise and have no fire, nor shew a light. Here, before the castle, two Paynim admirals are lodged, who have sworn that they will never go hence till they have us at their pleasure. We be here some

thirteen

thirteen persons, and with us a noble lady, wherefore I require you to let us come into your ship or else we be all lost. Fear not but you shall be well paid for your labour, you shall have gold and silver as much as you desire."

"Sir," quoth the captain, "you need not speak of any gold or silver, for this ship is yours to do therewith at your pleasure."

"I thank you for your courtesy," quoth Huon, "I pray you and your company come with me into the castle and I shall load your ship with gold and silver and rich jewels and precious stones, so that you and all yours shall be rich for ever. This must be done in haste before the Paynims here without perceive us, for if they perceive us we shall never get hence, they will at once send some of their ships and take this one."

"Sir," quoth the captain, "we are ready to obey your commandments;" so he and twenty-four mariners went with Huon into the castle and loaded themselves with all the treasure that was in it, and the riches that Huon and his companions had taken in the town; it was all borne into the ship, with victuals sufficient. Then Huon took Claramond by the hand all smiling, and said:

"Fair lady, one thing I ask of you, are you not grieved to leave the country and land where you were born?"

"Sir," quoth she, "I have long desired to see the

day

day that I now do see : well may we thank our Lord God that hath given us the grace to be taken ^D out of the hands of the enemies of the faith of Christ."

Then Huon and the fair Claramond and Gerames entered into the ship with all their company, so they were in number two score persons and with them was Mouflet the minstrel. When they were all entered into the ship, and it was charged with all things needful, they weighed up their anchors and hoisted up their sails. There was a good fresh wind, so that they were soon far from the lands of the two Saracen admirals. They sailed so well that before it was daylight they passed the coast of Rhodes, and so came by the Isle of Crete, and soon by the aid of God and a good wind they arrived at the port of Brindisi. About noon the admirals that were besieging the castle of Anfalerne wondered greatly that they could see no man stirring within the castle : then a Paynim said to Ivoryn :

" Sir, know for truth you shall find no man within the castle, for the Frenchmen have fled, but we cannot tell how."

When the two admirals heard that, they were sore troubled ; and they sent forth in haste a galley and thirty Paynims therein, commanding them to go to the port gate, which they did at once. When they came there they found neither man nor woman, but the gate was open ; so they entered the castle

Q and

and opened the broad gates and the two admirals entered in, sore displeased that the Frenchmen were escaped. Now let us leave speaking of them and return to Huon, who has arrived in safety at the port of Brindisi.

When Huon and his companions arrived at the port of Brindisi they issued out of their ship, and went devoutly to the church and there gave laud and thanks to our Lord God that had brought them thither in safety: then they went to the lodging of Garyn of St. Omer. When they were come into the house, his lady who was right sage and courteous, came to Huon and said:

"Sir, I am right joyous at your coming. But I pray you, where have you left Garyn my lord and husband? Seeing he is not with you my heart trembleth for fear lest he be dead or that some great misfortune has befallen him."

"Dame," quoth Huon, "to hide the truth from you cannot cause you to have him again, for it hath pleased God that he is departed out of this world; wherefore I counsel you, as much as you may, leave dolour and heaviness, for we must all come thereto. I repute you so sage that you well know that you cannot have him again for any sorrow or weeping that you can make."

When the lady heard Huon she fell down in a trance, more dead than alive, and Huon and his company set her up and comforted her as much as

they

they might.   Then Claramond took her and brought her into her chamber, and did so much with her fair and sweet words that she somewhat appeased her, so weeping sore she came to Huon and he said :

"Dame, appease yourself and pray for him, for we must all go by the same passage."

With these words and such other the lady was comforted, then they washed and went to dinner. After this Gerames and other of his company went into the town and bought horses and mules to ride on, and rich gowns all in one livery.   There they tarried eight days, and on the ninth day they paid the captain of the ship in such wise that he was rich ever after, and every mariner had a great reward, wherefore they thanked Huon and offered to do him any service.   After, Huon and Claramond with all their company took their leave of their hostess, whom they left in tears, and at their parting Huon gave her a rich gift, for which she humbly thanked him.   When they were all ready and their luggage tied up, they departed and took the way towards Rome with great joy and gladness.   But whosoever was joyful, Guyer the provost was doubly so, for he had found his lord Huon and his brother Gerames, and also because Huon his lord had fulfilled the message that King Charlemagne had charged him to do to the Admiral Gaudys.   At last on a morning they came to Rome and alighted at their lodgings, and then they all together went to hear divine

service

service, and as they came out of the church they met a servant of the Pope. Huon asked him what estate the Pope was in. "Sir," quoth the squire, "he is ready to hear service." Then Huon and his company leapt on their horses, and rode to the Pope's palace and there alighted, and Huon took the fair Claramond by the hand, and the good provost Guyer held his brother Gerames by the hand, and so all the other, two and two. They found the Pope seated on his throne talking with his cardinals, and Huon approached and saluted him humbly. When the Pope beheld Huon he knew him straightway, and came and embraced him and kissed his cheek, saying : " Fair son Huon, you are welcome ! I pray you shew me how it is with you, and tell me of your adventures."

"Sir," quoth Huon, " I have endured evil and trouble enough, and all these that are with me also, but thanked be God it is so now that I have brought with me the beard and great teeth of the Admiral Gaudys, and have also brought his daughter who is here present, and, Sir, I beg of you to give her Christendom and then I will wed her to my wife."

" Huon," quoth the Pope, "all this pleaseth me right well to do, and the rather seeing it is your pleasure ; I desire you to tarry here with me this night."

"Sir," quoth Huon, "your pleasure shall be mine."

That

That night Huon and his company tarried with the Pope and made great joy, and in the next morning a font was made ready wherein the fair Claramond was christened without changing her name, and Mouflet the minstrel was also christened there, and he was named Garyn. When the sacrament of baptism was finished the Pope himself said service; first he confessed Huon and assoiled him of his sins, and then he wedded him to Claramond. The divine service being ended, they all went with the Pope to his palace and there the marriage was celebrated. It would be tedious to rehearse the manner of the feast, the meat, the drink, the dress of the bride and bridegroom, but one thing will I say, such a rich and glorious feast had not been seen for a long time before, for the Pope treated them as though they had been his own brother and sister. The melody of the minstrels was so sweet and delectable that every man was satisfied with the hearing, and it was specially marvel to hear Garyn, the new christened minstrel, play, and he played so sweetly on his viol that it was joy to hear it. On the morrow they rose and heard service and then dined, their baggage was packed up, and their sumpners and mules were loaded, and their horses saddled; then Huon and Claramond went to take leave of the Pope and thanked him for the honour and great courtesy he had shewed them.

" Sir," quoth the Pope, " if it would please you to

tarry

tarry here with me, my goods and my house should be at your command."

" Sir," quoth Huon, " I cannot render thanks to your holiness for the good that you have done us. But I cannot longer tarry for the great desire that I have to accomplish the rest of my task, therefore, Sir, I recommend you to God."

The Pope kissed Huon, and touched Claramond by the hand, then they took their leave, and at their departure the Pope sent them a sumpner loaded with gold, and clothes of silk, and thus they departed from Rome.

They rode so long through cities, towns and valleys, that at last they saw afar off the steeples and towers of the city of Bordeaux, and when Huon caught sight of them he lifted up his hands to heaven, thanking God for His grace that He had brought him thither in safety, and then he said to Claramond :

" Fair lady, yonder you may see before you the city and country whereof you shall be lady and duchess, though it hath been before this time a realm."

"Sir," quoth Guyer the provost, "it is good you re-gard wisely your affairs which touch you right near : if you will do by my counsel, send first to an abbey that is here by, called the Abbey of St. Maurice, whose abbot is a notable clerk ; let him know of your coming, and that you will dine with him."

" Sir,"

"Sir," quoth Huon, "your counsel is to be believed," and he sent to the abbot informing him of his coming. When the abbot knew of Huon's return he was right joyful, for he loved him entirely and sore desired the sight of him; then he called all his convent, and charged them to dress them with cross and mitre and copes to receive Huon, "the rightful inheritor of the country of Bordeaux, though the Kings of France be our founders. But as to our good neighbour, we will do him this reverence, for honour is due to them that deserve it." The convent, as they were commanded, ordered themselves and went out of the abbey to meet Huon, who, when he saw them, alighted afoot, and also Claramond and Gerames and the others, and thus the abbot and his convent in rich copes came singing to meet Huon. When Huon came near he was right joyful, and the abbot, who knew him at once, came to Huon humbly and said:

"Sir Duke of Bordeaux, God be thanked that you have come home, for your presence hath long been desired."

Then they embraced each other, weeping tears for joy, and the abbot welcomed the provost Guyer and the others, but he knew not Gerames.

Thus the abbot and his convent brought Huon to their abbey in solemn procession, and Claramond and he followed on foot. When he came into the church he offered great gifts, and after their offerings

247   and

and prayers they went into the hall and sat down to dinner. How well they were served need not be rehearsed, suffice it to say they had every thing they needed. The abbot sat by Huon and said :

"Sir, I pray you shew me how you have done, and what was the end of the message you were charged with by King Charlemagne."

"Sir," quoth Huon, "thanked be God, I have accomplished all that I was commanded to do, for I have brought with me the beard and four of the greatest teeth of the Admiral Gaudys, and I have also brought with me his daughter, the fair Claramond, whom I have wedded in the city of Rome. To-morrow, by the grace of God, I will go to King Charlemagne my sovereign lord."

"Sir," quoth the abbot, "of that you tell me I am right joyous; but if it were your pleasure, I would send to your brother Gerard to inform him of your coming, that he might see you before you depart hence."

"Sir," quoth Huon, "I am content that you send for him."

Then the abbot commanded a squire of his to go for Duke Gerard, and he went and rested not till he came to Bordeaux to Duke Gerard, and said :

"Sir, if it be your pleasure to come to the Abbey of St. Maurice, you shall find there your brother Huon, who is come straight from beyond sea."

When Duke Gerard heard that his brother Huon was come to the Abbey of St. Maurice, he was so

overcome

overcome with ire and displeasure that his visage became like a flame of fire ; and he said to the messenger :

"Go and return, and say to my brother Huon that I will straightway come and visit him."

"Sir," quoth he, "I shall shew him of your coming ;" and so departed and came again to the abbey where he shewed Huon what his brother Gerard had said. When Duke Gerard saw that the messenger was departed he was sorrowful and pensive, and called to him his father-in-law, his wife's father, who was named Gybouars, the falsest traitor between the East and the West, and Gerard said to him :

"Sir, I pray you give me counsel in what I have to do, for my brother Huon is come from the parts beyond the sea, and is now present in the Abbey of St. Maurice. The abbot there hath sent me word thereof, and that I should come thither to speak with him, for on the morrow he will depart and go to Paris to the King. When he is come thither he will do so much that all his lands shall be returned to him, and I shall have never a foot of land left me but what you have given me with my wife, your daughter. Wherefore, dear father-in-law, I pray you to aid and counsel me in this great matter, or else I am but lost."

"Fair son," quoth Gybouars, "dismay you not, for unless my wit doth fail me, I shall play him
249   a turn

a turn that shall make him wish he had tarried
in the land from whence he comes, rather than to
travel hither to claim your land."

Then Gybouars said to Gerard :

" Fair son, go your way to your brother Huon,
and take with you but one squire. When you
come to him make him all the cheer you can, shew
him as great love as you may, and humble yourself
to him, so that he may not suspect you. When the
morning comes hasten his departure, and when you
come with him near such a little wood find some
vigorous words for him, and make as though you
were displeased with him. I shall be ready in
ambush in the wood with forty men-at-arms, and
when I see that there are words between you I shall
issue out and slay all those that are come with him,
so that none shall escape alive. Then take your
brother Huon and cast him into a prison in one of
the towers of your castle at Bordeaux, where he
shall miserably end his days. You shall then ride
in haste to Paris, but before you go there you shall
take from him the admiral's beard and teeth, and
you shall tell the King that Huon your brother is
returned without bringing with him either the beard
or the teeth of the Admiral Gaudys, and that for that
cause you have put him in prison. The King will
believe you, for he greatly hateth Huon because of
the death of his son Charlot whom he slew; for
the hate that the King hath to him in his heart

250   shall

shall never depart from him. Therefore, son, when you are with your brother ask him if he has the admiral's beard and teeth or not, and whether he bears them himself or who else : if he has them not he shall never have peace with the King, but he will be slain by an ill death, or hanged or drawn, for your brother laid hostage promising that he would never return without he brought with him the Admiral Gaudys' beard and teeth, and also he promised that he would not enter into his heritage till he had spoken to the King ; and this was enjoined him on pain of death." Thus, as you have heard, these two traitors devised and concluded the death of Huon.

"Gerard," quoth Gybouars, "think well of your business ; I shall go and assemble together forty of my most trustworthy servants to carry out this enterprise."

"Sir," quoth Gerard, " I shall go to the abbey to see my brother when it is a little nearer to the night."

When the hour came this false traitor departed from Bordeaux, taking with him but one squire, and so rode till he came to the abbey and there alighted. When he perceived his brother Huon he embraced him and kissed him with such a kiss as Judas gave, but when Huon saw Gerard his brother come with such humility, the water fell from his eyes for kindness, and he embraced and kissed him, saying :

" Right

"Right dear brother, I have great joy to see you; I pray you tell me how you have been since my departure."

"Sir," quoth Gerard, "right well, now I see you in good health."

"Brother," quoth Huon, "I have great marvel that you come thus alone without company."

"Sir," quoth Gerard, "I did it for the more humility, because I know not how you shall speed with the King, nor whether you shall have your land again or no. If God will that you shall have it, I shall assemble all the barons of the country to receive you, and make you cheer according: this I shall do till you return, for ofttimes these great princes are mutable and lightly believe false tales; for this cause, Sir, I am come to you secretly."

"Brother," quoth Huon, "your advice is good, I am content that you thus do, to-morrow betimes I will depart towards Paris;" then these two brethren took each other by the hand, making great joy.

"Brother," quoth Gerard, "I am right joyous when I see you thus returned in health and prosperity: have you accomplished the message that King Charles charged you with?"

"Brother," quoth Huon, "know for truth that I have the beard and teeth of the Admiral Gaudys, and besides that I have brought with me his daughter, the fair Claramond, whom I have taken to my wife and wedded her in the city of Rome;

also

also I have with me twenty sumpners loaded with gold and silver and rich jewels garnished with precious stones, whereof the half part shall be yours, and if I should shew you the pains, travails, and poverty I have endured since I saw you last, it should be over long to rehearse."

"Sir," quoth Gerard, "I believe you well, but, Sir, I pray you shew me by what means you brought your enterprise to an end."

"Brother," quoth Huon, "it was by a king of the fairies, called Oberon, who gave me such succour and aid that I came to my purpose and struck off the admiral's head, and so took his beard and teeth."

"Brother," quoth Gerard, "how do you keep them and where?"

"Brother," quoth Huon, "behold here Gerames, who hath them in his side. King Oberon did set them there."

"Sir," quoth Gerard, "which is Gerames?"

"Brother," quoth Huon, "you may see him before you ; he with the great hoary beard."

"Sir," quoth Gerard, "of what land is he?"

"He is one of the best friends I have," quoth Huon, "and he is brother to the good provost Guyer. You never heard speak of a nobler or truer man. I found him in a wood where he had dwelt forty years in penance. God aided me greatly when I found him, for if he had not been I could not have returned hither: much pain and poverty hath he

endured

endured for my sake. And now, brother, I pray you shew me how you have done since I departed from you. It hath been shewn me that you are richly married, I pray you where was your wife born, and of what lineage is she?"

"Sir," quoth Gerard, "she is daughter to Duke Gybouars of Sicily, who is a great lord, and hath wide lands and seigniories."

"Brother," quoth Huon, "I am sorry that you have taken such alliance, for I know him to be the greatest traitor that can be found, and the falsest."

"Sir," quoth Gerard, "you do ill to say so, for I take him for no such person."

As the two brothers were thus talking of Gybouars the abbot came to them and asked of them if it were his pleasure to go to supper.

"Sir," quoth Huon, "when it please you, my brother and I shall be ready."

The fair Claramond, who was weary of travel, was in her chamber apart, and divers other of her company with her, and there she supped and lay that night, and Huon was somewhat troubled because his brother had taken to wife the daughter of a traitor. They washed and sat down to supper where they were richly served, and at another table sat the provost Guyer, and Gerames his brother, and divers other barons. Gerard beheld the provost, whom he utterly hated because he went to seek for Huon, and he sware to himself that if he once went out of

254   the

the abbey, he should be the first to lose his life:
and he did eat and drink but little for thinking how
to accomplish his evil enterprise. When they had
supped, they rose from the board and their beds
were made ready. Then Huon called the abbot
apart, and said :

"Sir, I have in you great trust, and you know I
have brought hither with me great riches. I will
leave it here with you to keep till my return, and I
pray you for any manner of thing that may fall,
deliver it to no man living but to myself alone ; and
if God give me the grace to return, your part of it
shall be given you."

"Sir," quoth the abbot, "all that you give me
to keep shall be safely kept on your behoof, and I
shall do so that you shall be content."

Then he went to bed and Gerard with him, and
Gerard said : "Brother, if you think it good, I shall
call you betimes, for it seems that to-morrow the
day will be hot."

"Brother," quoth Huon, "I am content."

Thus they lay together in one bed, but the traitor
Gerard had no will to sleep, for the great desire that
he had to be avenged on his brother who had never
done him any harm. Alas I why did not Huon know
his plan? If he had the matter had not gone to
such a pass.

At last the hour came that the cocks began to
crow, and Gerard awoke Huon, saying :

"Brother,

"Brother, it were good for us to rise, for soon it will be day. It is good to ride in the cool."

Ah, the ill traitor; his thought was otherwise. When Huon heard his brother, he rose up and his companions, and every man made them ready.

"Sir," quoth Gerames, "how is it you are in such haste to depart hence? I pray you let me sleep a little longer."

"Sir," quoth Gerard, "that is ill said, for he that hath business to do that toucheth him near ought not to sleep nor rest till his business is finished."

"By my troth," quoth Huon, "my brother says truth, for I have good desire to speak with King Charlemagne."

So they took their horses, and the fair Claramond was ready mounted on a mule, and they all took their leaves of the abbot, who was right sorrowful that they departed so early: then the gates were opened and they departed fourteen in company, and Claramond made fifteen, and Gerard rode before to lead them on the way that he would have them to ride. Claramond, richly apparelled, rode very soberly and at last came to Huon and said :

"Sir, I cannot tell what aileth me, but my heart is so sore troubled that all my body trembles."

"Dame," quoth Huon, "be not dismayed and have no fear, for you are in a good country, where, by the grace of God, you shall be served like a princess and lady of the land."

With

With those words speaking her mule stumbled on one of the fore-feet so that she near hand had a great fall, then Huon approached her and caught the bridle in his hand and said: "Fair lady, have you any hurt?" "Sir," quoth she, "I had almost fallen." "By my faith," quoth Gerames, "we have done great folly in departing before daylight."

"Sirs," quoth Gerard, "I never saw men so fearful for so small a cause." "Sir," quoth Gerames, "I know not why, but if I might be believed, we should not go one foot further, but return again to the abbey till daylight." "It were great folly," quoth Gerard, "to return again for the stumbling of a mule: I never saw men so fearful. Let us ride forth and make good cheer, I see the day begins to break."

So they rode forth till they came to a cross where there were four ways, a league from the abbey. Then Huon stopped and said: "Lo, here is the border of the territory of the Abbey of St. Maurice, and this one way is to Bordeaux, which way I will not ride, for so have I promised to King Charlemagne, to whom I never broke my faith. This other way goeth to Rome, and this way before us is the right way into France, which way I will ride and no other."

Again they rode forth and all their company, and within a little while they were near the wood within a bow shot of where the traitor Gybouars lay in ambush. When Gerard saw his hour's time to speak to his brother Huon had come, he said:

257   R   "Brother,

"Brother, I see you are in mind to go into France to King Charlemagne to have your lands and seigniories which I am sure you shall have. It is a long space that I have kept it and maintained the country in peace and rest and good justice, and I have won but little and had small profit, not the value of one penny, and I am married to a noble lady, daughter to a great lord. It troubleth my heart sore when you repute him for a traitor; if he knew of it belike it might cost you dear. We believed that you should never have returned, therefore now I may say that I am not worth a penny: I would know of you how you will aid me, and what part I shall have at your return out of France."

"Brother," quoth Huon, "I have great marvel of this that you say, you know well that in the Abbey of St. Maurice I have left twenty sumpners loaded with fine gold, and I have said to you that your part shall be as much as mine therein, and I shall have no penny but one half of it shall be yours."

"Brother," quoth Gerard, "all this is not enough for me, for I would have part of the seigniory to maintain mine estate."

When Huon heard his brother, his blood rose in his face, for he saw well his brother was seeking to fall in debate with him, but Gerames who was sage and wise perceived at once that the matter was like to cause evil, and said to Huon:

"Sir,

"Sir, grant his demand to Gerard your brother. You are both young enough to conquer lands."

"Gerames," quoth Huon, "I am content that he shall have Bordeaux or Gironde, let him take which he list. Brother, show me which of these two you will have and I will have the other."

When this false traitor Gerard saw how his brother granted him his desire, and would in no wise strive with him, he was therewith so displeased, that he fell into a rage, and came to the provost Guyer and said : "Guyer, Guyer, false traitor, by thee and by thy deeds I am like to lose all my seigniories ; but by the faith I owe to God I shall strike off thy head before I die, nor shall any one hinder me from doing it." Therewith he cried out his word, and gave the sign, and Gybouars and his forty men hidden in the wood broke out with their spears in rest.

When Huon perceived them, it was no marvel that he was abashed, and humbly besought God to save his body from misfortune. Gladly would he have returned to the abbey, but he was so sore overlaid that he could not, so he drew out his sword and gave therewith such a stroke to the first that came that he clave his head to the teeth, and so he fell dead to the ground. Then Huon struck on the right hand and on the left, and whosoever he struck needed no surgeon. If he had been armed he would not have been taken without great loss, but his defence could not avail him, for he and all his company were

unarmed,

unarmed, while the forty were fully armed ; and they fought so cruelly that within a while twelve of Huon's men were slain in the place, and none escaped unhurt save Huon, who was beaten down to the earth and his hands bound. Then Gerard the traitor came to Gerames, who was beaten down by force, and cut open his right side, and took out thereof the Admiral Gaudys' beard and teeth, which were set there by King Oberon the fairy. Huon, seeing old Gerames left on the earth, said with a loud voice to Gerard :

"Ah, brother, I pray you show me the courtesy not to slay that old gentleman, but save his life."

"Brother," quoth Gerard, "let him keep what he has, he shall have no other such at this time."

Then they bound his eyes, and came to Claramond, who lay on the ground in a swoon, and bound her hands and eyes, and set her on a horse, whether she would or no, and Huon, as he was blindfold, heard the cries and weeping that she made. Then he said : "Brother Gerard, I pray you, for the love of God, suffer no ill to be done to that good lady, who is my wife, nor no dishonour." "Brother," quoth the traitor Gerard, "think on yourself and speak no more. I shall do as it pleases me."

So they set Huon and Gerames on two horses, and took the twelve dead bodies and cast them into the great river Garonne ; then they took the way to the city of Bordeaux, and led the three prisoners fast
bound

bound on three horses. Pity it was to hear the noble lady Claramond complain ; she said to Huon :

" Ah, Sir, you said to me that when we were once in your country of Bordeaux that you would cause me to be crowned with gold, but now I see well that we must pass the rest of our lives in great pain and misery. You have found here an ill brother, seeing he hath brought on you so much evil ; surely there is better faith and truth among the Saracens than among the people of the realm of France."

" Dame," quoth Huon, " your trouble more displeaseth me than my own. God send to my brother Gerard such reward as he deserves for the treason that he hath wrought."

Thus they complained and wist not whither they were carried, till they entered the city of Bordeaux one hour before day. The false Gerard brought them by dark bye-lanes to the palace so that they should not be perceived, and when they came to the palace they took Huon, Claramond, and Gerames, and put all three together in a deep prison, and ordained that they should have barley bread and water for food, and commanded the jailer not to allow man, woman or child to speak with them. The jailer promised to do so, for he was servant to Gybouars, and such as the master was, so was the servant. Now we will leave speaking of this piteous company suffering great sorrow in the horrible prison under the great tower of Bordeaux.

261   CHAP. XIII.

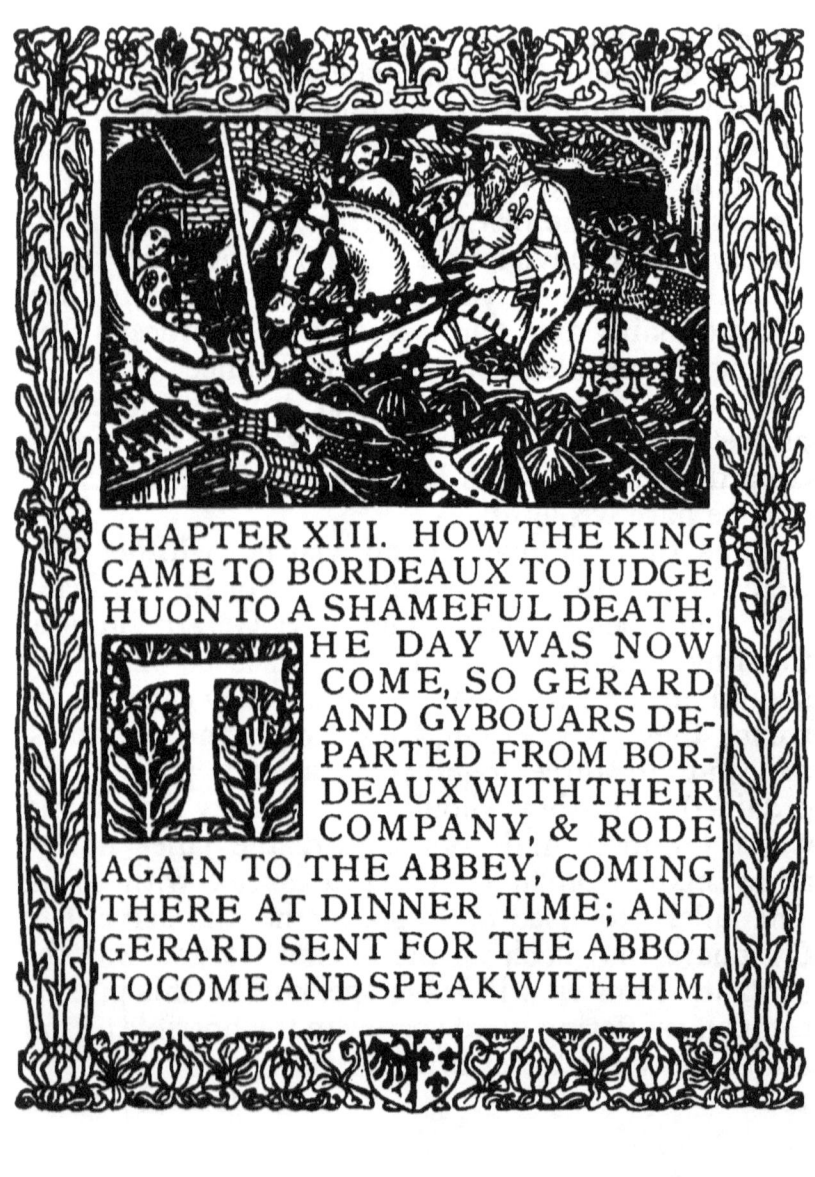

CHAPTER XIII. HOW THE KING
CAME TO BORDEAUX TO JUDGE
HUON TO A SHAMEFUL DEATH.
THE DAY WAS NOW
COME, SO GERARD
AND GYBOUARS DE-
PARTED FROM BOR-
DEAUX WITH THEIR
COMPANY, & RODE
AGAIN TO THE ABBEY, COMING
THERE AT DINNER TIME; AND
GERARD SENT FOR THE ABBOT
TO COME AND SPEAK WITH HIM.

When the abbot heard that Gerard was come again to the abbey, he marvelled greatly, and came to him saying:

"Sir, you be welcome. I pray you what adventure hath brought you hither again so quickly? I weened you were with your brother Huon."

"Sir," quoth the traitor, "after that my brother Huon departed hence, he thought that he should have need of his riches that he left with you to keep, because he would give gifts to the great princes and lords that be about Charlemagne, that his business may take the better effect. Therefore my brother hath sent me to you desiring you to send him his wealth by me."

"Sir," quoth the abbot, "when your brother Huon departed hence, it is true he left with me his riches to keep, but he charged me not to deliver it to any person living but only to himself in person. Therefore, Sir, by the faith I owe to my patron St. Maurice, I will not deliver you one penny."

When the traitor Gerard heard that answer, he said:

"Dan Abbot, thou liest. Whether thou wilt or not, I will have it, and no thanks to thee. And yet thou shalt also repent thy words."

Then Gerard suddenly caught the abbot by the hair of the head, and Gybouars took him by one arm, and struck him with a staff and bruised him, and then cast him to the earth so rudely that his

263   heart

heart burst in his body, and so he died. The monks had great fear when they saw their abbot slain, and fled away ; but the two traitors went after them sword in hand with sore threats, and when they saw they could not escape from the two traitors and their men, they tarried and fell down on their knees, praying them humbly to have pity and compassion on them, and they would shew them all the gold and silver that was in the house to do therewith at their pleasure, and the traitor Gybouars said that they had spoken well. When the monks saw that they had peace, they shewed the two traitors the place where the treasure was, and delivered them the keys, so they took away all the treasure that Huon had left there, and beside that, all the treasure of the Church, crosses, censers, chalices, copes, and candlesticks of silver, they took all and carried them away. In that house there was a monk who was a cousin of Gybouars, and him the two traitors made abbot of the place. When they had achieved their enterprise they departed with all their riches, wherewith they loaded fifteen strong sumpners, and left not in the abbey the value of a florin, for they took everything that was good with them. So they rode till they came to Bordeaux, and as they passed through the town they were greatly regarded by the burgesses of the city, who marvelled greatly from whence their lord had such great riches. These traitors passed on till they came to the palace, and there they un-
264   loaded

loaded their sumpners; then Gerard took the treasure that five of them did carry, and laid it in his chamber and coffers, and ordained that ten of them should be made ready to go to Paris, and sent them forward saying that he would follow soon after. Then he and Gybouars dined, and after meat they mounted their horses, and with them the new abbot, cousin to Gybouars, two squires, six other servants, and rode in haste to overtake their sumpners with their treasure, and caught them up within two leagues. So they all rode together until at last on a Wednesday they came to Paris, and there they lodged in the street next to the palace, in a good hostelry, and were well served, and there they remained till the morning. On the morrow they rose and apparelled them in fresh array, and led with them five of their sumpners with their riches, and two of them they presented to the Queen, and the other three to the King, wherefore they were received with great joy. Then after they gave great gifts to every lord in the Court, and especially to the officers, wherefore they were much praised. But whoever would take gifts the good Duke Naymes would take never a penny, for he thought that so much riches was not well gotten, and that they gave it to attain some false enterprise. This duke was a noble wise knight, and a true one, and of good counsel; he well perceived their malice.

Then the King commanded the three coffers to be set in his chamber, and would not look at them until he
265

he had spoken with Gerard, whom he caused to sit down by him, and likewise Gybouars and the new abbot, for it is a saying that they that give are always welcome.

"Gerard," quoth Charlemagne, "you are welcome. I pray you shew me the cause of your coming."

"Sir," quoth Gerard, "I shall shew you. Sir, the great business I have to do with you and your lords hath caused me to give these large gifts that I have given you ; and, Sir, I am sorrowful in my heart for what I must shew you. I had rather be beyond the sea than let you know that thing which I must needs open to you, yet it cannot avail me to hide it, yet never in all my life told I a thing with so ill a will, for I shall be blamed of many persons. Howbeit, I love to defend my honour better than all the world besides."

"Gerard," quoth the King, "you say truth, for it is better to shew the truth than to be still, seeing the matter toucheth your honour."

"Sir," quoth Gerard, "you made me knight, and beside that, I am your liege man, wherefore I am bound to guard your honour to my power, for I am certain I shall shew you such news that all that are in your Court will be sorrowful, and much more myself."

"Gerard," quoth Charles, "come to the point, and use no more of such sermons. I see by that that you have but evil news to tell me."

266   "Sir,"

"Sir," quoth he, "but late as I was in my house at Bordeaux, and with me divers lords and knights, as we were talking together, I saw my brother Huon enter into my house and two with him; the one was a young damsel, and the other an old man called Gerames."

When Duke Naymes of Bavaria heard Gerard, he had great marvel when he said that Gerames was one of them, and said:

"I hear what I can with pain believe, for if it be the same Gerames that I think it is, he and I were companions together at a tourney held at Chalons in Champagne, where he slew by misadventure the Earl Solomon."

"Sir," quoth Gerard, "I shall shew you as I have begun. When I saw my brother Huon I was greatly astonished, howbeit, I did him honour and made him good cheer, and made him and his company to dine. After dinner I reasoned with my brother, and asked of him if he had been at the Holy Sepulchre, and when he saw that I asked that of him he was so sore abashed that he wist not what to answer, and then I perceived by his words that he had not been there. Then, Sir, I next asked him if he had done your message to the Admiral Gaudys, but he could give me no answer nor say anything that I could believe, and when I saw that I could find no truth in any of his words I took him and set him in prison: howbeit it was

full

full sore against my will, but I considered in myself that I owe faith and fidelity to your Grace and that I am your man, and would not be found in any treason for any man living, though he were never so near of kin.   Therefore, Sir, I have retained my brother and his wife and his companion in my prison : and it is for you to do herein what it shall please you best."

When all the princes and lords that were there heard the words of Gerard that he had taken his brother Huon and set him in prison, there were none but were sorry thereof, and many began to weep, for the love of Huon.

Charlemagne, when he had heard Gerard, rose to his feet sore troubled and full of ire, for by Gerard's words the ancient hate and displeasure that he had to Huon for the death of Charles his son was renewed in his heart, and he said openly that every man might hear him :

"Lords that be here present, before you all I summon those that were pledges for Huon to deliver him into my hands to do with him my pleasure, and if he be not rendered I shall cause them to be hanged and drawn.   Let there be no man in my Court so bold as to speak or desire the contrary, or I shall make him die a shameful death."

When he had thus spoken he sat him down again and called Duke Naymes to him, and said :

" Sir

" Sir Duke, you have heard what Gerard hath said
of his brother Huon ? "

" Sir," quoth the duke, " I have well heard him,
but I believe that the matter is otherwise than he
hath said, for there is no man will say the contrary
but that all that Gerard hath said is done by false
treason : you shall find it so if the matter be wisely
inquired into."

" Sir," quoth Gerard, "you may say it pleases
you, but I take God to witness, and my father-in-
law Gybouars, and this good notable religious abbot
and his chaplain, that all that I have said is true, for
I would not for anything say that which is not just
and true."

Then Gybouars and the abbot and his chaplain
answered and said that what Gerard had said was
true.

" By my faith," quoth Duke Naymes, " all ye four
are false liars and thieves : the King is evil advised
if he believe you."

" Naymes," quoth the King, " I pray you how
seemeth this matter between these two brethren
unto you ? "

" Sir," quoth the duke, " it is a great matter : he
that is here before you is the accuser of his brother
and hath set him in prison, and now he is come
and accuseth him here before you because he
knoweth well he cannot come hither to defend
himself.   I should do a great evil if I had a brother
that

that was banished out of France, if he were to come
to me for refuge, and I were to take him and set him
fast in prison in my own house, and then after to
go and complain on him to the extent to cause his
death. I say there never was a noble man who
would think of so doing, and they that have done
thus are but false traitors. No noble man ought
to believe any such, and especially they that will
conceive such a deed against their own brother. I
know well all that they have imagined and done is
by false treason ; therefore I say according to the
right that all four are false traitors, and I judge for
my part that they are worthy to receive a shameful
death, for they are four false witnesses."

When Gerard heard Duke Naymes he changed
colour and waxed as white as snow, repenting in
himself the deed he hath done to his brother, and
cursed to himself Gybouars because he had followed
his counsel. Then he answered Duke Naymes, and
said : " Ah, Sir, you do me great wrong to owe me
your ill will."

" Gerard," quoth the duke, " it is for the evil that
is in you—you that wish to be one of the peers of
France. The King had certainly little need of such
a counsellor as you be. I had rather have lost one
of my hands than have consented thereto."

" Duke Naymes," quoth the King, " cause to come
before me all such as were pledges for Huon at his
departure."

The

The duke caused them to appear before the King's presence, of whom there were divers dukes and earls.

Then King Charlemagne said: "Sirs, you know well you are pledges for Huon of Bordeaux, and you know the pain that I laid on your heads if Huon did not accomplish my message that I gave him in charge, which he hath not fulfilled. Wherefore, if you do not deliver Huon into my hands, you shall not escape, but you shall all die."

"Sir," quoth Duke Naymes, "for God's sake I beg you to believe me at this time. I counsel you to take a good number of your notable men and send them to Bordeaux, and let them take Huon out of prison and bring him to you, and hear what he will say. If it be true what Gerard hath said, I desire you to have pity on him, but I believe surely you shall find the matter otherwise than Gerard his brother hath said."

"Naymes," quoth the King, "your saying is reasonable, I accord thereto. I will that he be sent for."

The King was so sore displeased with Huon that he would not wait till his messengers returned, but made himself ready to go thither himself with all his train. He commanded that the pledges should be set in prison till his return, but the good Duke Naymes became pledge for them all to be forthcoming, and so they went not to prison. When the King was ready he took with him his twelve peers

271   and

and set out on the way to Bordeaux. God aid Huon, for he was in peril of his life if God had no pity on him! Thus, as we have shewed you, King Charlemagne, nobly accompanied, rode so long on his journey that he came within sight of Bordeaux, and when he approached the city, Gerard came to the King and said : " Sir, if it please you, I would gladly ride before you into the city to make ready to receive you suitably."

" Gerard," quoth the King, " there is no need for you to go before to prepare for my coming ; there are others that shall go before, you shall not go till I go myself."

When Duke Naymes heard the King's answer he said to him : " Sir, you have answered like a noble prince, blessed be he that counselled you so to say."

So the King rode forth without giving any notice of his coming, and entered into the city of Bordeaux and rode to the palace and there alighted, and the dinner was made ready. The King sat down and Duke Naymes with him. At the other boards the other lords and knights, and all were richly served. Great was the noise in the palace, so that Huon in his prison marvelled at what he heard, and asked of the jailer what noise was that he heard above in the palace. The jailer answered with great pride and contempt, saying : " You need not have asked, for you are like to know too soon, but seeing you wish to know, I will tell you the truth : it is King

Charlemagne and his barons who are come hither to judge you to be hanged."

"Go thy way, false traitor," quoth Huon, "canst thou not shew me any other tidings but that?"

Thus Huon answered the jailer. There was as great confusion in the city as there was in the palace from the lodging of the King's men, and the commons and burgesses of the city of Bordeaux wondered greatly why the King came thither at that time so suddenly.

The King sitting at the table made good cheer, but Duke Naymes who sat by him began to weep and could neither eat nor drink; he rose up so suddenly that he overthrew the cups and dishes upon the table.

"Naymes," quoth the King, "you have done ill thus to do."

"Sir," quoth the Duke Naymes, "I have good cause thus to do, and I have wondrous great marvel that I see you thus doted, nay I am in such sorrow thereby that I am near hand out of my wits. How is it that you are come into the city of Bordeaux to eat and drink and to take your ease? You need not have gone out of France for that, for you had meat and good wine sufficient at home in your own house. Ah, right noble and worthy emperor, what think you to do? It is no small matter to judge to death one of your twelve peers, and it is not possible to give any true judgment when you and we are full

of wine and spices. But Sir," said the duke, "by
the Lord that formed me, whosoever this day doth
eat or drink wine shall be my foe as long as the life
is in my body."

"Naymes," quoth the King, "I am content with
your will."

Then the King commanded that all men should
rise from the tables, and that Huon should straightway be taken out of prison and brought before him.
They that had the commission to do it went to the
prison and took out from it Huon and his wife
Claramond, and the old Gerames, and brought them
all three before the King and his barons. When
they came in Huon saw where the King Charlemagne sat among all his lords, and they all arose
when they saw Huon and his company, though they
were pale and discoloured by reason of the evil prison
that his brother had put them in, and Claramond and
the old Gerames were greatly looked at. When the
pledges saw Huon before the King they said: "Sir,
now you may see Huon for whom we are pledges,
we trust to be quit and discharged of our pledge: it
lieth now in you to do with him at your pleasure."

"Sir," quoth the King, "I hold you quit; you
may go from hence where you list, for Huon cannot
now escape our hands."

Huon kneeled down right humbly before the
King and when the Duke Naymes saw him, the
drops fell from his eyes, and he said to the King:

274   "Sir,

"Sir, I pray you give Huon audience, and hear what he will say."

"I am content," quoth the King, "let him say what he will."

Then Huon, still kneeling on his knees, said:

"Sir, in the honour of our Lord I cry for mercy to God, and to you, and to all your barons. I complain of the false traitor that I see there who was my brother if there had been either faith or truth in him, but I believe there cannot be found so cruel and false a traitor in all the world, for Cain that slew his brother Abel was not so false nor so cruel."

When all the lords heard Huon they began to mourn, saying to each other:

"Where is the beauty gone that was wont to be in Huon? We have seen him so fair that none could pass him in beauty, and now we see him pale and lean and discoloured: it appeareth well that he hath not been always in ladies' chambers nor among damsels to sport and play him."

Thus they talked of Huon and took no notice of Gerard who was by them. Then Huon spake again and said to the King:

"Sir, true it is that I have done at length the message that you commanded me to do to the Admiral Gaudys as you commanded me. I have passed the sea and come to Babylon to the Admiral Gaudys, and there I required of him, in the presence of all his lords, his beard and teeth. When he had

275   heard

heard my demand he took it for a great folly and so he forthwith cast me into prison where I should have died for famine if the admiral's daughter, whom you may see sitting by the pillar yonder, had not saved me, and if I had not been aided by the good King Oberon whom I ought greatly to love. He is a right powerful king of the fairies, and dwells in the city of Montmure. When he knew of the peril I was in he had pity on me and came and succoured me in such wise that he slew all the men in Babylon who would not believe in the faith of our Lord. Then he took me out of prison and we entered the palace, and slew all such as we found there, and I went to the Admiral Gaudys and struck off his head, I cut off his beard and opened his mouth and drew out four of his greatest teeth. When I had them I desired King Oberon to help me to find a means to bring the beard and teeth in safety to your presence, and to show me where I might best keep them, thereupon the good King Oberon, by the grace of our Lord God and by the power He had given him, closed them within the side of Gerames so that they could not be perceived. When I saw that I had finished your message I returned and took with me the fair lady Claramond, daughter to the aforesaid Admiral Gaudys, and the twelve gentlemen out of France who have always been with me. If I should show you, Sir, the great pain and poverty that I and they have suffered it would be too long to rehearse,

276   but

but I may well say that but for the grace of God I had never come hither again, if I had had ten lives I could not have escaped death. After all these pains and travails that I and they that are with me suffered, we came to Rome, where the holy father the Pope received me with great joy, and there wedded me to Claramond, the admiral's daughter, whom you may see yonder all desolate and full of displeasure, and not without cause."

When the barons that were there heard the piteous complaints of Huon, every man looked on the lady, who, pale and discoloured, sat sore weeping, so that such as looked on her were constrained to take part in her sorrow. There was no man there but began to weep, and Huon, who was before the King, was sorry to see his wife make so great grief. Then he said aloud to the King:

"Sir, if you will not believe my word, send to Rome to the Pope to know the truth: if you find my words untruthful I submit myself to receive such death as you and your barons can devise, if the Pope does not bear witness to what I have said. God forbid that I should tell you anything else than the truth, and he shall give you tokens that all I have said is the truth: I could say more if I would, but it is not needful that I should make a long sermon. But, Sir, as I have told you, I returned from the place that you sent me unto, and, Sir, know for truth I came not so unprovided but that I

brought

brought great plenty of gold and silver with me, and all my companions came with me, and I was in purpose not to rest in any place till I had spoken with your grace for the great desire that I had to see you. So I rode along till I came to an abbey nearly four leagues hence, called St. Maurice, because the abbey is of your foundation and not pertaining to the land of Bordeaux, for I would not have entered into this town because of the commandment that you gave me, and I came and lodged in the abbey. The abbot received me with great joy, and sent word of my being there to my brother Gerard. The traitor came to me like a false traitor and brought with him but one squire, whereby now I may perceive that there was nothing in him but falsehood and treason."

"Huon," quoth Duke Naymes, "your reason is good, for if he had been true as he ought to have been he ought to assemble the barons and lords of the country, and so to have come with them and have received you with reverence and honour."

"Sir," quoth Huon, "it is true; but the traitor did otherwise, for when he was come to me, by great subtlety he demanded how I had sped in my journey and whether I had spoken with the Admiral Gaudys or not, and declared to him your message, and if I had brought with me his beard and great teeth. I told him I had accomplished all your commandment, and the unhappy traitor

278   asked

asked where I kept them, and I told him, for I had no mistrust of him. On that he exhorted me so that he made me arise hastily at the hour of midnight and made me and all my companions ready, and so we leaped on our horses and rode forth on our way. When we came to a cross way and he saw that I took the way into France, he began to speak rigorously to have some occasion of strife between us. Near thereto there was a little wood, where Gybouars lay in ambush, and forty men of arms well armed with him, and they came and ran at me; but my companions and I were unarmed, and they met with but little resistance from us, so the twelve gentlemen that were with me were soon slain and hewn to pieces, and they took their dead bodies and cast them into the river Garonne. Then they struck me to earth, and bound my feet and hands fast and blindfolded my eyes, and they treated my wife in like manner. Then they came to Gerames, and the traitor my brother came to him and opened his side with a sharp knife, taking out from it the beard and the teeth of the Admiral Gaudys which were set there by King Oberon. The false traitor knew the place where they were, because I had shewed him thereof before. Would to God that when he came to do that cruel deed to Gerames that the old Gerames had been armed: I am sure the false traitor durst not have looked towards him to have done him any evil. But, Sir,

279   when

when he had taken out the beard and teeth he bound Gerames' hands and feet, hurt as he was, and, Sir, you may know the truth by him."

Then Gerames stepped forth and lifted up his cloak and shewed the King the wound in his side, which every man might see was there."

"Sir," quoth Huon to the King, "when he had done all this he set us on three lean horses and so brought us into this town, bound hands and feet, and then set us in a deep prison, and so has kept us hitherto with bread and water, and hath taken from us all the riches that we brought with us. Sir, if he be so hardy as to say the contrary, that what I have said is not true, let him and Gybouars, like traitors as they be, arm themselves and I shall fight against them both. If I can conquer them both, whereof I have no doubt with the aid of our Lord God, then let them have as they have deserved, and if I cannot overcome them nor make them shew the truth, then straightway cause me to be drawn and hanged."

"By my faith," quoth Duke Naymes, "Sir Huon cannot say nor offer anything more, for he offereth to prove the contrary of what Gerard hath said."

"Sir," quoth Gerard, "my brother speaks at his pleasure because he knows well that I will not strive against him, since he is my elder brother. Let the king do as it shall please him : as for me, I never consented to do so cruel a deed as is now laid to my charge."

"Ah,"

"Ah," quoth Duke Naymes, "how the false traitor can cloak and cover his wickedness!"

"Huon," quoth Charlemagne, "I cannot tell what you have done, but I will that you shew me the beard and four great teeth of the Admiral Gaudys."

"Sir," quoth Huon, "I cry you mercy: I have shewn you how they were taken from me by the false traitor my brother Gerard."

"Huon," quoth the King, "you know well that at your departure out of France I charged you upon pain of your life that if by chance you returned again into France you should not be so bold as to enter into this city of Bordeaux until you had spoken first with me, and you delivered hostages to me that you would keep your promise, which hostages I have released since I have you in my hands. It lieth now in my power either to hang you or draw you, or to pass any other judgment on you, for it was agreed at your departure that I should do so. By the faith I owe to St. Denis, before night I shall cause thee to be hanged and drawn, and no man living shall hinder me from doing it, for now I have found you in your own house."

"Sir," quoth Huon, "God forbid that a king of France should do so great a cruelty. I cry you mercy: for God's sake do not so great a wrong to me, for you may know right well that I was brought

here

here perforce.   Therefore, Sir King, I demand that you let me have rightful and true judgment."

"By my faith, Huon," quoth Duke Naymes, "it is but a small request that you make, for your right is so clear that if justice may be shewed to you there is no man can say the contrary but that your lands ought to be rendered to you frank and free, and your brother Gerard hanged and strangled."

Then the duke said to the King, "Sir, I require you have pity on Huon and do nothing to him but right; and, Sir, you shall do great sin unless you do him justice."

"Naymes," quoth the King, "you know well it is in my power to cause Huon to die ; but seeing that he is one of my peers I will order him to judgment."

When the lords and other knights heard the King say so they were right joyful, for then they believed that the King would have mercy on Huon, but Duke Naymes was not content, and said to the King, "Sir, by what I see and hear you bear Huon but small love, seeing you will put him to judgment, considering his deeds and sayings to be true, and especially since he offers to prove it by our holy father the Pope."

So Huon drew back, and leaned him against a pillar hard by.   Then the King called all his peers and lords to him and said : "Sirs, I require you, by the faith and truth and homage that you owe to me,

that

that you aid not Huon against me, nor say nor do any falsehood, but do the most rightful judgment that you can. I charge you give true judgment without favour or partiality."

When the lords heard the King speak thus to them, conjuring them so sorely to do right and justice, they well perceived that he greatly hated Huon and that the death of his son Charlot was not forgotten out of his mind. So they drew apart all together into a chamber right pensive and mourning, and sat down on benches looking into each other's faces without speaking of any word for a long space. When Duke Naymes saw that he rose upon his feet and said : " Sirs, ye have heard how the King hath charged us to say the truth : we may well perceive by his manner that he beareth great hate to Huon, who is one of our companions. Therefore, Sirs, I request you that every man by himself will say his mind as he thinks."

Then there rose up a knight called Walter, he was of the family of Ganelon, one of the Peers of France, and he said : " Sirs, as for me, seeing the case is as it is, I say that Huon by right judgment ought to be hanged and drawn, for as you well know the King hath found him in the city of Bordeaux. Therefore I say that the King may, without doing any sin, put him to death ; and, Sirs, if you think that I have spoken reason, agree to the same and let Gerard his brother be lord and master of all the

lands

lands and seigniories that should pertain to Huon. I consent and will, as much as toucheth my part, that Gerard be one of the peers of France in the place of Huon his brother."

When Walter had ended his judgment, Harry of St. Omers spake and said :

"Sir Walter, go and sit down, your words can bear no effect for they be of no worth. But, Sirs," quoth he, "shortly to speak and righteously to judge, I say that it is reason that Huon be restored to all his lands, for his deed is well proved and by good witnesses, as our holy father the Pope. We may surely believe that Gerard his brother, that hath thus betrayed him, hath done it by false covetousness. Therefore I say and judge that Gerard be drawn at horses' tails and then hanged till he is dead." Then he said no more but sat down again.

When Harry of St. Omers had given his judgment the Earl of Flanders rose up and said to Harry :

"All that you have said I will not consent to, but I will shew you my advice as to what ought to be done. Sirs, you all know well the world, which is now of little worth, since nowadays true friends cannot be found as they used to be, as well you may see by these two brethren. The strife that is between them is foul and dishonest, and we should do well if we could by any manner of means find a

way

way to appease them ; therefore I counsel you, let us go all together to the King, and desire him to have mercy and pity on both these two brethren, and that it may please him to appease them, and render to Huon all his lands. If we could bring it to this point, it would be a good deed."

After the Earl of Flanders had spoken, the Earl of Chalons rose up and said :

" Sir Earl of Flanders, your judgment is good and you have spoken like a noble man, but I know surely that the King will do nothing at our desires. But, Sirs, if you think it good, let us all put the whole matter upon Duke Naymes of Bavaria, and all that he shall say let us agree thereto."

Then all the lords accorded together and said that the Earl of Chalons had spoken well. Then they came to the Duke Naymes, and desired him that he would take the charge of that matter on himself and whatsoever he did they were all agreed thereto. When the Duke heard them he stood still a certain space, and took all the ten peers to counsel with him. When the fair Claramond saw Huon her husband in such danger among those with whom he should have been in joy, she began to weep sore and said :

" Ah, Huon, I see here great poverty, when in the very town where you ought to be lord you are in this danger, and besides that you are not believed of any man that is here for any proof or witness that you can offer or shew. King Charlemagne will

not

not believe that you have been in the city of Babylon, and yet surely you have been, for I saw you there slay my father the Admiral Gaudys, and take his beard, and draw out of his mouth four of his greatest teeth. Great pity it shall be if you should die for your truth and faithfulness. The thing that most feareth one is that I see none that be here likely to be a noble man, especially the King who is chief of all other; methinks he is full of falsehood, for I see nothing else than that he seeks your death. But I promise to God that if He suffer you to have this wrong thus to die, I say then that as for my part Mahound is better worth than your God Jesus Christ. If it be so that you receive death without cause, I shall never more believe in Jesus Christ but renounce His law and believe in Mahound."

There were many lords and knights that heard the lady's words, and had such pity thereof that the most part of them began to weep. When Huon heard his wife he turned his face toward her and said :

" Lady, I desire you to leave your sorrow and trust in God Almighty, Who so oft hath succoured us. You know not what He will do; let us be content with His good pleasure."

With such words Huon appeased the fair Claramond.

CHAP. XIV.

CHAPTER XIV. HOW HUON WAS
KEPT FROM DEATH BY OBERON.

AFTER THIS WAS SAID,
DUKE NAYMES, WHO
WAS SITTING WITH
THE OTHER PEERS,
SAID TO THEM, "SIRS,
I HAVE GREAT PITY AT MY
HEART BECAUSE OF THESE
TWO BRETHREN, SO THAT I

cannot tell what counsel to find. I desire you all in this weighty matter to counsel me and show me your opinion therein."

"Sir," quoth the lords, "other counsel you shall not have of us, for we have laid all the matter upon you to do therein what it shall please you."

"Sirs," quoth the duke, "to dissemble the matter availeth not, seeing that Huon must pass by judgment; how say you, shall he be hanged or drawn?"

"Sir," quoth Walter, who was the first speaker, "methinks he cannot escape."

"Ah, traitor," quoth the duke, "thou liest falsely, for it shall not follow after thy counsel, whether thou wilt or not; there is no man this day that shall be so bold as to judge him to die. Therefore, Sirs, shew me again whether you will all agree to my counsel."

"Sir," quoth they, "we have laid the charge on you, and we will all bide by you."

But whosoever was glad, Walter was sorrowful and angry, for he would have consented to the death of Huon. Then all the barons, right sad and pensive, went out of the council chamber, and they could find no manner of way to save Huon, but they all prayed to God to aid and succour him. Huon, seeing the barons coming so sadly together, thought the matter was not at a good point and began to weep sore. When Claramond and Gerames saw the sorrow that Huon made they had great pity on him. Then Huon looked on Duke Naymes, for
288   he

he knew well all the matter lay in his hands, and he feared greatly for the judgment that should be passed upon him, and said :

"Ah, very God and man, as Thou didst die on the holy cross to redeem us all, I beg Thee humbly in this my great need to succour me as truly as I am in the right, for more wrong can no man have."

So Duke Naymes of Bavaria came to the King and said : "Sir, will it please you to hear what we have been speaking of?"

"Yea," quoth the King, "I desire nothing else than to know it."

"Well, Sir," quoth the duke, "then I ask of you in what place of your country think you that you ought to judge of the peers of France?"

"Naymes," quoth the King, "I know well you are a noble man, and all that you say is to deliver Huon of Bordeaux : but I will that you know all this shall not profit him."

Then the duke said : "Sir, to say so you do great wrong. Therefore, Sir, look well in what place you will have one of your peers judged. If you know not where it ought to be done I will show you. In your realm there are but three places to do it in. The first is the town of St. Omers, the second is Orleans, and the third is Paris. Therefore, Sir, if you will proceed against Huon by justice, it is convenient that it be done in one of these three places, for here in this town he cannot be judged."

"Naymes," quoth the King, "I understand well why you say this : I see well and perceive that you seek no other end but to deliver Huon unscathed. I had thought to have treated him by the order of justice to the intent that none of you should have reproved me, therefore I ordained that he should be judged by you, the Peers of France. I see well you have done nothing therein, and therefore as long as you live you shall meddle no more with that matter ; but by the beard that I bear on my chin I shall never dine nor eat meat after this dinner till I see him hanged and drawn, for all your support of him against me."

Then he commanded the tables to be set. When Gerard heard the King he was joyful thereof in his heart, but he made no semblance of joy because of the lords that were there present ; but when Huon and Claramond heard how the King had sworn his death, the dolorous weeping and tears they shed were so extreme that it were hard to declare it. Claramond said to Huon :

"Ah, Sir, now I see well that the parting of us two shall be great pity. If I had a knife I would not abide your death, but slay myself first before this false and untrue king."

Her complaints were so pitiful that most part of the lords wept for grief, and the old Gerames wept sore and said :

"Ah, Lord God, in what an hour was I born ! in

great

great dolour and pain have I spent my youth, and now in my old age thus shamefully to die!"

Thus all three made such moan that it would have made a hard heart lament, and thought none otherwise than to die because they heard King Charlemagne make such an oath ; but when God will aid no man can hinder, for if God favour the good King Oberon King Charlemagne shall be forsworn, as you shall presently hear. Now let us leave speaking of this piteous company and speak of the noble King Oberon of Fairyland, who was then in his wood.

You have heard before how King Oberon was displeased with Huon because he had broken his commandment ; but when Huon had been at Rome and confessed all his sins and been forgiven, King Oberon was content, and in his heart forgave all the ill-will that he had to Huon. Now on this day as he sat at dinner, he began to weep, and when his servants saw that they marvelled and said to him :

" Sir, we desire you to show us why you weep and are so troubled ; there is some displeasure done to you ; therefore, Sir, for the love of our Lord we desire you not to hide it from us."

" Sirs," quoth Oberon, " I remember now the unhappy Huon of Bordeaux, who is returned from far parts, and hath passed by Rome and there hath taken Claramond in marriage, and hath been forgiven for his sins, for the which he hath been sore punished

by

by me.   But it is time now to aid him if ever I will
do him any good, and succour him against King
Charlemagne, for he hath sworn never to go to bed
till he has hanged and drawn the poor Huon.   By
the grace of God, Charlemagne shall be forsworn,
for at this time I shall succour and aid him, for he
is now in such a danger that death is near him if he
be not succoured straightway.   Never in his life was
he in such peril.   He is now in the palace at Bordeaux, with his wife the fair Claramond, and the old
Gerames, bound with fetters on their feet, in great
sorrow.   Charlemagne is sitting at dinner, and hath
made his oath to hang Huon, but yet whether he
will or not he shall be perjured, for I will go to
my friend Huon and help him in his need.   Therefore I wish my table and all that is thereon near to
King Charlemagne's table and about two feet higher
than it; and because I have heard that ofttimes of a
little thing comes a greater, I will that on my table
be set my cup and horn and harness, the which Huon
conquered from the giant Angolafer, and also I wish
with me a hundred thousand men-at-arms, such as I
was wont to have in battle."

He had no sooner said the words than by the will
of God and the might of fairydom his table, with all
that he had wished on it, was set just by King
Charlemagne's table, higher and greater than his was.
When Charlemagne saw the table and the cup and
horn and coat of mail he had great marvel and said
to

to Duke Naymes: "Sir Duke, I believe you have enchanted me." "Sir," quoth the duke, "never in my life did I meddle with such a matter."

The lords and all such as were there were greatly abashed to tell how that matter came to pass, but Gerames, who sat near to Huon, when he saw the table, and the cup and horn of ivory, and the harness on it, knew them well and said to Huon:

"Sir, be not dismayed, for on yonder table that you may see is your cup and horn of ivory and coat of mail. I perceive well that you shall be succoured by King Oberon."

Huon looked up and beheld the table and had great joy when he saw it; then he lifted up his hands to heaven and thanked our Lord God that He would visit such a poor sinner as he was.

"Ah, King Oberon," quoth he, "in many great needs have you succoured me."

Therewith arrived King Oberon in the city, whereof the burgesses and the commons were greatly abashed, when they saw such a number of men-at-arms enter their city without their knowledge. When King Oberon was within the town and all his company, he said to his lords:

"Sirs, look that you set good watch at every gate, so that no man go out:" the which they did diligently, for at every gate they set a thousand men, and the city was full of men-at-arms. Then King Oberon took the way to the palace, and at the gate

he

he set ten thousand men, commanding them on pain
of their lives not to suffer any man to pass out, and
also he commanded that if they heard him blow his
horn of ivory they should forthwith come into the
palace to him and slay all such as they should find
there, and they promised him so to do. Then King
Oberon went up into the palace and many of his
lords with him. He was richly apparelled in cloth
of gold, and the border of his robe was fretted with
precious stones; goodly was it to behold, for a
fairer little person could not be found. He passed
by King Charlemagne without speaking a word, and
went so near to him and shouldered him so rudely
that his bonnet fell from his head. "Ah," quoth
Charlemagne, " I have great marvel what this dwarf
may be that hath so rudely shouldered me, and
almost overthrown my table. He is fierce indeed
when he thinks scorn to speak to me; howbeit I will
see what he will do. I cannot tell what he thinketh
to do : as me seemeth he is right joyful, the fairest
creature that ever I saw."

When Oberon had passed by he came to the
prisoners, and wished the fetters from off their feet,
and took them by the hands and led them before
Charlemagne without speaking a word, and caused
them to sit down at his own table that he had wished
thither, and he sat down with them. He took his cup
and made thereon three crosses and forthwith the cup
was full of wine. Then King Oberon took it and
gave

gave it to Claramond to drink, and then to Huon and so to Gerames and when they had all three well drunk he said to Huon : "Friend, arise up and take this cup and bear it to King Charlemagne. Say unto him that he drink to you in the name of good peace ; if he refuse it he did never such folly in his life."

King Charlemagne, who sat near to them at his own table, heard King Oberon's words and wist not what to think, so he sat still and durst speak no word for the great marvels that he saw there, and no more durst any of his men, for they were so abashed that there was none there but would gladly have been a hundred leagues off, and each man looked on his fellow in wonder. But whosoever was afraid, Gerard was not well assured. Then Huon rose from King Oberon's table, and took the cup and went with it to King Charlemagne and delivered it to him. The King took it, for he durst not refuse it, but as soon as it was in his hands it became dry and empty, with not a drop of wine therein.

"Fellow," quoth the King, "you have enchanted me." "Sir," quoth King Oberon, "it is because you are full of sin; for the cup is of such dignity that none can drink thereof without he be a noble man, and clear from any deadly sin. I know one that you did not long ago of which you have never repented, and if it were not to your shame I should tell it here openly, that every man should hear it."

And when the Emperor Charlemagne heard King

Oberon

Oberon he was abashed and afraid lest he should be openly shamed. Then Huon took again the cup and straightway it was again full of wine, so he bore it to Duke Naymes, who sat next to Charlemagne, and Naymes took the cup and drank thereof at his pleasure ; but all other could not drink of the cup, they were so full of sin. Then Huon returned to King Oberon, and sat down by him at his table ; the which Duke Naymes did and durst not say him nay. Then Oberon said to him : "Sir Duke Naymes, I give you thanks that you have been so true to Huon. For you, King Charlemagne, Emperor of the Romans, behold here Huon whom you have wrongfully and without cause disinherited, and would take from him his lands. He is a noble man and true, and besides that, I say to you for truth he hath done your message to the Admiral Gaudys, and I aided him to bring him to his death. He took out of his mouth four of his great teeth, and did cut off his white beard, and I did close them in the side of Gerames by the will of God. This that I say you may believe surely, for I was present at all these deeds. See yonder false traitor Gerard, who, driven by his malicious spirit, hath done this treason. To the end that you may know the matter more surely, you shall hear it confessed by his own mouth."

Then Oberon said to Gerard : " I conjure thee by the divine power that God hath given me, here before King Charlemagne and all his lords, shew

and

and declare the truth of this treason that thou hast wrought against Huon thy brother."

When Gerard heard Oberon he was in such fear that he trembled for dread, for he felt in himself no power to conceal the truth about his treason, then he said: "Sir, I see well that hiding the truth cannot avail me: therefore true it is I went to the Abbey of St. Maurice to see my brother Huon, and Gybouars went with me, accompanied by forty men-at-arms. We departed from this city and laid our ambush in a little wood about two leagues hence, to watch when my brother Huon should pass by that way."

"Gerard," quoth King Oberon, "speak out higher, that you may be better heard, that every man may know the treason and falseness you have wrought to your brother."

"Sir," quoth Gerard, "I wot not what to say, for I have done so evilly and falsely against my brother that I could not have done worse; I am ashamed to recount it. But, to speak truly, before it was midnight I made my brother rise and depart from the abbey, and when we came near the place where my father-in-law Gybouars was with his ambush, I began to strive with my brother so loudly that Gybouars could hear me. When he heard me speak he broke out of his ambush, ran at my brother's company, and slew them all except these three that be here. Then we took the dead bodies

297   and

and cast them into the river Gironde, and bound
Huon and his wife and the old Gerames, hands and
feet, and blindfolded their eyes, and so we brought
them on three poor horses into the city, and I took
out of the side of Gerames the beard and four great
teeth, which, if it please you, I can fetch from
where I left them."

"Gerard," quoth Oberon, "you shall not need to
take the trouble, for when it pleases me I can have
them without you."

"Well, Sir," quoth Gerard, "when I had set
them in prison I went back again to the abbey and
demanded of the abbot and his monks where the
treasure was that my brother had left there, and
bade him deliver it to me, telling him that my
brother Huon had sent for it. The good abbot
would not deliver it to me, wherefore Gybouars and
I slew him, and then we made this monk here
abbot, who is near of kin to Gybouars, to the end
that he should aid to bear us witness, and to justify
our sayings. Next we took all the treasure that
was there and brought it hither ; and I loaded ten
sumpners which I had with me for King Charlemagne's Court at Paris, of which treasure I gave
part to the King and to others by whom I expected
to be helped to perform my unhappy enterprise. I
believed surely that by reason of the riches I gave
that my brother would have been condemned to
death, and I thereby have become lord and master
298 of

of all his lands and seigniories. Sir, this treason that I have shewed you Gybouars caused me to do it, or else I had never thought of it."

" Gerard," quoth King Oberon, " if it please our Lord, you and he shall both be hanged by the necks ; there is no man living shall save you. Sir Emperor Charlemagne, you have heard well the confession of Gerard concerning the great treason that Gybouars and he have wrought against Huon. Both they two and the abbot and his chaplain shall be hanged for their false witness."

" By the faith that I owe to St. Denis," quoth King Charlemagne, " they cannot escape it." "Sir," quoth Naymes, " it is great sin to trouble a noble man ; you shall do well if all four are hanged."

When all the lords heard Gerard confess the great treason he had wrought against his brother, they wondered at the treachery of one brother to another ; but King Oberon thought on the beard and teeth, and said : " I wish them here on this table."

He had no sooner formed this wish than they were set on the table, to the great marvel of all such as were there. Then Huon knelt humbly before King Oberon and said : "Sir, I request of your Grace you will pardon my brother Gerard all the evil he hath done against me, for he did it by Gybouars' advice : as for me here, I pardon him before God, and, Sir, if you will do so, I shall be content therewith, and to the end that we may spend

our

our lives henceforth in good peace and love, I will give him the half of my lands and seigniories. Sir, in the honour of our Lord, have pity on him."

When the lords there present heard Huon, they all began to weep for pity, and said among themselves that Huon was a noble knight, and that it had been pity if the matter had turned otherwise. "Sir Huon," quoth Oberon, "it is not fitting to request this of me, for all the gold in the world should not respite them from death. I wish, by the power that I have among the fairies, and by my dignity, that here beneath in the meadow, there be a pair of gallows and all four hanged thereon."

Forthwith it was done and all four hanged : thus, as you have heard, the traitors were paid their deserts. When King Charlemagne had seen the great marvels that were done at the commandment of King Oberon, he said to his lords :

"Sirs, I believe this must be God Himself, for no mortal man can do this that he hath done."

When Oberon heard the Emperor he said :

"Sir, know for truth I am not God, but a mortal man as you are. I was born of a woman, as you are, and my father was Julius Cæsar, my mother the Lady of the Secret Isle. When I was born there were with my mother many ladies of the fairies, and by them I had many gifts. Sir, know for truth above all things God loveth faith and truth when it is in man, as it is here in Huon, and

because

because I know for certain that he is true and
faithful, therefore have I always loved him."

After that King Oberon had ended his words and shewed the Emperor Charlemagne all his estate, he called Huon and said : "Arise up and take the beard and the teeth and bear them to King Charlemagne, and desire him to render you your lands as he promised." "Sir," quoth Huon, "I ought so to do."

Then Huon came to King Charlemagne and said : " Sir, by your grace, and if it may please you, receive here the beard and teeth of the Admiral Gaudys."

" Huon," quoth the King, " I hold you quit and I render to you all your lands and seigniories, and pardon you of all my ill will, and put all rancour from me, and from henceforth I retain you as one of my peers." " Sir," quoth Huon, " for this I thank God and your Grace."

Then the Emperor Charlemagne embraced Huon and kissed him in token of peace and love, and the lords who saw it wept for joy and thanked God that the peace was made, and Duke Naymes was most joyful of all ; and within a while many of the lords departed from the Court.

After this King Oberon called Huon to him and said : " Sir, I command you, as dearly as you love me, that this same day four years hence you come into my city of Montmure, for I will give you all my realm and my dignity, which I may lawfully do, for at my birth it was granted me to give it where I like
best.

best. Because I love you so entirely I shall set the crown on your head and you shall be king of my realm. I will that then you give Gerames all your lands and seigniories in these parts, for he hath well deserved it. With you and for your love he hath suffered many great troubles."

" Sir," quoth Huon, " seeing this is your pleasure, I ought to be well pleased therewith ; I shall accomplish your commandments."

" Huon," quoth Oberon, " know for truth I shall not abide long in this world, for so is the pleasure of God. I shall soon go to my place in Paradise ; in fairyland I shall abide no longer. But beware, as dearly as you love your life, that you fail not to be with me at the day that I have appointed ; beware that you forget it not, for if you fail I shall cause you to die an ill death, and therefore remember it well." When Huon heard King Oberon he was right joyous and stooped down to kiss his feet, but Gloriant and Malabron took him up. Then said Huon : "Sir, for this great gift I thank you."

When King Oberon had said to Huon as much as he would of what he ought to do, he told Huon that he would depart, and took leave of him and sweetly kissed him. Then Oberon stood still a season and looked on Huon and began to weep. Huon was sorry at heart when he saw that, and said :

"Ah, Sir King, I desire you to show me why you make this sorrow at your departure?"

" Huon,"

"Huon," quoth Oberon, "I shall show you; it is for pity that I have on you. I swear to you that before I shall see thee again thou shalt suffer so much pain, travail, poverty, hunger, thirst, fear, and adversity, that there is no tongue alive can tell it, and thy good wife shall suffer so that no creature shall see her without having great pity on her."

"Ah Sir," quoth Huon, "then I require you to aid and comfort me."

"Huon," quoth Oberon, "what comfort would you have of me?"

"Sir," quoth Huon, "I desire you let me have your horn of ivory to the intent that you may succour me if I have need; for so well I know you that I am sure you will come and succour me."

"Huon," quoth Oberon, "seeing I have made your peace with Charlemagne, trust not to be succoured in any of your needs by me; be content with the gift I have given you of all my realm and power, look for no other help from me."

"Sir, I am sorry thereof," quoth Huon, "that it may not be otherwise."

Then King Oberon took leave of King Charlemagne and of Duke Naymes, and of all the other lords there present, and then he went to Huon and embraced him and took his leave of him and also the fair lady Claramond and of old Gerames, and said to the fair Claramond : "I commend you to God, and I desire you, if you have done well hitherto,

to

to persevere ever better and better, and bear always faith and honour to your husband."

"Sir," quoth she, "I pray God I live no longer than I should do the contrary."

Thus King Oberon departed, and after his departure King Charlemagne made ready his company, and took leave of Huon and Claramond and Gerames, and they brought the King two leagues on his way, and then took their leave of the King and Duke Naymes and all the lords. Then the King said :

"Huon, if any war be moved against you, or if you have any great affairs to do, let me have knowledge thereof and I shall come and succour you, or send you such aid as shall be sufficient."

"Sir," quoth Huon, "I thank your Grace," and so took leave of the King and returned to Bordeaux, where he was received with great honour and lived in much joy.

NOW LET US LEAVE SPEAKING OF HUON AND CLARAMOND AND THEIR ADVENTURES AT THIS TIME.

FINISHED THIS THIRTIETH DAY OF MAY 1895 BY ME, ROBERT STEELE, AND PRINTED BY BALLANTYNE & HANSON FOR GEORGE ALLEN, OF LONDON.